MONSTER HUNTRESS

DAVID WILEY

WITHDRAWN

JOHNSTON PUBLIC LIBRARY
6700 MERLE HAY RD
JOHNSTON IA 50131-1269

Monster Huntress
OWS Ink, LLC Press, United States
Published by Catterfly Publishing
Copyright © 2018 by OWS Ink LLC
Cover credit: Rebecca Keeler

All rights reserved. Printed in the United States of America. No part of this book may be used or reproduced in any manner whatsoever without written permission except in the case of brief quotations embodied in critical articles or reviews.

This book is a work of fiction. Names, characters, businesses, organizations, places, events and incidents either are the product of the author's imagination or are used fictitiously. Any resemblance to actual persons, living or dead, events, or locales is entirely coincidental.

For information contact:

OWS Ink, LLC

1603 Capitol Ave.

Cheyenne, WY 82001

http://ourwriteside.com

ISBN ebook: 978-1-946382-26-9

ISBN print: 978-1-946382-27-6

First Edition: April 2018

Dedication:

To my wife, Nicole, for always believing in me and pushing me to pursue the dream of becoming a writer.

To J.R.R. Tolkien, whose work continues to inspire new generations of readers and writers. Your fingerprints are all over my writing, even though we'll never meet on this side of Heaven.

To Stephanie Ayers, for taking a chance on an old writing friend. For believing in Ava's story and for wanting to see it in print.

PROLOGUE

Death was stalking her tonight, lingering in the depths of the shadows, stirring under the cover of the cloudless night. She could feel it in the very fiber of her being; the presence of something ominous approaching. She welcomed the challenge but feared for her family. Her husband was an ignorant nobleman at heart still. He enjoyed dressing up in fancy clothes and attending lavish parties that they couldn't afford, coming home with the rising of the sun. He was no match for the corrupt evil that was hunting her, nor did he care most nights about its presence in the 13 kingdoms. Her daughter was only three and could hardly be expected to fight, although she showed early signs of possessing the natural instincts a huntress would require. The woman was prepared to face her fate, to pay any price it required of her, so long as her family escaped unscathed.

She dropped to her knees, bowing her head in prayer to Eodran. Her ringlets of red hair were radiant in the candlelight. The dim light masked the streaks of gray that threatened to overrun the vibrant color of her youth. She heard the familiar sound of her husband's footsteps long before he stepped into the doorframe behind her. Over the past six months, his gait had grown uneven, a mixture of shuffling and stumbling that a trained ear could hear a mile away. Every time she heard it, the sound broke her heart because she knew what it signaled. It was another night that he had sought comfort in the bottle instead of finding it in her arms.

"Why do you insist on following that foolish ritual," he asked in a tone that matched the frigid air. "When has this Eodran ever answered your prayers?"

"Every day, Tristan," she said, rising to her feet. She brushed the dirt from the knees of her black breeches as she turned to face him. He had that look in his eyes again that confirmed, without needing to smell it, that he had been out drinking. "Every day that you and Ava are still alive is another day that I count my prayers as answered."

He said nothing, swaying as he stared at her. He was younger than her by a handful of years and his black hair was still free from signs of age. She wondered, as she had many times over the past few months, when he stopped being intrigued by her profession and routines, stopped being excited about her adventures, and stopped loving her. Her prayers never bothered him in the early years of their marriage, neither had her hunting, but in the past months he had drifted further apart from her. She knew without asking that their daughter would not be raised as a huntress if she died tonight. But she still clung to her hope that Ava would come to know her ways someday, and perhaps even follow in her footsteps.

She dragged her mind back to the task at hand. "Tristan," she said, "you need to take Ava and leave. Tonight."

"Kicking us out, Kenna? I knew you'd do it sooner or later," he slurred, advancing toward her. He had been swaying in the doorway, waiting for something to latch onto and get belligerent about. She handed him the excuse he sought, even if her intentions were wholly for his own benefit. She didn't have much time left--certainly not enough time to engage him in a drunken spat--so she needed to be swift in convincing him to leave. No matter the cost.

"I'm doing it to protect you," Kenna answered, wishing he would listen to her like he used to. Three years ago he would have nodded and started packing without needing an explanation or an argument. Not anymore. He was still too attached to his rich upbringing, still too caught up in living the life of luxury in the midst of the king's court in Hárborg. Kenna had hoped moving to a more isolated countryside location just outside the castle walls would have helped him to break free, but instead it thrust him deeper into their society.

"I'm starting to think what they say is true," Tristan said, "that you hunters are in league with the abominations. That it's all some big ploy and pretend to belong to the Order of the Light but really are sworn to the Order of Might. The king said so himself at the dinner feast tonight and not a person there objected."

"You really believe that?" she asked, hurt flashing in her eyes. He knew what she did was real. She had taken him on hunts, showed him the threat of the monsters and other dark creatures in the land. How could he believe such unfounded rumors of black magic and monster-loving, after experiencing the truth for years?

"Why else would you want us gone?"

"Because I want you safe. Is that such a horrible thing--to want you and our daughter to be alive? There is something coming here. Tonight. It is hunting me, and I don't know if I am strong enough to kill it."

His expression sobered. She had said the right words to break him free from the spell of alcohol. "Kenna," he said in a soft voice, "why don't you come with us if you think it can kill you?"

"It is better to face it now, on my terms, than on the run. If I flee I might survive the night, yes, but I would have to live in fear and paranoia for the remainder of my days. I would be constantly looking back over my shoulder until either I killed it, or it killed me." She also knew that slaying it would prevent the demon from going after her daughter. That little girl was her hope for the future. Kenna drew her sword and rubbed the blade with an oiled cloth. Tristan stood a few feet away from her. He watched her labor away at the task without saying a word. He knew that it was one of her habits, something she did obsessively, habitually, whenever she was nervous or scared. "Go, you fool," she said, not bothering to glance up from the blade.

He turned to leave and stopped in the doorway leading to their daughter's room. He looked back and saw she was sharpening one of her daggers now. He cleared his throat and she looked up, eyebrows arching over her emerald eyes. "I'm sorry for what I said," Tristan told her. "Please be careful."

"I always am," she answered, "which is why I am still alive."

They rode away from the house, his daughter clutching the folds of his cloak. Her twig-like arms were too small to wrap around his waist, but she made a valiant attempt as she pressed in hard against him. He was feeling remorse for his actions, aware that his drinking caused most of it. Tristan knew he still loved Kenna, even though they had drifted apart since Avalina's birth. It was slow at first, but the past few months their relationship had spiraled out of control. He wanted her to leave the monster hunting in her past, to settle into society like he did and find a respectable trade, something that didn't involve risking her life every day.

But he knew, long before Avalina, that she would never do that. It was one of the many things he admired about his wife, even if he wouldn't always admit it. She had a deep-rooted, unshakable faith and believed that her profession did more to help this world than any other she could choose. She was convinced that she was called to use her talents to fight off the evil spreading throughout the world. Kenna also had a fierce, rebellious streak in her and it was a trait his daughter had already inherited. He knew that fatherhood would not be a simple task if she continued to take after her mother. She had her mother's eyes, her mother's hair, and her mother's sense of adventure. Everything about Avalina reminded him of Kenna, and she was only three. He could only imagine what she would be like as she grew older and more independent.

The clouds above cast dark shadows on the ground as Tristan and Ava rode on. The wind whistled through the valleys between the hills and whipped Ava's fiery hair into his face. Kenna had taught him to observe the weather over the years, how to read the signs in the clouds and the wind. Tonight it seemed a sinister storm was rolling in. Yet something about it felt off. This wasn't a typical summer storm that was sweeping mindlessly across the continent. The atmosphere was thick with evil, a dread overture for the night. As if it were cover for devilish deeds to be done.

"Mommy," Ava whimpered, stretching a thin arm toward her home, fingers wiggling as she tried to grasp the house in the distance. Tristan looked back and his eyes followed the line of Ava's arm. A large shadow, nearly imperceptible, slipped around the side of the building and disappeared into the doorway. Tristan tugged on the reins, stopping the horse at a crossroads. Going left would loop back around; going right would take him along to the next village. He knew Kenna would be furious with him if he went back now. The smart thing to do was to do as she asked and head onward. He was no warrior, and he had to consider the protection of their daughter. He could already hear her lecture about needing to trust her and how his chivalrous notion needlessly placed Ava in danger.

None of that mattered when he heard Kenna scream.

He turned the horse along the left path and dug his knees into its sides. The steed burst into a gallop that consumed the distance between them and the house. But it wasn't going to be fast enough. Death resonated in that scream. He had heard the sound dozens of times, coming from the monsters Kenna hunted, but it had never given him chills before. Not until tonight. He knew the sound would haunt his dreams for years. He just hoped he was fast enough to catch whatever it was that killed his wife and avenge her by killing it. That would be the proper course of action and would allow Kenna to sail into the distant beyond and rest in peace for eternity.

Ava clung to his neck as he dismounted from the horse. She made it clear that she was unwilling to be left behind. He dropped to the ground with a loud thud and wondered how Kenna had always been silent and graceful in her dismounts. He had no weapon with him, but he gave no thought to the madness of his actions-- the sheer insanity of being unarmed and unskilled, when facing the monster that killed his armed and skilled wife.

He burst into the house and his eyes quickly took in the grisly sight. Kenna lay on the floor, her right leg twisted at an unnatural angle. The tattered fragment of a black cloak was clutched in the pallid fingers of her left hand. Thick, crimson blood pooled beneath her body, seeping into the cracks between the wood panels of the floor. Her sword rested inches from her right hand, the steel blade coated with a black, vitriolic liquid that smelled like a corpse left out in the sun for weeks. Ava, pale at the sight, screamed and sobbed as she backed into a corner. Tristan looked around the room but didn't see the killer. He rushed over to Kenna's side, kneeling in the expanding pool of blood as he cradled her in his arms. He didn't even care that the blood was ruining his expensive, fancy clothes. His wife needed him and he was there for her.

"Kenna," he cried, smoothing her hair back as tears ran down his cheeks. "You can't die on me. Our daughter needs you." He kissed her forehead. "I need you," he said.

Her eyes fluttered open for a brief moment. Her breathing was ragged and laboured, and it wounded his heart to hear the weakness in his strong wife. "Tristan," she whispered, "bring me the white jar on the third shelf. And Avalina." He rose up to do as she bade without argument or hesitation, sensing that her time was short. The tears welled in the corners of his eyes but refused to fall, blurring the peripherals of his vision. His limbs moved mechanically, responding as though submerged in a pool of water. He could hear a liquid sloshing around inside the jar, smell the fragrant aroma of frankincense, myrrh, and cinnamon seeping from under the lid. Silky liquid ran down the back of his hands as some escaped its canister. He had always wondered what was in this jar and now he knew.

Kenna took the jar from him with shaky hands. More of the oil spilled on her arms and into her lap, but she ignored that, setting it beside her. Ava wracked with sobs as she stepped into her mother's embrace and the two of them cried together for a minute. And then Kenna forced herself up onto her knees. "Kneel, Avalina, and bow your head. This was to be done when you were older, on your thirteenth name day, but it appears Eodran has called me into His Kingdom, the 14th Kingdom." Kenna set the lid aside and dipped a hand into the jar, the blood on her skin mingling with the oil. She took a deep breath and let the oil drizzle over Ava's head. The liquid ran through Ava's red ringlets and dripped down her cheeks and along the back of her neck.

And then Kenna began speaking in the language of the 14th Kingdom, in words rarely heard by human ears, as she anointed her daughter and bestowed blessings of strength, courage, and honor upon her. When she was finished, Kenna fell to the ground and her breathing grew even more shallow than before. Her face was pale, bereft of color. She smiled at her daughter.

"You are destined for great deeds, my child. May Eodran's Spirit fill you and guide you in times of need, give you strength when you have none left, and light your way even though the path may be in darkness. I love you."

Tristan moved forward, taking Kenna in his arms. Her eyelids fluttered and her body trembled from the effort of breathing. Her lips were moving, yet he could hear no sound. He leaned close, placing his ear to her lips, and heard her final words, softly spoken. "Take care of her. Our Avalina. I love--"

She fell limp in his arms, and her head rolled back. His daughter cried even harder, and Tristan felt the life depart from Kenna's body. He had no idea how long he sat there, holding the lifeless body with tears streaming down his face, but he realized that his daughter was hugging him and trying to comfort him. The tears on her face dried already, her green eyes searching his as she placed a tiny hand on his cheek. She needed him. And he realized that he needed her just as much. Perhaps more.

"I'll take care of her," he whispered to Kenna, "and raise a daughter that you would be proud of. She'll be strong, just like you always were." Tristan eased Kenna to the ground and took Ava in his arms.

"Avalina," he said as he knelt down and looked into her eyes with a sad smile, handing her two things. "This book is yours now. It will guide your steps like it did for your mother. And this dagger will protect you as you grow stronger and battle with the darkness.. Do not be afraid, for Eodran is with you and will protect you wherever you go. Help me dig a hole tonight, dear one, and tomorrow I'll teach you to pray like your mother did."

CHAPTER ONE
Monsters and Spies

She crouched low to the ground, feeling the warmth radiate off the sand as she followed the prints left by her quarry. As she crested the dune, she knew this trail would lead one of them to their death. The wind hadn't done enough to cover its path, meaning she was close. Her emerald eyes studied the tracks as she hurried along, deciphering clues about her prey. The prints were getting closer together, a sign that it was running out of energy. It would have to rest soon, most likely stopping near a source of flowing water. There was only one place in the area where that could be found. She smiled, breaking into a light jog as she headed toward the river. Her hunt was close to its end. She would be the bringer of death to this beast, for she was a famous monster huntress, just like her father.

Sand blazed against the soles of her feet with every soft step, as the grains wiggled their way between her toes. She wiped a trail of sweat off her cheek with a dusty hand, leaving a smear of dirt upon her tanned face that begged to be scratched. The discomfort would have to be tolerated, though, because she was close now. She knew this land well, having lived in the area since she was four. The monster was at a disadvantage because she had stalked and hunted and roamed throughout the area for nine years. Her hand reached down to grip the hilt of her sword and she took cover behind a large boulder. The pond was on the other side and, if her deduction was accurate, so was her target.

It was her first time hunting a black-tailed warg, the most ferocious predator within fifty miles of Tirgoth. Her father had killed one last month, bringing home its massive pelt as a trophy. The black-tailed warg were extremely rare around their village, but she was a skilled hunter and tracker. Just like her father. She knew that the bigger and meaner the monster, the better the prize at the end of the hunt. This would become the crown jewel in her collection so far.

She poked her head around the edge of the stone. Her prey was bent over the small river, taking a sip of the cool water. A thick black stripe, the distinguishing mark of the monster, ran through its matted, sand-coated, gray fur. The monster was massive, likely three heads taller than her father. Pale yellow eyes looked around, alert and afraid. Black lips were pulled back in a low snarl that revealed fangs as long as her arm. It was trapped now. Ava slowly drew her blade from its sheath. Tension fled from her body with every breath she took, as she sought the calm of the warrior within herself. She silently prayed to Eodran that the the bright sun would not reflect off the blade and tip off the beast. She tip-toed through the sand in a crouch and closed the distance with practiced stealth. And then the monster lifted its head and sniffed the air. It tensed and showed signs of wanting to flee.

The warg spun around. She raised her sword to strike it with a lethal blow. Fear danced in its yellow eyes, and it cowered backward. Ava brought her blade down, driving it deep into the sand. The warg tumbled backwards into the calm shallows of the pond. It resurfaced, spitting water from its mouth and gasping for air, as she pulled her sword from the sand.

"Why am I always the monster when we play monster hunter?" asked a young boy, as he swam toward the river bank.

"Because," the girl said, "my father is a monster hunter and yours isn't." She turned away, the evening sunlight reflecting brilliant hues of pinks and reds off her fiery hair. The boy pulled himself out of the water and shook himself off like a dog, spraying Ava.

"I'm tired of running away, hiding, and dying, Ava," he complained. He attempted to smooth his sandy blonde hair. "I want excitement and adventure for a change. Next time, I get to be the hunter."

Ava scowled at the boy, sighing. "Fine, Edgar. But you make a much better monster."

Edgar laughed and snatched the wooden sword from her hands. He ran back toward the village while challenging her to try and catch him. She dug her toes deep into the sand, crouching low to the ground before taking off into a sprint. The distance between them closed. Her lungs ached as she gasped for air, but she pressed on, determined to catch Edgar. He was only a few strides ahead now. She could almost reach out and grab his shoulder. She matched his rhythm while elongating her own stride, mentally preparing to drive him to the ground with a tackle. Sensing her plan, Edgar cut north, away from their village and toward the mountains. A joyful giggle burst from her and she gave chase.

They both slowed a bit yet neither gave up. She was further behind him now, having lost ground when her feet slipped in the sand with the sudden changes in direction. His zigging and zagging, and sureness on his feet as he shifted his path ahead of her, was one of the reasons he made the better monster. The wind felt refreshing as it rushed over her skin, providing a temporary relief from the afternoon sun. Her hair waved and danced in the breeze. The grains of sand beneath her feet disappeared, replaced by rocky dirt and poky patches of brown grass. She let out a hearty laugh and leaped with all her might, tackling Edgar to the ground. They rolled along the dirt, a cloud of dust forming in their wake as each one tried to wrest the wooden sword from the other's grip. Arms and legs tangled together as they struggled to gain mastery of the weapon. Their skin grew slick with sweat and became coated in dirt, making it harder keep a firm grip. A sharp stab of pain bit into Ava's thumb from a small splinter but she ignored the sensation and redoubled her effort to win the battle over her blade. Both of them were laughing gaily by the time Ava pulled it free from Edgar's hands.

Their merriment was cut short by a deep grumble. It sounded distant but the noise was so out of place in the area that it made them both pause. Ava raised a hand, signaling for silence while turning toward the sound. The grumble repeated a few moments later, answered by a higher-pitched whistling sound. Ava slipped a knife from her belt, handing it to Edgar before unsheathing another knife for herself. She motioned for Edgar to follow as she crept toward the noises.

They ducked behind a large rock. They stood still for a moment, not breathing as they listened for a change in the noise. She stood in silence, motionless, eyes closed, taking in the pattern of the sounds. Hearing nothing out of the ordinary, Ava peeked around the edge. "Goblins," she whispered to Edgar. "Two of them are asleep in the clearing. They must be a scouting party."

"Scouting what?"

"I bet they are checking out the village, to see if we're undefended now that father and his men are gone on a mission. We can't let them report back, or we'll have the whole horde swarming down on us before dawn breaks."

"But how are we supposed to keep them from telling the other goblins?"

"I guess we'll just have to kill them," Ava said, hoping her voice didn't carry any of the fear and uncertainty she felt welling up inside her.

"I've never killed a monster before," Edgar whispered back. "What if I miss, and it claws my eyes out or rips my heart from my chest?"

"It is sleeping. It'll be dead before it knows we're attacking. We have no choice, Edgar. The elders need to be warned, but they will never believe us without proof."

"But they are alive, Ava," Edgar said. She could see he was wrestling with the morality of the task. It was an issue she struggled with as well, even though she had been training to become a hunter of monsters for her entire life. Ava knew she had to act fearless, to be firm in her conviction like a member of the Order of the Light, if they were to protect the village. Any sign of weakness and the goblins could escape to raise the alarm. If that happened, everyone in Tirgoth would be in danger so they needed to do this in order to save more lives. Edgar needed to arrive at that same conclusion, and fast, otherwise the goblins could wake and present even greater danger to themselves and the village.

"So are silvertails, but that doesn't stop us from catching and cooking them for food. This isn't much different. You take the left one and I'll take out the one on the right." Edgar numbly nodded his agreement and the matter was settled. A chill ran down Ava's spine, she wasn't sure that it was because of the cool breeze.

Ava motioned for Edgar to circle around the rock. She clutched her knife in her hand and snuck toward the sleeping goblins. As she moved she recited a prayer she heard her father use before. "Eodran, ruler of the 14th Kingdom and Father to us all, I ask that you would guide my blade and let it strike true. Lead me as I encounter this trial before me, and guide me to safety. Amen." A warm calm washed over her as she ended the prayer and turned her focus toward the monsters in front of her.

The goblins were as hideous and disfigured as she imagined every time her father described them. Their skin was black as obsidian and looked like rough, bumpy leather that had cured in the sun for too long. Their joints were knobby and stuck out at angles that looked painful. Thick, pointy ears stretched above the crown of their heads and a long, crooked nose jutted from their face. The goblin nostrils seemed to be wide enough to fit her hand inside. She watched one snoring, its mouth open to expose the rows of small, sharp teeth that could tear the flesh off a man with ease. Small patches of wispy yellow hair were matted down atop their heads, failing to conceal the pattern baldness common among their species.

Things were going as planned. She was over halfway to her goblin, and she knew Edgar should be close to his by now. Her father would be proud that she used her wits to win in her first true monster encounter. She imagined his warm embrace, the rapt attention as he listened to her recount the tale and the proud look in his eye as he promised to take her as an apprentice on his next hunt.

A sharp cry of surprise shattered her thoughts and froze her in place. Ava glanced back to see Edgar sprawled on the ground. He had tripped over something and cried out. Two pairs of beady black eyes flashed open and Ava recoiled from their gaze. The larger of the goblins let out a shrill screech and grabbed its weapon. It was slow getting to its feet, but it stood as tall as Ava. The other goblin scrambled to its feet immediately, standing about chest-height. She watched it process the ambush before turning and running away. Ava begrudgingly let it escape. She was too far away to chase after it, and she still had the large goblin to concern herself with.

She looked back in time to see the remaining goblin approach her. She stepped to her left, avoiding the swipe of its black, claw-like nails. She thrust with her knife and was rewarded by scoring a shallow cut on its arm. It bounded back a few paces and crouched low to the ground, snarling at her. It drew a short, curved sword made from bleached bone and cackled at her as it advanced.

She stood her ground as it approached. Panic and fear mixed with the excitement and adrenaline of the moment. The goblin gripped the smooth bone hilt of its sword in both hands and raised it for a powerful overhead cut. Ava seized the window of opportunity and threw her knife at the exposed body of the goblin. She missed her mark and the blade grazed along its side. A small trickle of black blood welled on the surface of its skin but the goblin seemed unfazed by the cut. Ava jumped back as its sword came down, evading the attack. She drew her wooden sword, aware that it was going to prove an ineffective weapon against the goblin's bone blade, and stood ready for its next move.

The next strike came quickly. The goblin brought its sword in an upward arc across its body. Ava blocked the sword mid-swing with her own, halting it as bone clashed with hard oak. They tested their might against each other and found each other as equal in strength as they were in size. Ava's arms shook from the strain, her arms still not used to meeting such strong resistance. This goblin was far stronger than Edgar. Seeing its opening, the goblin flung some loose dirt in her face. Their swords unlocked, and Ava staggered back, rubbing her eyes with her left hand. The monster strode forward, thrusting its sword while she was blinded. Before the sword could find its mark she was tackled to the ground by Edgar.

They landed hard on the grass below, caught in a tangle of arms and legs. Ava shoved him off with her free arm, bringing the wooden sword up in time to catch another swing. The goblin pressed its sword down hard, adding its weight to the effort. Ava angled her sword as it inched closer to her body. She strained to keep the blade from reaching her, and her arms quivered. She could feel the wood of her sword cracking beneath the pressure and knew it was a matter of time before her weapon broke in two. Edgar was back on his feet and pushed the goblin aside, sending the monster tumbling to the ground. He had his dagger in one trembling hand, staring down the monster. Ava scrambled back to her feet and shifted in front of Edgar as the beast rose again.

Edgar winced as the blades clashed mid-strike again, but this time the impact shattered both blades. She had expected her own to break, but the destruction of the goblin blade took her by surprise. Ava sidestepped a thrust from its fractured weapon and punched the goblin with all her might. She could feel the bone of its nose break under the impact and the monster staggered, dazed and dripping with blood as dark as its evil heart. Ava turned and swiped the knife free from Edgar's hand and attacked the monster with a swift slash that sliced the goblin open from shoulder to abdomen. Thick, black blood oozed from the wound as the monster staggered backward, clutching the gash with both clawed hands. She thrust the knife into its throat, cutting short its wail of pain. The rotten egg scent of sulfur filled the air from the corpse and made Ava nauseous. Edgar sat down on a fallen log, pale with fear. She turned away as he retched in the grass.

"We can't rest now, Edgar," Ava snapped as she wiped her blade clean on the grass. "We've got to get back and warn the village. One escaped, which means we might have an army of goblins besieging the village by nightfall."

Ava retrieved a token from the dead goblin's belongings and another from the abandoned pile of stuff belonging to Edgar's escaped goblin. The latter had left behind a bag made of thick hide and tied with a thick cord. She opened the bag, reached inside, and squeezed her eyes shut as her hand grazed something wet and gooey. She dumped the contents out and crinkled her nose at the gelatinous glob radiating on the grass. Did goblins really eat that? Gross. She snagged a brass helmet from the midst of the goo and wiped it on the ground. The relics would be proof of the encounter for the village elders and her father. She ran back toward the village with Edgar trailing behind.

CHAPTER TWO
The Council of Elders

In Ava's mind there was only one place they could go to submit their case since her father was gone: the Council of Elders. There were always five men on the council, and they were the ones who ruled over Tirgoth's daily affairs. The main requirement, apart from being born a male, was the ability to cast magic, and so anyone born with even a hint of magical talent spent years learning laws and rituals of magic so they could one day join the Council of Elders in Tirgoth. When one of the five died another from the village was elected to take their place.

Nothing exciting ever really seemed to happen in Tirgoth, at least not since they had appointed Ava's father, Tristan, as honorary protector of the village. That title had been bestowed during a time of despair. That was when the invasion of monsters appeared to be imminent and the village lived in constant fear of monster attacks during the day and the night. They had erected makeshift walls, formed from a mixture of mud and clay and standing about waist-high, on the outskirts of the village, but it hardly seemed to help keep the monsters at bay. Ava's father hand-selected and trained a small band of men and women who were willing to fight back and they had eliminated all nearby threats and brought about almost six years of relative peace in Tirgoth. After the defeat of the monster threat, the Order of Light also gained a foothold in Tirgoth, a small sect of men and women who were preaching how monsters are creatures of Darkness to be executed without exception.

The years of peace for Tirgoth appeared to be at an end, thanks to those goblins. Ava knew that the elders needed to be informed and involved whenever there was a major decision about the village. If they thought sporadic droughts and wind-damaged huts were important enough to listen to and respond to, then she assumed they would certainly be swift in executing some manner of defense after hearing her story. Goblin invasions were far more serious than damaged huts.

They approached the Council of Elders. The five men were seated in the center of the village on stumps and stones indented and worn from years of overuse. The elders formed a half-circle and were in the middle of a heated debate when the children approached.

"The time has come for the village's funds to go toward something more productive," one of the elders said.

"Agreed, there hasn't been a genuine monster threat to the village in years," the head elder replied.

"But what if those monsters return once we disband those protectors?" another chimed in. Ava coughed but none of them looked her way.

"Nonsense," the first elder said, "Tristan and his men have been going on much longer expeditions for a year now. Clearly they have to travel a long way to encounter any sort of monsters. He's clearing the borders for places other than Tirgoth, mark my words. I bet he's being paid by them, as well, and hoarding gold for himself."

"Do you remember what it was like, all those years ago?" an elder in blue said, standing up. "Back before Tristan was here, things were terrible. Tirgoth was nearly wiped off the map before he arrived. Even if he is pulling in double pay somewhere, I say he's earned it ten times over. Without him, we would not be here arguing over the village's funds."

The head elder opened his mouth to respond and then stopped, his gaze focusing on Ava and Edgar. Silence hovered in the air. Ava bit her lip, not knowing what to say. They wanted to stop having her father defend the village? Well, she would change that stance when they heard about her goblin encounter.

"What are you doing here?" the elder in red said, his face brightening to match his robes.

"I have something that you need to hear," Ava answered.

"It can wait, child," the head elder said. "We are in the middle of discussing important village business. Send a formal request to meet the council and we'll hear your tale." The elders stared at her with arms crossed. Ava sighed and took a step back. But no, they were wrong. They needed to hear this and to hear it now. They couldn't wait days or even hours. It had to be now.

"You don't understand. We're going to be under attack." She held her breath, waiting for them to dismiss her again. The head elder sighed and waved her forward.

"You can't be serious," the one in red snapped. "She's a child. Send her home and tell her father to make sure she doesn't intrude on council business again."

"Silence, Bartz. Even a child's tale can hold merit for those who care to listen. Speak, child, and be quick about it."

Ava took a deep breath and recounted the events of their day. At the end of her tale she stepped toward the five elders, and placed two goblin trinkets in front of them as concrete evidence of her story. She stepped back beside

Edgar and waited expectantly for the swift order to rally the defenses of the village.

The man in the center of the half-circle of elders raised a gnarled finger in the air. All eyes turned to him, awaiting his words. He was dressed in a robe of four colors: red, blue, green, and yellow. There was no pattern to the way the colors merged within the fabric, and it lent the clothing a chaotic appearance. Ava had never understood why the head elder would wear such silly clothing. The other four wore plain robes that bore one of the colors found on the head elder's robe. Ava always wondered if the elder's robe was really made from patches of the other four robes that were sewn together into one garment. But she had never been able to get close enough to look for the stitching to prove or disprove her theory.

Ava fidgeted while they watched the elder inspect the trinkets. The torch light gleamed as it was reflected off the grimy brass of the goblin horn she stole from the first goblin. Runes from an ancient tongue were chiseled into the bone mouthpiece and it felt like the elder spent ages studying those characters, tracing them over and over again with his finger. Ava exhaled with relief when he set it aside, hoping to hear his judgment, but he picked up the second trophy instead.

She knew there could be no doubt that this one belonged to a goblin. The brass helmet was poorly forged, held together in places with rusting bolts, and its shape could only fit upon a goblin's head. Most of their helmets had slits for their ears, but this one was designed to provide an armored cover for the delicate goblin ears. Ava realized how was lucky it was that she caught these goblins sleeping, otherwise her battle would have been against a fully armored goblin, armed with a wooden sword and a small knife. Her mind wandered while the elder observed the helmet, and she found herself wondering if the goblin armies had mounted knights like humans did and, if so, what they rode into battle. Surely a horse was too large and a pony was more likely to be prey than a mount. Maybe they rode on the backs of tigers or small bears? The thought of facing a goblin atop a great black bear gave her chills and she banished the thought from her mind.

The head elder licked his cracked lips and looked up at Ava and Edgar, beckoning them to move into the center of the circle. Ava was disappointed to note, as she knelt in front of him, that his robe was not made from patches of other robes but was expertly woven into that mesmerizing pattern of colors. He spoke in a raspy voice, saying, "Children, I have considered your story with great care. While these appear to be authentic goblin possessions, your tale is too far-fetched for me to believe."

"But we did fight the goblins," Edgar insisted. "Well, Ava really did the fighting, but we're telling you true. She has scrapes to prove it."

"Edgar," the elder answered with a small smile, "We all know how rough you and Ava get when playing your imaginary games. Would your mother believe such a tale?"

"Well," Edgar began, frowning at his feet, but the head elder cut him off by asking for silence. The tips of Edgar's ears turned red and blotchy spots broke out on his cheeks.

"And Ava, what would your father make of these claims?"

"He'd believe me," she answered without hesitation, "and you're just a bunch of old fools if you do not! The Order of Light would believe me. Maybe I should go to them, instead."

Murmurs of surprise rose from the others, but they were silenced by the head elder. "Old we may be, but fools we are not. Ava, there hasn't been a goblin sighted in these parts for nearly six years. Your own father was the one who led the expedition that purged them, along with all other monsters, from the surrounding areas. It is on that basis that we are forced to dismiss your story as a fabrication and you will find that all others in this village will agree with our perspective on the matter. Now tell me true, child, you found these when you were playing in your father's room, yes?"

"I took them off the goblin that I killed," Ava shouted. She rose to her feet and clenched her hands into fists at her sides. "You need to assemble the guard, post sentries along the outskirts of the village, and fortify the perimeter. They are coming."

"Enough," the head elder said. He shot her a sad look. "You have worn my patience with these half-truths. Go back to your homes and do not mention goblins again unless it is to confess the falseness of this story."

Ava spun on her heels and stormed away from the gathered elders. She murmured under her breath about how foolish and old they were. She wished her father was there to help convince them. He would believe her, wouldn't he? As much as she wanted to believe that he would, she knew he would still voice his own doubts. He would have offered some of the same criticisms as the elders. The peacetime had grown too long around the village and they were growing complacent in their attitudes towards the monsters. But they were all wrong. The elders would have believed the tale if it had been an adult or someone within their inner circle bringing it before them. It wasn't her fault that she was only thirteen and a girl and non-magical.

She cut through the village toward the largest of buildings. The thatched roof was covered with a layer of crescent-shaped clay tiles and the walls were reinforced with fresh-mined stones from the mountain and the twin doors were made from hearty oak with strips of iron running horizontally across the surface. Heavy brass rings gleamed in the sunlight and a trickle of incense smoke trailed out of the cracks around the doors. Ava could hear the muffled sounds of a woman speaking inside the building and the occasional chant or cheer that followed. The children pulled the stout door open and slipped inside.

Cinnamon and clove wafted into her nostrils, the initial wave making them both cough. A half dozen heads turned to stare at them and Ava felt the heat rushing to her face. Her bare feet padded across the velvet runner along the stone floor, the softness a welcome sensation. The woman at the front was dressed in ivory robes that trailed behind her, trimmed with gold threads that glimmered in the torchlight. Four men and a woman knelt on the ground at the woman's feet. Ava suspected they were the usual bunch that gathered here, praying for the prophesied scourge to come and sweep the monsters free from the 13 kingdoms.

"Yes, my children?" the old woman asked. Her voice was flat and her gaze froze them to the ground.

"You teach us that all monsters should be eliminated, right?" Ava asked. The woman's mouth turned up in a slight smile.

"Yes, my child. The day will come when the Child of Light will fight back the Darkness, but until that day we must battle the monsters on our own."

"We fought goblins," Edgar blurted out. Ava sighed and made a mental note to talk to this boy about tactfulness.

"Where? When?" the kneeling woman asked. All eyes had turned to the woman at the head of the room, whose expression had not changed.

"We fought two of them not more than an hour ago, off to the north. We caught them sleeping, killing one while the other escaped."

"Ava thinks they are going to lead an invasion," Edgar chimed in.

"Child, what proof have you of this?" the woman asked, folding her arms tight across her chest.

"We had proof, but the Council of Elders took them and didn't give them back."

"And so the Council is preparing for this unexpected invasion?"

"Well, no. They didn't believe me."

"And so you expect me to accomplish what, dear child?"

"You need to rally the village. Get them to build the defenses. To prepare for the goblins to come!"

The woman stood like a statue at the front of the room. The men and woman kneeling before her had their heads upon the stone floor, muttering inaudible prayers. Ava could tell, before the woman spoke again, what the answer was going to be. She couldn't believe how blind adults could be to the dangers surrounding them.

"My brothers and I have no authority to call the village to such an action. And even if we did, my child, we would need more proof than the word of a young one to go off. Now be gone before you waste any more of the time of the Order of Light."

Ava spun on her heels and stormed out of the building, leaving the door flung wide open. Her knuckles were white and a single tear trickled down her cheek.

Edgar caught up to her, matching her stride as he fell in beside her. He wore his disappointment on his face, but his voice masked his frustration. "Maybe they won't come," he said.

"You're as big a fool as they are if you believe that," Ava answered without looking at Edgar.

"But what do we do now? We can't go and meet a goblin horde by ourselves. We should ride after your father and convince him to return. He would know what to do."

"No. He would tell us the same things they did. It is no use trying to convince anyone that the goblins are coming, so we need to do what my father would do if he had seen them."

"What is that?" Edgar asked.

"We're going prepare for battle," Ava said.

Ava and Edgar had the attention of the entire village that night as they took turns patrolling atop the tower. The villagers spoke in whispered hushes as the two of them placed sharpened stakes around Tirgoth's perimeter. Many women brought them dried fruits and meats and one even brought some fresh baked bread. Even Hazel, Ava's neighbor and her usual caretaker when her father was gone, appeared to support her cause by bringing food and warm clothes for the night. But she was also quick to point out that Ava should come inside when she was "done playing at this foolish game." They feasted that night before keeping watch in shifts beneath the stars.

They still had some sympathetic onlookers the second day, but only Hazel brought them food. Instead of smiles and kind words, they received silent frowns and shaking heads. Edgar tried to talk her out of their vigil twice that day. Both times the argument ended in hours of silence between them. But he still stayed with her. Hunger gnawed at them as they lay atop the tower that night and it prevented either of them from getting a restful sleep beneath the clouded night sky.

Ava and Edgar were both weary and irritable by noon on the third day. She stared out into the distance and tried hard to ignore the sight of Edgar walking into his house. She failed miserably. Her blasted peripherals caught every step he took away from the tower and witnessed him disappearing through the doorway into his house. He promised to bring her some food later, but Ava knew that was only an afterthought.

She suspected the real reason he was going home. He didn't believe her conclusion anymore, even though he had been there to see the goblin scouts. And, worst of all, he didn't think what she was doing was important or would make a difference. His words from this morning echoed in her mind, the claims that he was tired of taking orders from a silly girl with a wooden sword. She knew the whole village thought that by now; the elders, Hazel, the villagers passing by beneath her, even the Order of Light. And now Edgar had said as much. If the rest of them weren't saying it in her presence they were whispering it when she wasn't around.

Ava missed her father and tried to think about what he would do in her place. She knew it had been like this for him in the beginning.

They all believed his stories when they moved eight years ago, and they all thought it was tragic how his wife died during a monster attack, but none of them could be convinced that the monsters were a threat to them. He had told her, once, about that first week in Tirgoth. She thought back to his tale now, struggling to remember the details.

He told her it had been the thought of her safety that kept him going in the face of the criticism. He confessed that he would have found a way back to his post atop the tower if they had succeeded in removing him against his will. It was his love for her that allowed him to endure the long nights. Ava just needed to figure out whose love would keep her here. The head elder and the rest of the five didn't deserve her love. They had a chance to believe her and chose to ignore the facts. Her neighbor, Hazel, always had been kind to her and even gave her sweets sometimes. She watched over Ava when her father was gone, protecting her even though Ava didn't really need that protection. It was funny, when she considered it, that Hazel was supposed to be protecting Ava when her father was gone. But here she was protecting Hazel in the face of all this criticism. Ava didn't think she deserved to die, but she didn't love Hazel's constant chiding about her father's love life and the need for a sensible woman around the house to raise her the right way. Or her idea that Ava should be brought up as a "proper lady". No, she didn't love her enough to endure the long nights on Hazel's behalf.

Edgar's face came to mind, unbidden. She brushed that crazy notion aside and thought about some of the other people she knew in the village. Edgar kept looking like the better choice compared to the rest of them. It was obvious that he loved her. Even at thirteen Ava knew he was smitten. But to her, he was still the boy that had to be the monster because he wasn't a good hunter. It was his fault that she was up here, after all, because he fell down and let his goblin escape.

Her anger increased the more she thought about that last point. It was entirely his fault that she was suffering alone atop this tower. And he had the nerve to go run home and eat a hot meal and take a nap in his bed and play with his brothers. Ava picked up a rock and threw it as hard as she could. It kicked up a little dust as it slid along the road and the exertion from throwing it made Ava feel better so she threw another. And one more, chucking it as hard as she could into the distance.

Then she noticed the two clouds of dust stirring from the ground, one in the west and the other to the north. The smaller cloud was coming from the desert in the west and was much closer to Tirgoth. The one to the north, moving down a mountain, was large enough to worry her. She hadn't ever seen an army marching but she had heard enough stories to understand that there were a lot of people coming from that direction. Or a lot of goblins.

CHAPTER THREE
Preparations for War

Ava hurried down the tower as fast as she could. As she moved, she debated whether she should wake Edgar first or tell the elders. They needed to know and would know what to do to get ready and they needed to be told as soon as possible. But she didn't want to talk to them alone. It had been only a few days since they rejected her story of the goblin encounter outright and she was still upset about that. If she went alone, they might do it again, and then everyone would get hurt. But Edgar had also abandoned her and left her to keep watch alone, so he didn't really deserve to help spread the news. By the time her feet hit the ground she had made up her mind. She would get Edgar first, even if he was the clumsy boy that caused this trouble in the first place.

The residents of Tirgoth were going about their daily lives as though there wasn't a clear threat about to descend upon them. She passed by the rickety old carts with hawkers selling their wares, bronze-skinned farmhands tilling the ground in desperate attempts to get something to grow, dark-skinned young women balancing buckets of water on either end of a wooden pole; Ava couldn't believe they were so blind to the danger around them. Had they grown so complacent in the years since her father drove off the monsters? Were the old spinsters baking fresh bread in the hopes of offering the monsters a welcoming feast? Grownups were so blind! An invasion was descending upon them! Their priority should be on preparations to meet the enemy force, or else all those fields would be torn apart by the goblins, and the bakeries and market carts would be burned to the ground.

Ava did her best to put those thoughts out of her mind. She rounded a corner on the dirt path. Edgar's house was up ahead, a shabby two-story wood house encircled by a rotting fence. It was one of the many houses with the scent of baked goods pouring into the air through an open window. Any other day, Ava would succumb to her grumbling stomach and beg for a slice of hot bread slathered in fresh-churned butter and dripping with warm honey. But she had more important matters to attend to. She heard Edgar's snoring as soon as she entered his house. It was a sound that would have infuriated her if she wasn't in such a hurry to tell the elders what she saw. Every minute she wasted on this impossibly clumsy boy could be the difference between life and death for them all.

Edgar was sprawled out in his bed at the back of the house, arms and legs tangled in a heavy wool blanket. A small clay cup of water was on the table beside the bed. Ava tiptoed closer, formulating in her mind an unpleasant wake-up call for Edgar. She grabbed the cup and dipped a pinky in to test the water's temperature. She was pleased to discover that it was still quite cold with tiny shavings of ice still circulating along the top. He would be mad, of course, but he deserved at least this much as a punishment for deserting her during the watch.

Ava emptied the contents of the cup onto his face. The cold liquid splattered on his skin and soaked his bed and shirt as well. Edgar tried to jump to his feet but his arms and legs were entwined in the blanket. His limbs flailed around as he crashed onto the floor. Ava laughed at him and set the cup back on the table while he scrambled out of his blanket.

"What'd you do that for?" Edgar snapped as he wiped water from his eyes with the first hand he untangled from the blankets.

"You need to come with me," Ava said as she grabbed his arm. She tried to drag him along but Edgar wouldn't budge. While she was faster than him, he was still the stronger of the two.

"I can't keep patrolling with you, Ava," Edgar said. "Mother has forbidden it."

"I don't want you to come keep watch."

"I said... wait, what?"

"I need you to come with me to talk to the elders again."

"They already said no. If that is all you wanted I'm going back to bed." Edgar sat down upon his mattress and started wringing the water from his blanket.

Ava sighed and reminded herself that Edgar didn't know about the approaching horde yet, just like the rest of the villagers. "I saw something. Two somethings, actually, and they are coming this way. The elders need to know so we can be ready to meet whatever is coming, friend or foe."

"You're certain?" he asked while scratching his damp head. A few droplets of water sloshed onto her forehead but she ignored them.

"I wouldn't be wasting my time with you if I wasn't. Now come on," she said, turning to walk out of his house. Edgar called for her to wait up just as she stepped outside. A hint of a smile crept on her face and she slowed down a little so he could catch up. It seemed right to have him at her side once more.

All five of the elders stopped their discussions and frowned when they noticed Ava and Edgar approaching them. Two of frowns deepened into scowls when the children stepped into the center of their half-circle. It was not the reception Ava hoped to receive but it was the one she expected. Maybe this was even a warmer welcome than she had expected from these fuddy old men. Suddenly she was thankful she had decided to bring Edgar along.

"Let me guess," one of the younger elders, Damien, called out, "you have some new relic to show us that you dug up somewhere? In your father's basement, perhaps? Or maybe this one came from under his bed?" A few light chuckles trailed on the heels of those comments but Damien folded his arms across his chest and glared at her. The elders still thought she was making things up, like in the stories where Analise told her parents that a griguar was under her bed. But while Analise finally told the truth the last time and no one believed her, Ava had been telling the truth the whole time but the adults wouldn't listen. Maybe these elders would become a story that kids would tell to remind adults to listen to their children more often.

Ava answered his scowl with a forced smile, wishing she could make his thick robe catch on fire. He wouldn't talk to her that way if she was older, or a boy. Or if she could do magic like they could. "We're going to be under attack before sunset," she said, turning her focus to the head elder.

"Where is your proof, child," he asked her, wheezing as he struggled to fight back a hacking cough.

"If you come up onto the tower I could show you," she answered. "There are signs of two different groups advancing toward town. One of them seems like it should be a small group and the other looks like an army marching."

"You have both seen this?"

Ava looked down at her feet, shifting uncomfortably under his gaze. She raised her head and brushed her red curls aside with a hand. She had to admit the truth of the matter. It was a punishable offense to lie to an elder and all the children knew that the elder's magic was able to detect lies.

"Aye, we both saw it," Edgar answered. Ava blinked. She was shocked to hear Edgar backing up her story. Ava had never heard him lie to an adult before, much less the circle of elders. The head elder looked at Edgar and studied him with a critical eye. Ava bit her lip as she imagined the silent incantations the elder must be performing to discern the truth. He would see right through Edgar's lie, and that would doom them both. But to Ava's surprise he nodded, looking at the four elders gathered around him.

"We will send someone up with these children to see if their story is true. If there are strangers approaching, monsters or otherwise, we would be wise to be prepared to meet them."

Ava watched the flurry of activity going on in the village with a smile on her face. She could picture the look of disbelief that must have been on the faces of a few of the elders when they heard confirmation of her story from Damien. Within minutes the five elders had spread throughout the village. Men, women, and children rushed throughout the village to complete the tasks being assigned to them. The elders even convinced a few of the devoted from the Order of Light to help prepare the village. Ava hadn't seen any of the elders move so fast.

As the forces of Tirgoth gathered together, Ava thought they formed an interesting line of defense: more than half of the men were wielding pitchforks and scythes rather than swords or spears. A few tried to piece together makeshift armor, throwing on rusty patches of iron to protect a shoulder or to cover a leg. Ava was pretty sure she saw at least one man wearing a tin pot on his head but no one else seemed to think the sight was amusing. A real army descending upon the village would laugh at the sight of them and brush aside the possibility of real resistance. Would a goblin army see the humor in this line of defense or would they be discouraged by even a hodgepodge force like this? Ava hoped to find out when she was standing on the front line of the battle, brandishing one of her father's swords in her hands as the first wave rode into town.

She had been busy ever since finally convincing the elders of the danger. Ava and Edgar went to her house in order to get suited for the upcoming battle. Her house was identical to many of the others in the village. It was formed from a combination of wood and clay with a thatched grass roof. To an outsider, it would be impossible to distinguish who lived in each house, but Ava had lived here for nearly eight years now and, to her, there was no other house exactly like hers. She couldn't even remember where they had lived before moving to the village of Tirgoth because she had been too young. As she got closer, she could see deep gashes in the sides of the building, scars from her imagined duals with hordes of monsters from her father's stories. She had been lashed when her father realized she had dulled the blade of his favorite sword by hacking into the clay bricks and wooden posts. He had forced her to spend hours sharpening and polishing the steel blade until he deemed it restored to its original condition. It was a lesson she never forgot and the bricks served as a daily reminder to take more care when she snuck out with her father's weapons. She hadn't been caught since. Nor had she treated them so recklessly.

She raided every room of their house in search of armor that mostly fit her. She had on a layer of black leather armor, complete with greaves for her legs that were a little too long. She tried to fit into a suit of plate mail but it was far too heavy for her to stand without assistance. Edgar laughed for a long time before helping her back onto her feet. His laughter died quickly once she smacked him upside the head. Ava settled for a coat of chain mail instead which was heavy, but still allowed her to move enough to fight. None of her father's gauntlets fit her small hands, but she found some leather gloves that were secure enough to work once she stuffed them with old rags. She finished off the armor with a half helm of steel that nearly covered her eyes even with a cloth bundled in the top. She wore a thick hide belt around her waist with a slender dagger sheathed on her right side and a long sword on her left. The tip of the sword dragged along the ground as she walked but she didn't plan on that weapon remaining in its sheath for long once the battle began. A short bow was slung over her shoulder, accompanied by a small quiver of arrows. She was no markswoman with a bow, but she was determined to try and take a few goblins down before they reached the village.

She had offered to arm Edgar in a similar manner but he had opted instead for an old set of leather training armor with a leather helm. He had a short sword strapped to his back and a recurve bow in his hands. Ava knew that he was clumsy and slow with the sword but he was a decent marksman with a bow. Far better than she was, although she would never confess that in range of his hearing. He had made shots that she could only marvel at and could usually duplicate any impressive shot. She made sure he had plenty of arrows to fire because she knew each one was likely to claim the life of a goblin.

Ava wove her way through the line of villagers, wanting to get a close look at the approaching figures. The smaller group had been making good time. They emerged from the desert an hour before Ava anticipated. She could see the outlines of men atop horses as they neared the village but they were still too far to be recognizable and the waning sun cast them as dark figures on the horizon. Hushed whispers buzzed through the air as everyone weighed in with an opinion on their identities, ranging from Ava's father to a dispatch from the King's army to disguised lizardmen, known as Drakhari. She squinted, straining her eyes to try and see who these men were and was rewarded by being the first to identify them. Ava let out a squeal of delight and ran along the road to greet them. Her father returned home in time to fight the goblins with her!

His face was haggard and gaunt and his clothes were rent in a dozen places. He had an empty sheath on his back and many of his weapons had been chipped or cracked over the course of his adventure. He had a curved horn, coated with dried blood, strapped to the saddle of his horse. Ava wondered which monster he vanquished to earn that new trophy. She couldn't wait to get home and hear him tell her all about it, but she knew that he needed to hear her adventure first. There would be time for storytelling later that night once the goblin invasion had been repelled.

He pulled her up into the saddle with him and took in her appearance with a curious stare. It was unusual attire, even for her, and he was almost certain to guess there was a story to accompany her appearance. But even that could wait. She wrapped her arms around his torso and hugged him tight. For a few moments neither one said a word, choosing to enjoy the reunion. Finally he broke the silence and spoke in a quiet voice.

"Avalina, why in Eodran's name are you dressed for war?"

"Father," she answered, "you'll never believe what happened. Edgar and I found a goblin patrol and I killed one of them, but one got away and now there is a horde descending down upon the village."

"Goblins? Near the village? There hasn't been a goblin sighting in years. We drove them off for good and made sure they knew the consequences of returning to disturb Tirgoth."

"That is what the elders said but I proved them wrong. I stood watch, just like you did when we first came here, and I showed them proof of their incursion. The goblins should be here before sundown."

Her father uttered a curse under his breath and urged his horse into a gallop. The villagers scattered as Ava and her father raced past. She was pleased to see that he was riding straight to their house. He believed her! Of course she always knew he would, but it was nice to have something turn out as it should for a change.

Her father dismounted outside of their house, pausing only to lend a hand to Ava so she could dismount as well. She was pretty certain she would have fallen without his help, encumbered as she was by the oversized armor. He limped as he crossed the threshold of the doorway, and then paused to hold it open for her. The stress from his job had added lines to his face that made him appear much older than his thirty seven years. Flecks of white peppered his short beard and his eyes were as gray as the steel of his sword. His face masked all expression as he watched her approach and he stepped aside to let Ava into the house. He had more weapons strapped to his body then he usually wore; most days he had a sword on his back and a pair of long knives in his belt. Today his armament included a bow and two quivers of arrows, a dozen short daggers concealed in various places, a spiked mace, a hand ax, two swords and a coil of rope. On most men this would look ridiculous, but not on her father. He looked menacing, like he was ready to wage a one-man war. In a way, that was exactly what he had just done on his hunt. And what he was about to do again tonight with the goblin horde. He stripped off the layers of battle-worn clothing as soon as he stepped in the door. Ava noticed there were large tears in the armor underneath. She gasped when she saw a giant gash in his side. He stopped and looked at her with a tired smile.

"The hrundtboar put up a mighty battle, but no monster is a match for your father. You'll enjoy hearing the tale once we ward off these goblins. And it sounds like you have a tale to tell to rival it."

"Don't you want to go on the tower and see proof that there are goblins coming?"

"I've heard and seen all the proof I need with you," he answered as he wrapped some linen over his wound and deftly tied it with one hand. "How long before they will arrive?"

"They were a little farther from here than you were when I saw them. And they were going slower. There are probably a few eager ones ahead of the main group and I think we'd see those within the hour. The rest of them shortly after."

"Good. Let's prepare a surprise for them." He walked over to the table and picked up a small bundle of mauve-colored cloth. "This is for you, Avalina," he said as he handed the bundle to her. "I was going to wait until you were a little older but it seems wise to give it to you now."

She bit her lip and reached for the bundle. She could feel something hard and heavy inside. The shape and weight seemed somewhat familiar. Ava peeled away the layers of fabric and squealed in delight at the treasure in her possession. She grasped the hilt of the sword and could feel the symbols engraved in the leather pressing into her skin. The sheath was made of the same tanned leather as the hilt. The guard was formed from polished bronze that reflected the sunlight peeking through the windows. She pulled the sword free, a soft ringing sound filling the air as the weapon slid free from the leather. She recognized some of the ancient glyphs engraved along the length of the steel blade. Her father had shown her the same symbols of strength, victory, and protection on some of his own swords. The other side contained a single glyph. She knew from her father's swords that it would be the name of the blade so that the foes might know the means of their demise. But she didn't recognize this symbol.

"This sword belongs to you now, Avalina," her father said. He brushed a strand of her red hair aside with a calloused hand. "Do you remember what I taught you about the tenets of a swordsman?"

"Yes, Father," she replied, sighing.

"Let's hear them."

"A swordsman is a weapon unto himself, the sword is merely a tool. A swordsman uses his sword to ward evil, never to cause injustice. A swordsman keeps... but father, I'm not a swordsman. I'm a swordswoman!"

His hearty laugh in response warmed Ava more than any fire in a hearth and soon they were both laughing without control. Her father wiped tears from his eyes as he regained a serious demeanor. "Do not torment that boy with your sword, Avalina. Remember all that I have taught you because you will be a protector for this village, and for those anywhere you go who are unable to defend themselves against the creatures of darkness. It is a serious and sacred task, one entrusted to me for years. Now it is your time to join me in this vigil." He took the sword from her and traced his finger along the name of the sword. "The sword is named

Seraphina, which means 'burning fire'. Let it be the torch that guides your path and keeps our home safe."

He handed the sword back to her and she stared at the glyph. Ava marveled over the intricate design that represented its name. *Seraphina*, she thought as a smile crept onto her face. She bowed her head and said a prayer asking for the sword to be blessed, to grant her the ability to serve and protect the ones she loved and cared about. Her father watched in silence, his slate eyes full of warmth. He pulled her into an embrace after she finished the prayer. The bare metal of *Seraphina* felt cool against her naked arm as it pressed into her. Ava didn't want him to let go but she staved off the urge to tell him so. She needed to be strong in front of him. A proper swordswoman doesn't need hugs from her father and she was a proper swordswoman now that she had a sword of her own.

"Help me with this, Avalina." He said. He was pointing to his spare armor on the wall. She walked over and helped him put on a gleaming coat of plate armor. The edges of the metal were sharp and pressed painfully into her fingers but she didn't utter a word of complaint while helping dress her father. By the time he was finished he was armored as well as any knight, weighed down by thick metal that covered his entire body. Ava felt quite silly in comparison with her odd ensemble of armor.

"When do we go to meet them?" Ava asked her father as he strapped on a second brace of knives.

"We aren't going to meet them," he answered. "I am going to meet them. You are staying with Hazel."

"But Father!"

"There is no point in arguing the matter, Avalina. You and Edgar are far too young to be parading around the village during an attack. You could get hurt in the battle or cause someone else to lose focus and get hurt. I gave you *Seraphina* so that you can protect yourself in dire need. Not so you could go rushing headlong into danger. You will both stay away from the battle until we come and get you. Is that understood?"

"But I was the one who saw them. And I killed one goblin already."

"I know," he said as he tried to hug her through the stiff armor, "and I am proud of what you have done. But I can't risk losing you to this goblin horde. We have enough men to ward them off but if it looks like we're losing I will send for you."

"Promise?" she asked him, a hint of a smile creeping on her face.

"I promise. Now go and head over to Hazel's with Edgar and try to have some fun with the boy. Maybe you should let him be the hunter for a change." He flashed her a smile and ruffled her hair.

"He is supposed to be, but I don't think he'll be very good at it. He makes a much better monster." Her father's laugh lifted her spirits, and he ushered her to Hazel's house.

CHAPTER FOUR
Goblin Invasion

"Would you like some tea, dears?" Hazel asked them for the seventh time in the past hour. Ava smiled at the kind old woman, shriveled and bent with age. This woman had helped Ava and her father through their first years in Tirgoth by looking after Ava constantly while her father was off battling monsters in faraway lands. The house still smelled the same as it did all those years ago, the aroma of a dozen varied dried herbs thick in the air mingling with a musty smell that seemed to hover around the house of every old person in the village. It was enough to make Ava's stomach queasy every time she walked in the door, though her senses usually adapted within a few minutes. It still made for an uncomfortable first few minutes, suffering through her body's reaction to the smell as well as Hazel's sloppy kisses. At least this time it had been worth suffering through to see Edgar turn red to his hairline when Hazel kissed him. Her side still ached from the fits of laughter.

"No, thank you," Ava said while shaking her head, "you have done enough already."

The old woman looked at her with the deep almond eyes that suited her name and returned the smile before shuffling into the other room. The children resumed their imaginary battle, trading blows with each other. They were still wearing armor, although they set aside their weapons for willow switches. They had dipped the tips in red paint so that they could see the hits that the armor absorbed. Dueling while wearing the heavy chain mail made her strikes slower, allowing Edgar to hold his own against her, even though he still wore more red marks than she did. But Ava thought the armor made it feel like she was fighting in a real battle instead of playing with her friend while the goblins attacked her father and the rest of the village outside. Ava and Edgar stopped mid-strike when they heard the trumpeting of horn blasts outside, two short blasts followed by a long blow.

"What does that horn mean?" Edgar asked.

"It is a signal to fall back," Ava answered, "but I don't know if it is the goblins or the village that is being told to fall back."

"Does that mean we're losing?" Edgar asked while pacing across the room.

"Father would never lose."

"Even your father can't fight the whole horde alone."

"You're right," Ava answered. Edgar stopped his pacing, his eyes wide as he stared. "I know, Edgar, but you can't always be wrong about everything. We need to do something."

"But how?" Edgar asked, motioning toward the front room where Hazel kept watch. "It is no use trying to get past her. We've already tried that twice and she saw us with her secret eyes that see everything. Besides, your father didn't want us to leave, remember? And he told her that, so she'll never let us out that front door."

"He doesn't know that I know a secret passage," Ava said. She grabbed her weapons and headed into an adjoining room, motioning for Edgar to follow.

"Are you sure we should be in here?" Edgar asked, frozen in the doorway of the room.

"Of course we should. They need our help, and that is far more important than following some command about staying inside the house. My father has told me dozens of stories about soldiers disobeying commands and saving the day because they chose to act instead of obey. Those men were the heroes of the story, and this is my chance to be a heroine, swooping in to drive back the goblin horde just as the battle looked bleak. The bards will be called in from the 13 kingdoms to write this story."

Ava moved a warg-skin rug from the floor to reveal a small wooden trapdoor with a black iron ring underneath. Together they pulled on the iron handle, opening the door with a creak that made them cringe. Ava held her breath and counted to twenty but she heard no sign of Hazel stirring in the other room. Looking down, she saw that there was enough sunlight shining into the tunnel below so that Ava could see the handholds carved into the stone wall. She nodded to Edgar and descended down into the tunnel. When she reached the bottom she ran toward the exit, not bothering to wait for Edgar to climb down first. Seconds delayed might mean the death of her father, and she could never bear that burden.

Smoke and chaos accompanied the sounds of battle as Ava stepped out into the village. People that she had grown up with lay dead or dying in the middle of the roads. There seemed to be two dead goblins for every slain villager yet the goblin force was still numerous. It looked like every goblin alive in the 13 kingdoms was attacking her village.

The goblins swarmed buildings and people, gnashing sharp teeth and hacking with blades of bone and bronze. Most of them were small in stature compared to the men of the village, the tallest standing about as high as Edgar, and all of them unpleasing to the eye. Her father once told her that goblins were small, slow, stupid, and easy to defeat alone; that explained why they usually moved as a horde, descending in great numbers to overrun superior forces. A thin stream of flames danced through the air. The flames lit a trio of goblins on fire. Ava looked over and saw one of the elders send another wave of flames toward the goblins. These elders were finally good for something more than lie detecting and sitting around being bossy. They could be efficient warriors, in their own way, when it came down to it. If she happened to see someone from the Order of Light out here next she would know things were truly serious.

Edgar caught up to her, doubling over as he struggled to catch his breath. His face blanched as he took in the carnage in the village and the bow fell to the ground. Ava turned toward Edgar and he met her eyes. His skin was pallid, but he nodded and picked his weapon off the ground. He raised his bow as he pulled an arrow free from the quiver. In one smooth motion he took aim at a goblin chasing one of the neighbors and loosed the projectile. The arrow pierced its gnarled shoulder, driving deep into the leathery skin. The goblin turned, howling in pain, and Ava drove *Seraphina* deep into its chest. The monster made a feeble attempt to rake at her with its claws but its arms were too short to reach her.

They snuck across the village as much as possible, crouching to avoid notice. Edgar stopped to shoot at any goblins that took notice of them, which was usually enough to discourage them from pursuing the children when more vulnerable prey could be found. Ava stabbed goblins in the back whenever she could help save one of the villagers. She knew she needed to head toward where the battle was thickest if she wanted to help her father. No doubt that was where he would position himself. The children battled and crept and fled across the village. They both bore a number of cuts and bruises before Ava finally spotted her father. He was locked in a duel with the biggest goblin she had ever seen. It stood as tall as her father and was covered from head to toe with armor. Every other goblin had rusty and rotten armor that was made from incomplete sets, but this goblin wore a full set of polished armor. That in itself marked it as the leader of this band of monsters. Ava watched as their swords clashed over and over as man and monster both struggled to gain the upper hand. The villagers and goblins gave the pair a wide berth but Ava noticed several black goblins creeping in behind her father. She shouted to get his attention but her father either did not hear her or was ignoring her.

"Edgar," Ava said as she turned back to her friend, "shoot them!"

"They are too far away," he said, turning to take aim at a closer target. His arrow whizzed through the air and took the goblin in its shoulder. That moment of distraction was enough to allow a villager to run it through.

"Stay here," she said. She cut across the battlefield, weaving through the combat. She moved with stealth and took care to avoid any chance of confrontation, drawing *Seraphina* from her sheath so she could use it if needed. She needed to get there fast if she was to save her father from the ambush. Along the way a goblin tried to cross swords with her and she ducked under its slash. A spout of flames flashed onto the goblin from behind, engulfing the monster. Ava nodded at the head elder and hurried along toward her father.

Her sword intercepted a pair of weapons as the black goblins swung their brass blades at her father. Sparks stirred as their weapons slid down the length of *Seraphina* and the two goblins snarled and snapped at her in a guttural tongue. Tristan glanced back long enough to notice her presence and then he renewed his attack on the goblin king with increased fervor. Ava ducked under a slash, countering with a thrust of her own. She stumbled as she struck, missing her mark but catching a goblin in its chest. The other goblin's blade sped down at her extended arms. She released the hilt then stepped back to avoid the attack. The brass blade sliced into the ground. The impact sent dirt flying into the air. She spun to kick the goblin in the head while it was bent over but the weight of her armor prevented her leg from reaching above its waist. The goblin staggered a little to the side from the blow but was otherwise unharmed by her kick.

Her father was losing ground in his own battle, edging toward her with each parried blow. He bumped into her and they stood back to back, each facing their enemy. Ava reached back, grabbing a knife from her father's belt, brandishing it in an aggressive stance.

"I told you to stay safe," her father said as he blocked a sword strike. Ava countered a thrust from her goblin, slashing at its arm as it backed away.

"I'm nearly a woman grown, father," she answered. "I want to help." The goblin struck at her again. Its blade grazed her arm. She let out an involuntary yelp of pain and blood trickled down her forearm. Her father glanced back and the goblin leader snuck in an attack, the blow ineffectively clanging off his armor.

"You were helping by staying safe," he answered. He charged the goblin leader, unleashing a flurry of swift strikes that left the leader wounded in multiple places.

The goblin pressed its advantage, striking from a distance with its sword. Ava tried to parry a strike but the knife was too small to force the blow aside. Pain flared in her side and the goblin licked its lips, sensing victory. Tears welled in her eyes, but Ava fought down the pain. A huntress wouldn't let that wound affect her during battle, and she was a huntress.

Ava feinted an attack at her monster and pivoted to circle around it to retrieve her sword from the corpse of the other goblin. Her foe snarled in response to seeing the weapon in her hands and moved back a step. It spun around, brass blade arcing toward her father. Ava's reflexes from training took over and her arms moved faster than she thought possible. She intercepted its attack with *Seraphina*. The impact rattled them both but Ava regained her composure and responded with an attack of her own. The goblin snapped its fangs at her and lifted its sword in defense but was too slow. *Seraphina* cut through flesh and tendons as it sunk into its neck.

"I'm perfectly capable of defending myself," Ava said, panting as she strained to pull her sword free from the goblin. Real battle turned out to be a lot more exhausting than any imaginary battle she had encountered with Edgar. It didn't help that there were just so many goblins. For every one they killed there were still more to replace it.

"What about the boy?" her father answered as he landed another successful blow on the goblin king. Ava turned to look for Edgar and spotted him backing into a corner. He was alone and struggling to fend off a large, misshapen goblin. Ava cursed and left her father to finish his fight.

Ava struggled to dart around the lingering battles in the village. She seemed to get blocked by every goblin along the way. Some she managed to get around, but one she slew while it was grunting challenges to her. It seemed like she was still miles away when she saw Edgar get disarmed. His sword kicked up a cloud of dust upon impact. He sidestepped a thrust but wasn't expecting a second strike. Ava ran faster as she watched Edgar fall to the ground, a gash on his face from the goblin's sharp claws. The monster stood over the fallen boy. It raised its sword.

Ava leapt. She crashed into the goblin, tackling it to the ground. Her fists struck its exposed face again and again. She pounded into the leathery flesh while hot tears streamed down her face. She grabbed the knife she stole from her father's belt and drove it to the hilt into the goblin's chest and a sob wracked her whole body.

Edgar lay motionless in a shallow pool of blood. The crimson liquid was still running down his face. All color had departed from his complexion and his breathing was shallow. Ava rushed over to him, struggling to lift him in her arms. She prayed to her god, Eodran, for her friend's life and the strength to carry him to safety and protection from further harm. Ava felt an odd calm wash over her and she bent down and performed a feat of strength far beyond her by picking Edgar up and carrying him in his armor. The hot blood was slick but she maintained her grip as she carried him toward the nearest home. Every time she thought she was going to have to stop and fight, a blast of flame or an arrow would strike down the goblin. Ava thanked Eodran as she barged into the nearest house without any further harm coming to Edgar. She laid him on the bed and ran to the nearest well, filling a bucket of cold water while the battle wound down around her and the goblins started to withdraw. Her mind was only on the wounded boy.

Unbidden tears streamed down her face as she washed the blood from his cheek. She didn't understand why she was crying when she was so mad at him for going and getting himself hurt. Possibly even killed. It wasn't fair of him to do that to her, to die on her. Who would get to be the monster if he wasn't there anymore? Who would sit with her for days on a tower, looking for signs of an invasion? Who would lie to the elders for her to convince them to believe her?

He simply couldn't die on her. Not now.
Not ever.

CHAPTER FIVE
A Tearful Farewell

Ava woke up a few hours later with a damp cloth still clutched in her hand. It was stained crimson and stuck to her hand when she tried to drop it. She lay there for a few moments longer and listened to the reassuring sound of Edgar's beating heart. His breathing was still intermittent and ragged but he was alive and the wound had finally clotted over properly. He would have a nasty scar--she had seen enough of her father's wounds to recognize the consequences--but at least the boy would live. Ava sat back up, brushing a tear from her cheek as she smiled and said a soft prayer of thanks to Eodran.

"What happened?" Edgar whispered, his eyes blinking open.

"You nearly got yourself killed," Ava answered, "but I killed it first."

"My face hurts," Edgar said and he winced as he touched the scabbed wound. "How did I get here?"

"You were carried."

"Did we win?"

"We did," her father answered as he stepped into the room, "and now you need to rest. The healer will be over soon to see to your wound, Edgar."

"I'll wait here until he gets here," Ava said.

"No, you'll come with me," her father said. "You've done enough for him already by carrying him to safety."

"Ava carried me?"

"Aye, she did. And washed your wound with her tears from what I hear."

"You cried for me?" Edgar asked.

"I did not!" Ava said as she rose from her chair. Her face burned and she hoped Edgar didn't notice. She turned away from him and walked toward the door. "Let's go, father, so that this silly boy can rest. He is getting delirious if he thinks I cried over him."

"But he just said..." Edgar started. Ava spun on her heels to face him. She had a reputation to maintain. She was a swordswoman and a monster huntress and could not afford to show emotion. That was weakness and weakness would get you killed.

"I never cry. And if I did, I certainly wouldn't cry for you." Ava said and then she stormed out of the room and ran back home. It seemed impossible to suppress the torrent of emotion flooding through her. There was no choice but to succumb to the tears and a sob burst from her as she dashed into the house. Ava slammed the door behind her and crawled into her bed and under her blanket to hide from her father for a few hours. It wasn't more than a few minutes before she felt him sit beside her on the bed. She braced herself for his reprimand. She knew that she would be in trouble for disobeying his wishes and for how she treated Edgar. She deserved to hear the lecture, even if she didn't want to hear it right now.

"Avalina," he said, his voice soft and gentle and nothing like how she imagined it would be right now. She lifted the blanket enough to peek out at him. He smiled at her and reached under the blanket to muss her red hair. "You taught me something today."

"I did?" she asked, poking her head out from under the blanket. She looked up at his face to see if he was tricking her but his face bore no hint of a smile.

"Aye, you taught me that you are indeed almost a woman grown. And more like your father than he'd care to admit." He placed his hand on her shoulder and pulled her close. "I'm proud of you. You kept watch over the village. You took the mission seriously. You fought a goblin patrol, tried to convince the elders of the danger and took charge of defending the village when they didn't believe you."

"You know about all of that?"

"Aye, the head elder told me all about it after the battle was over."

"But I disobeyed your orders."

Her father did the last thing she expected: he laughed. "And I know that I would have done the same thing if it had been me. I can hardly fault you for that, can I? Not only that, but you saved my life." He paused, looking into her eyes. "And Edgar's life."

"So I'm not in trouble?" Ava asked.

"Oh, you're in trouble all right. But not the kind you think. You are almost a woman grown, as you reminded me earlier. And it is obvious to everyone that you want to enter into the trade of monster hunting. It is past time that you were trusted with some responsibility and it is past time that I moved on. Tirgoth was never intended to be a permanent home for me. It was supposed to be a place to stop and wait for you to grow older."

"You mean I get to go on hunts with you now? And train with all the weapons? And get to see big castles?" Ava asked, her eyes growing wide and a grin spreading across her face. Her father shook his head and the grin faded from Ava's face.

"No, Avalina. Your place is here, in Tirgoth, taking my post as the defender of the city. It is a job for which you are more than capable and today helped me to realize that. But it is time for me to move on at last and to accomplish the things I have been avoiding for years."

Her heart skipped a beat after hearing his words. How could her father be saying this? After all this time spent idolizing him, dreaming of the day that he would take her with him on one of his adventures, he told her to stay in boring old Tirgoth and do the unappreciated job he had toiled in for years. He couldn't even get the Council of Elders and the Order of Light to rally together for a common cause, so what made him think she could do any better in this role? Why not promote one of the villagers who had been with him for years? "Why can't I come with you instead?" she asked.

Her father shook his head. "You can't come with me on this. What I am going to seek is far too dangerous for you. Perhaps even for me. Plus, Edgar needs you here. If you leave now do you think he won't come riding after you and try to follow? He isn't suited for the life and all three of us know it." He placed his hand on Ava's shoulder. "But he will live and that should be the important thing right now. Because of you, his life continues. And who knows, in a few years you may find that there is a life you prefer over hunting monsters with your father. If you come with me, you may never be able to make that decision for yourself, my little Avalina."

Ava slumped down on the bed and crossed her arms, looking away from her father. "When do you leave, Father?"

"Soon," he answered, rising from the bed. "I caught a glimpse of something I hadn't seen since... the night your mother died. That is why I must not delay, not even to help them rebuild. Tirgoth will recover and prosper, I dare say. The elders might even give up some of their hoarded gold and hire a small army from the king to keep guard now. And maybe the Order of Light will do something more than talk about eradicating monsters for a change." He stopped, taking a deep breath. "And don't you worry for one moment about me. I will be fine. Even more so, knowing you are safe here and helping them to rebuild and set proper defenses. You know that I am more than a match for any monster that crosses my path."

Ava got up and fell into his arms, wrapping him in a tight embrace. Tears flowed freely down their faces and all she could whisper, over and over, was that she loved him. He ruffled her hair and kissed her hair but the sound of horses outside their home ended their embrace. Her father stood up and smiled at her as he reached for his pack of supplies. He touched the hilt of his sword, a habit that Ava had seen him do a hundred times, before he stepped outside. Three horses waited for him, fully saddled and each with packs of food and a dozen weapons strapped to them. A tear rolled down Ava's cheek in spite of her attempt to be brave for her father. She tried to call out to him as he slid into the saddle but a sob burst out instead.

"I love you," her father said, "my brave little Avalina. I'll be back before you know it, once this business is ended. When I return I will train you properly if this is still the life you wish to choose. I promise." He dug his heels into the sides of his horse and took off. Ava tried to call out to him, but the words caught in her throat. Tears streamed down her face and she watched him disappear into the distance. He turned in his saddle at the gate, waving one last time.

"I love you, too," Ava whispered, waving back. And then he was gone.

It didn't take long for Ava to understand that she had to go after him. She understood why her father decided to leave her behind but he was wrong. She didn't need to stay in Tirgoth; she should be there with him so she could protect him. She had heard the stories of the night her mother died a hundred times. Her father still burned with a desire for vengeance.

And based on his comments he must have seen it, or thought he saw it, during the battle.

Whatever killed her mother was strong and dangerous. Her mother had died trying to face it alone. She wouldn't lose her father in the same way. She was old enough and strong enough to help him even if he didn't realize it yet. But if she gave him a head start, took a few days to catch up to him, by then he would have time to realize his mistake and would welcome her presence.

Edgar was sleeping again when she arrived, so she sat down beside him and watched him for a while. He looked so peaceful while he slumbered, all traces of pain gone from his expression. The healer had done a good job of patching him up and Ava thought he almost looked normal. Well, as long as she ignored the giant poultice plastered on his face. He would likely have a scar there for the rest of his life. Would it be a reminder to him of the good times he shared with her, or would it be a constant source of anger toward the reckless girl that almost got him killed? Ava prayed it would be the former. She wanted him to remember her fondly when he grew into his new life without her.

The next thing Ava knew, she was crying again. She had been good at hiding her emotions for years but today it seemed that she was crying over every little thing. At least the boy was still sleeping so he could not see her tears.

"So you have been healing me with your tears?" Edgar asked. His voice was weak and light but his eyes were suddenly open and staring straight at her.

"Have not," Ava retorted, turning her head away. She rubbed her arm across her face before turning back to him. "Anyone who says otherwise will wish the goblins killed them before I'm done with them."

"Don't worry, Ava," Edgar said, brushing her arm with his fingers before his arm fell back by his side, "your secret is safe with me. They always have been."

"It changes nothing," Ava said.

"I didn't expect it to."

"Father is leaving again soon."

"Oh," Edgar said, "so I suppose you'll be back to patrolling instead of having fun?"

Ava shook her head, not sure of whether to smile or frown. "I'm going with him this time."

"He is taking you with him?"

"Well, not exactly," Ava said. "But he needs my help, even if he doesn't know it yet. I'm going to follow him."

Edgar closed his eyes, sighing. He lay motionless for a long time. Ava watched his chest rise and fall with each breath. She counted them in the silence to occupy her mind. At last he opened his eyes and looked at her. "I suppose I knew this day would come sooner or later. I just always assumed it would be later."

"I," Ava stammered, "I'll miss you."

"I know," he said, forcing a grin on his face. A tear rolled down his cheek and she leaned in to brush it away. He sat up and kissed her cheek, turning red as he fell back into the bed. "I've been meaning to do that for a long time," he said.

"Breathe a word of it and you'll wish you hadn't," Ava said with a slight smile on her face.

"You'll come back in a few weeks, right?"

"I don't think father means to. I think this time he is leaving Tirgoth for good."

"Oh," Edgar said.

"And I should be getting ready to follow him before his trail grows cold. I just wanted you to know," Ava said. She rose to her feet and turned to leave but Edgar grabbed her wrist.

"Take care of yourself, Ava. I mean that. And someday, if you can, come back and see me."

"I will try," she promised as he released his grip. "Just don't go getting yourself killed without me."

Edgar didn't answer, so Ava walked out the door and headed home, tears streaming down her cheeks after facing another farewell.

Ava woke up a few hours before dawn. She already had a horse loaded up and saddled. She slipped into the traveling clothes her father had bought for her, a green tunic and brown breeches. She strapped *Seraphina* to her back and grabbed a light brown cloak before heading out the door.

The whole village was still asleep as she mounted up. Ava's mind raced as she thought about all of the adventures she had heard about. She imagined all of the exciting quests that were waiting for her outside these village walls. It was a new day, a new start to the next chapter in her life. Even though she would miss this old life she knew she was ready to become an apprentice monster hunter. She had dreamed of this day for years and she knew her father would finally agree to train her when she caught up to him. He had to.

She urged her horse into a slow walk, not wanting to wake anyone with her departure. She reached the western edge of the village and stared out at the vast expanse of desert ahead of her. And then Ava heard a shout behind her.

She turned in the saddle and spotted Edgar a little ways back, leaning heavily on a thick staff, waving. She smiled and waved back. She was going to miss that boy but she had a feeling they would meet again someday. Ava urged her horse into a trot and rode off into the distance knowing that Edgar would still be standing there, in spite of the pain, waving until he couldn't see her anymore.

CHAPTER SIX
Picking up the Trail

The miles of desert sand around him shifted into grassland as he rode west along the road. He saw it there, in Tirgoth, in the heat of the battle with the goblins. The monster that had slain his wife so many years ago. It hovered along the outskirts of the skirmish, barely visible, taunting him for his laziness. For letting the trail run cold for so long. He had hunted it relentlessly after Kenna's death, driving himself to the brink of obsession. Only his daughter had been able to bring him back.

The miles passed by as Tristan rode along the road at a slow trot with a pair of spare horses tethered to his mount. The grass grew thicker and groups of trees clustered around the road. He was in no hurry to rush headlong into whatever trap the shadowy fiend had in store for him. So far, the trail had been obvious, pointing the direction he should ride. Even a drunk ogre could have tracked this quarry to this point. Which made Tristan nervous. He was used to its habits by now. The monster had frustrated and deceived him with false trails, ambushes, and perilous terrain in the past. He couldn't begin to count the number of times he had felt like he was on the heels of the monster only to have every sign disappear like an extensive illusion. What hunter could maintain their sanity in such a hunt?

Kenna had. Somehow she knew, when the time came, that it was actually hunting her rather than the other way around. At least Ava was safe, back at home. She would be furious about being left behind, but it was for her protection. Tristan couldn't drag his daughter into this hunt. It was his responsibility to avenge his wife.

The sound of horse hooves jarred him from his thoughts. The horse was coming at a slow, plodding pace to the south but was headed straight toward him. His instincts took over, and his hand moved to the hilt of his sword, checking to make sure it was loose in its scabbard and ready to be drawn. He repeated the same motion with a few of his knives before grabbing his bow. He didn't think an ambush likely, but years of hunting taught him to rule nothing out. Better to prepare for the worst and be wrong than to be caught off guard.

He stopped his horses thirty yards from a crossroads. He could still hear the horse hooves clattering along the road but it hadn't crested the hill yet. The dark shadow of a figure was still obscured by tree branches and hilltops. Tristan pulled his bow free and strung it. He notched an arrow and shifted in his saddle so that he might have a clean shot when the rider came into view. If danger was riding toward him, it would not find him unprepared.

The tension on the drawstring increased in proportion to his nerves. Whoever was approaching had slowed down. Had he been spotted? It was likely. He was sitting in the open, atop a horse with two others saddled beside him. Tristan glanced to either side, peering into the shadows of the trees. The darkness there was thick, providing the perfect place for an ambush. The thought flashed in his mind and simmered in his thoughts. He bit his lip and a bead of sweat trickled down his forehead. His eyes flickered to the sides again but saw nothing. He glanced over his shoulder and saw that no one was sneaking up on him.

The rider crested the final hill and was now in clear view. It was a merchant that Tristan had seen several times in Tirgoth peddling assorted wares. He relaxed his draw and set his bow and arrow aside, urging his horses along the road. Tristan waved as he approached the crossroads but the other man, Larch was his name, didn't wave back. The closer Tristan got to the merchant the more concerned he became. Larch's azuline eyes were a duller shade of slate today and his skin was pallid, his face ashen. He didn't raise his head to meet Tristan's gaze. He merely hunched over the saddle as his horse plodded on. Something was wrong.

The sound of a crossbow bolt clicking into place brought Tristan crashing into reality. He dove off the saddle of his horse without thinking about his actions and rolled as he hit the ground. A crossbow bolt clattered off the dirt road. Tristan drew his sword in a fluid motion as he rose from the ground but Larch was gone. How had he vanished so fast? Sinister laughter echoed, a laugh he had tried to block out of his nightmares for years. Was this new or merely a phantom menace from the past? The laughter simply echoed over and over again until it pressed him toward the brink of madness. A madness he remembered far too well from the last time he hunted this fiend. He pressed his hands over his ears, his fingers digging into his temples. The last time it dominated his thoughts like this he had been lost in it.

Out of all the monster hunting skills that her father possessed, he taught Ava the most about tracking. It was something they practiced together for as long as she could remember. It gave Ava an edge when playing Monster Hunter with Edgar and the other children in Tirgoth because there was nowhere they could hide that she couldn't eventually follow. Stealth had been a skill that paired perfectly with tracking, an essential aspect if she ever wanted to get close enough to see her quarry. Both of these skills, honed and sharpened for the past ten years of her life, served her well today.

The desert disappeared behind her much sooner than she anticipated. It always seemed to stretch on for days, but she crossed it in a matter of hours at a steady trot. She stopped on the other side and cleaned the sand from her horse's hooves and treated it with a fresh apple. Her horse needed to stay strong and fresh if she was going to be traveling the world to hunt monsters, and the last thing she needed was for her horse to go lame or to get irritated with her. Besides, she was not in any hurry to catch up to her father. He would command her to go back to Tirgoth, perhaps even escort her back himself and make certain she would not be able to follow. She would be able to follow the subtle signs left by her father so long as the good weather held. One good storm might make the tracking a more difficult task, but Ava believed that luck was on her side right now.

She rode onward, past rolling plains, until large hills crested to the north and the south. Dense trees, so tall that she had to crane her neck to see the tops, surrounded the road to the north, south, and west. Ava always believed the trees to the west of Tirgoth were a forest, but the dense foliage surrounding her proved how naive that belief had been. She had never seen such vibrant, verdant greens in her life. There were trees of varying sizes and shapes, each one thick with leaves of various hues of green in a variety of shapes. Colorful fruits hung from some of the branches and Ava stopped several times to pluck a new variety when she spotted one within reach. An hour later her hands stuck to the leather of the reins from the dried juices. She moaned and shut her eyes as she felt her stomach trying to expand. There were still a few hours of daylight remaining but she needed to stop and set up camp soon. The jostling canter of the horse was shaking things up and, if this continued, she was certain that her insides would explode.

※

The next morning she set back out at first light. Ava knew she had lost precious miles by camping so early, but she had been in no shape to continue riding after her father. Vibrant shades of pink and orange blossomed on the horizon, giving her just enough light to see the road she travelled upon. The wind danced in her hair as she rode along, sending chill bumps down the back of her neck. It was a revitalizing moment, a taste of freedom on this crisp spring morning. She didn't need to look for tracks right now because there was only one way her father could have gone, so far as she was concerned. So she let her steed have its head for a while and covered the ground at a brisk pace.

She slowed her horse as she approached a crossroads. She didn't want to miss signs of the direction her father took and, if she wasn't careful, she could spend hours riding in the wrong direction. The crossroads were quiet without a soul in sight but, as she studied the horse tracks below, she was confused. It appeared her father stopped here for some reason. It was almost as though he anticipated an attack, and then dove off his horse in order to avoid an oncoming projectile. But there were no other fresh tracks to be seen at the crossroads. Ava dismounted and moved through the scene to be certain. Her father's tracks were the only ones to pass through in the last week. Ava wondered what could have caused his erratic behavior. Did he realize she was following him and was trying to confuse her to cover his trail? She decided to spend even more time searching around this area, hunting for clues. Her father wouldn't do something unusual unless there were a reason, and she wanted to try and puzzle out this mystery because it might be important. Besides, she was still wary about catching up too soon and him insisting on sending her back. Better to lose a few hours so they would be further from Tirgoth.

Ava crawled around the area on hands and knees, inspecting the ground with a fierce scrutiny. She wished she tracked things more often, as she was certain that she was overlooking something obvious. A more experienced eye would find a clue to this mystery that would unlock the answers to her questions. She decided to expand her search, moving along the north and the south path of the crossroads for a hundred paces. The dirt of the road irritated her hands and she stopped, glancing at both palms. When had she scraped them so bad? Ava sighed and wrapped some linen around each palm and then resumed her search. She crawled along the grass to the west and then circled back and checked the grass near where her father had stopped. Her fingers brushed up against something cold and hard just north of where her father had stopped. She gripped it and her body recoiled. Whatever this thing was it felt... evil. Tainted. It made her skin flush and a cold sweat beaded on her forehead. The one thing she knew for certain, she did not want to handle this object with her bare hands. She flattened the grass in the area surrounding the object and went back to where she had tethered her horse. She still had the cloth her father used to encase *Seraphina*. She went back over and used it to pull the object free. A hollow void filled the pit of her stomach but she willed herself to remove the object, whatever it might be, from the ground. It may prove to be the key to solving this mystery.

It was as long as her forearm and the thickness of her index finger. The shaft was blacker than the night, absorbing the light surrounding it. Three barbed prongs converged into a point that could pierce leather as though it was made of churned butter. On the back end, a pair of vanes fanned out, the fletching made from the feathers of a crow. The presence of this bolt bore down upon Ava and her limbs moved as if submerged in mud. But she rose to her feet, wrapping the bolt multiple times in the cloth. She was thankful that she hadn't pricked her finger on the barbs of that head, suspecting that it might be coated in some vile poison that could bring about a slow, agonizing death. Each step back toward her horse was an effort that demanded her full concentration and twice she found herself looking at the uncovered bolt.

The impulse to touch it raged inside of her but a distant voice compelled her to cover it again and continue moving toward the horse.

Her horse craned its neck to watch her with big, unblinking eyes. Ava stood there frozen, arm extended over the open saddlebag. The cloth around the bolt loosened more and more with each tremor that traveled through her arm. Black clouds circled overhead, casting deep shadows of trees and bushes. The wind tossed her hair about her face and still she stood there, unable to take the final step and drop the bolt into the bag. She wanted to unwrap the cloth and see it again, to look upon the slender black perfection. To feel the cold metal in her hand, to test the sharpness of the point and see if it still retained its edge. She wanted to toss the bolt aside and run far away from this spot. To place great distance between herself and this manipulative object. Her body and mind were locked in a stalemate and, with every inch of cloth lost she was one step closer to touching the bolt and feeling the raw, unfiltered sensations that rippled through her before. She knew not what else to do. A hint of black appeared, the tip of the fletching poking out beneath the lip of the cloth. In desperation, Ava cried out mentally in prayer.

Eodran, please help. I cannot overcome this temptation with my power alone. I'm begging you, help me to release this bolt from my grasp.

Ava shook her head and rubbed her eyes. Her head felt clear and her limbs could move once more. The deep shadows had receded with the resurgent appearance of the sun overhead and the saddlebag in front of her was closed and fastened. How had that happened? She shook her head again, feeling as though she had spent half the day running across the desert sand wearing a full suit of chainmail. Every muscle ached, yet she knew that she should continue on the trail. The black clouds were gone for now, but if a storm came too soon it might wash away the signs of her father's passage. And suddenly, she no longer worried if her father would send her back to Tirgoth or not. She just wanted to be in his presence, to be certain he was all right and take comfort and strength from his company. So Ava slipped back in the saddle and followed his trail north.

Tristan felt a wave of exhaustion ripple through his body. His mind was on high alert for hours. He allowed the horses to walk along the road, so his eyes could watch for any signs of a second ambush. Every sound seemed out of place. The madness was returning. It took him so long to drive it off when he arrived at Tirgoth, but it came back and eagerly embraced him like a lost lover. He still had a few hours of light remaining, but his mental stimulation had taxed his body too much. He was going to need to rest.

Tristan dismounted and unlatched his sleep roll from behind the saddle. If he was going to sleep, he might as well get started now. In a few hours he could get a fire going to keep warm. He brushed a spot in the dirt with his boot, clearing away rocks and twigs. The last thing he needed was to sleep with a pebble pressing into his back. Tristan stifled a massive yawn and slipped his boots off. Yes, sleep was exactly what he needed.

She could tell that she was gaining on her father. There was almost as much instinct as evidence for her conclusion, but she knew that he was riding at a much slower pace than her. He hadn't even stopped to change horses yet, another sure sign that his pace was bound to be scarcely faster than a light trot. Horses couldn't run forever with the burden of his heavy weapons and armor and she was very aware of that fact. She checked the speed of her own horse, aware that the daylight was quickly fading and that her father was likely to be considering making a camp soon.

A trio of horses standing up ahead was the first sign that she had caught up to her father. Ava slowed her own steed's pace and dismounted, walking it the last stretch toward the three horses. She could see various weapons and pieces of armor that belonged to her father strapped onto the horses, but she could see no sign of him in the immediate vicinity. She spotted signs that he had headed deeper into the forest to the west, and whatever he had seen must have been urgent. He hadn't even tethered his horses, and Ava knew that it was a matter of time before even these domesticated horses would figure that out and wander off. She tied all four of the horses' reins to nearby trees and then stalked into the woods after her father.

Ava found blades of grass trampled and dry twigs broken everywhere she looked. The footprints zigged and zagged, cutting one way and then back another before cutting straight back to the previous point. She had grown up around her father and ventured into the sparse woods west of Tirgoth many times with him. She always wished that someday she could move like him, leaving almost no obvious trace of his passage. He certainly never snapped a twig underfoot. She had memories of cringing beneath his stare every time she had done so on those trips. So for him to leave such an obvious trail, breaking dozens of twigs while moving in such an erratic fashion, was beyond unusual. Ava bit her lip as she studied the aftermath of his passage. She followed her father because she needed him to train her to be a monster huntress, yet in that moment she was convinced that he needed her, too. Perhaps even more than she needed him.

He was crawling through the grass in a small clearing. His hair was soaked in sweat and clung to his forehead. Snapped fragments of twigs jutted out from his beard and brambles clung to his cloak, which contained more than a few tears in it from snagging on branches and bushes. Dirt coated his fingertips and was smeared along his cheeks and nose and forehead. His eyes were dilated and he frantically moved around on hands and knees in the clearing.

"Father," Ava shouted. He didn't even pause in his movement. She shouted even louder with equal effect, "Father, please look at me!"

She could hear him muttering something as he moved around, flush and frenzied, but the words were foreign to her. Tears trickled down her cheek and Ava rushed across the clearing toward her father. She grabbed his shoulder and he shrugged her aside. She caught back up to him and grabbed his arm and his eyes turned toward her. The unblinking gaze made her take a step backward and her grip loosened. Her father pulled his arm away but she grabbed it again. His shove broke her grip free and sent her tumbling into the tall grass. A sob wracked her body and she cried out his name, over and over, but he never looked her way again.

Ava's throat grew raw from the crying and shouting and she fell to her knees at last, clasping her hands. Words caught in her throat and she wept and stammered and the only word she managed to get out was "Eodran". In that next moment, her tears ran dry and the hollow pit inside of her vanished and she felt a warmth radiating through her. There were no words, but somehow she sensed that Eodran had heard her and understood her prayer. She looked up and her father lay slumped on the ground and he was snoring within moments.

Ava was cooking a pair of rabbits over a campfire when her father woke from his rest. The stars filled the sky overhead, a grand masterpiece painted by Eodran. She marveled at its beauty while he slept and she tethered, watered, and brushed their horses. Ava also started a small fire and set traps to catch dinner. Ava smiled at her father, who blinked in surprise.

"What are you doing here, Avalina?" he asked in a quiet tone. She studied his face to try and read his reaction to her presence.

"Someone has to take care of you," she answered with a smile. "Your horses nearly got away because you didn't tether them to a tree. You might even have frozen to death when the sun went down. Not to mention how hungry you'd be if I weren't here."

Her father sighed and shook his head. She didn't know if it was from wonder at her efficiency or in frustration at her disobedience. She hoped for the former. "I suppose this means you said your goodbyes to the boy?"

"Edgar? Yes, Father," Ava answered. She didn't expected that question.

"And you brought *Seraphina* with you?"

"Of course. How could I leave such a beautiful sword behind?"

"I had hoped to give you another year or two to grow before beginning your training. But it appears I have little choice, since you are determined to follow me into danger whether I allow it or not. Better for you to travel with me than to sneak around behind me, which is what you'd do if I sent you home, right?"

Ava nodded. Was it merely a guess it or was it that obvious? She didn't care. He was going to take her with him on an adventure! It would be just like she always dreamed, full of excitement and a little bit of danger (but not much, for what monster was a match for her father?) and people cheering during their triumphant return.

"We had best eat a good meal and get a good night of rest, dear one. We have a few days of travel still to reach our first destination."

"Where are we going?" Ava asked.

"To Dunharrow, to gather information," he said. She was about to ask him what they were hunting when he said, "No more questions tonight, Avalina. Pass me one of those coneys and let's get some rest. Tomorrow will be a long day."

CHAPTER SEVEN
The Storming Stallion

They reached the neighboring town of Dunharrow three days later as the sun set in the sky, casting pink and violet hues of light in the horizon. Many new sights and smells overwhelmed Ava's senses: the cobbled roads under the horses' hooves, noble-looking men and women strolling arm-in-arm, the overpowering scent of their perfume as they passed by those nobles, fragrant flower gardens surrounding a burbling stone fountain. Yet amidst the unfamiliar were also the smells and sounds and sights she knew well: baking bread, the clanging of a blacksmith hammer, women hanging tunics and breeches out to dry on the line, boys chasing small animals through the streets and down dark alleys.

They had ridden for more hours than Ava could count to get here, pressing along the road long after the moon rose each day. That first night they only stopped because she fell from the saddle, unable to remain upright any longer. Her thighs ached, her back throbbed, and she had dirt in her disheveled hair. So far, the glamorous life of a monster hunter wasn't quite living up to her expectations but she knew that would all change now that they were in a town. Here she would see the townspeople herald her father as a hero and hear stories told in admiration of his feats at monster killing, keeping the entire kingdom safe by tracking down wargs and hrundtboars and many other minions of darkness.

Her father led them through the streets, navigating the town with familiarity. A few peddlers remained out along the cobbled roads and they seemed desperate to end their day of sales on a high note. Ava watched their eyes initially light up at seeing a pair of travelers. She guessed they expected to be able to wheedle the newcomers into parting with a few pieces of copper or silver. That glimmer of hope faded as soon as they recognized her father. His reputation was apparently known among them all. But what that reputation was Ava could only guess at, although it was definitely not for being generous enough with his gold to buy trinkets and treasures at their stands.

Her father stopped his horse in front of a rickety old building that was half-covered in peeling white paint. Many of the windows were either broken or boarded up and the remainder were coated with so much dirt that no light would ever be able to shine through. A faded sign hung over the door frame depicting a thick thundercloud over a rearing black horse. The name of the place, The Storming Stallion, was painted in dark azure letters beneath the steed. She trusted her father to know what he was doing but she still thought it would have been nice to stay at one of the other, nicer-looking inns they passed on the other side of town with unique names like The Lucky Lady or The Tenacious Troubadour.

A wiry boy, his face gaunt with deep bags beneath his eyes, came to lead their horses to the stable. Her father slipped him a copper in return. The boy's face brightened and the coin disappeared up his sleeve in a flash. He stammered out his thanks, bowing half a dozen times before disappearing around back. Ava's father strode toward the building and stopped just short of the door.

"Avalina," he said, turning toward her, "I will be sending your supper up to our room. This tavern is not the best place for young eyes and ears."

"But Father," she complained but he raised his hand to silence her.

"I'll not be swayed from my thoughts, dear one. I need both your trust and your complete obedience in this tonight. The crowd is bound to be the unsavory sort and they don't take kindly to hunters around here."

"But why would anyone not like monster hunters?" Ava asked, furrowing her brow. "We help protect them from the threat of the monsters that prowl the lands around them."

"Not everyone understands us, just like the elders back home," her father answered. "Common folk tend to fear what they don't understand. They fabricate stories about hunters, vilifying them and casting them as monster lovers."

"That makes no sense, Father, because it isn't true."

"Which is exactly why I want you upstairs, safe and away from these brigands."

Ava still wanted to be with him even though she understood his concern for her safety. But she knew that he was not likely to change his mind. And she also knew ways of hearing conversations that were meant to remain private. Her curious nature had taught her to eavesdrop at an early age because tongues tended to speak more freely when they thought she was not around.

"I'll sup in my room, then," Ava said with a mock curtsy that made her father smile. He mussed her hair and shook his head at her. Bright torchlight burst from the opening as her father opened the dingy door. Ava could hear the buzz of a dozen conversations, most of them raucous and loud enough to be heard outside the building. The room inside was full with commoners crowded around the tables, dressed in jerkins stained brown with liquor, or tunics with frayed sleeves. A few men sat quietly with a bowl of stew, but most held massive tankards in their hands. Ava could tell that some of the patrons had begun the night's festivities a little early from the blotches of red in their faces. There had been men and a few women in Tirgoth who were the same way and she had learned quite early to avoid them as soon as they showed sign of being affected by their drink.

Ava stayed on her father's heels as he crossed over to the owner of The Storming Stallion. The man towered over everyone as he stood behind a counter, polishing bowls with a grimy rag. The silver in his hair marked him as older than her father but Ava never saw someone his age that looked so strong. He wore no shirt, his physique bearing a silent message to all who aimed to cause mischief in his establishment. There was a large cudgel hooked on his belt for those who didn't understand the first message. Even Ava, who hadn't traveled outside of Tirgoth since she remember, could grasp the meaning behind his menacing appearance. He would not tolerate the mistreatment of his patrons nor the reckless destruction of his property. He eyed the two of them warily as her father approached the counter.

"We're full," the man said in a gruff voice. He looked back down at the bowl he was cleaning. Ava noticed that particular bowl had one small spot that was shinier than the rest, as though the man frequently polished the same bowl in the same spot for hours each day. But she dismissed that as ridiculous because no one would waste their time on such a meaningless task

"I'm certain you'll find that a room has opened up," her father said as he slid a gold coin across the counter, "if you are willing to look hard enough."

The man took the coin and held it up, looking at both sides. He frowned and bit the coin, gently pressing his teeth into the metal. He nodded his head upon seeing the slight indents in the metal and slipped it into his apron. Ava wondered what it tasted like; she was determined to attempt it the next time she had a chance. "Aye," the owner said at last, "I recall one of the patrons leaving earlier. I'll have Bessie show your girl to the room." Her father nodded and turned away and find a table but the man reached across, grabbing his arm. Her father turned around and the owner gave him a hard look. "I expect peace while you are under my roof. I want no hunter trouble, you hear? First sign of mischief in here and you'll be sent packing with a few lumps to encourage you to steer clear of here in the future."

"Understood," her father said with a slight incline of his head. He looked down as a maid only a few years older than Ava and dressed in a plain blue dress came over toward them.

"Remember what I told you," her father said to her, "I'll be up once I have some information." Ava hesitated. A small part of her wanted to rebel and stay but another glance at the cudgel convinced her to comply. The maid's dress swished to and fro as she led Ava around the crowded tables, deftly avoiding the probing hands of the drunks. Ava frowned at this display, wondering why the men were trying to reach her. Did they need their mugs filled? She didn't have much time to ponder before they were headed up a small stairway. The maid took the stairs two at a time as she chattered mindlessly to Ava about which patrons she loathed the most and, therefore, Ava should take care to avoid. But Ava was only half-listening. Her mind was already coming up with fanciful adventures that might arise in this town. She was certain they'd have a monster or three to track by morning.

"Mind yer head," the maid said as she ducked under a low plank of wood at the top of the stairs. Ava's forehead thumped into the thick wood, having failed to register the advice fast enough to avoid the obstacle. The maid turned to her, cheeks puffed in a pouty expression that made her look like a chipmunk. "I said," she huffed, emphasizing the latter word, "to mind yer head. Ye okay, lass?"

Ava nodded and followed the maid. She wanted to rub her forehead but was determined to be tough in front of the girl. Ava thought she heard the maid mutter something like "Daft country girls" under her breath as she whisked around a corner. Ava puzzled at what that could mean as she followed. At last, the maid stopped in front of a door that was as plain as the rest, with a small brass knob on one side. The door was opened and Ava shuffled past the maid.

"I'll have yer supper up in a bit," the maid said with a stiff curtsey, "let me know if yer needing aught else." And then the door shut and the maid was gone, probably rushing back down the stairs to navigate the rowdy crowd.

※

Her steaming bowl of stew sat untouched on a wooden table that had one leg shorter than the others. Ava was busy sitting on the floor with a dagger in hand, working to pry a loose board free. The problem with grown-ups, she learned with Edgar years ago, is that they never look up, a fact that allowed her to eavesdrop on countless conversations that her father thought to be private. Her efforts tonight were just as likely to pass by unnoticed by anyone, so long as no one heard the sound of her dagger sliding under the wood. She worked the nails loose with practiced effort that was both silent and efficient.

Ava was coated with a light sheen of sweat by the time she had freed the board from the floor. There were rafters running perpendicular to the board she removed. This provided her with better cover from the occasional upward glance. She draped a brown cloak over most of the hole, lying down to peer through the small opening that remained uncovered. She could see her father sitting alone in the corner, sipping a frothy drink from his tankard. She noticed a few of the drunken men eyeing him from time to time and sensed they were the trouble her father wanted to keep her away from. After a while, the occasional stranger would get up from their table and head over toward her father, speaking to him in hushed tones. Ava was disappointed to learn that she couldn't hear those private conversations, as her father was too far away and they spoke too soft to be heard over the raucous crowd. Yet she could see the shine of silver every time a coin was exchanged. It seemed like her father was having some luck tonight.

Her father rose from his table and dusted a few stray breadcrumbs off his cloak. He was definitely having some luck tonight if he was turning in already. She scrambled to grab the board but stopped when she heard the belligerent shouting begin down below.

"Hey you, monster lover," one of the drunk men slurred, "why you leaving so soon?" Ava repositioned herself, peering down to see a small gang of the men crossing the room. At the front of the gang was a man dressed in tattered clothes that were brown with stains from booze. His skin was stretched thin across his angled face and his green eyes had a distant, glassy look. He didn't appear to be armed but the burly trio behind him had weapons sheathed in their belts. Her father had paused where he was, his right hand under his cloak. Ava knew he was clutching the hilt of his sword, anticipating trouble. "You haven't given us our silver yet," the drunk continued. "And I got some choice words to share with you and that little wench of yours."

"I have all the information I need," her father said. He inclined his head in a hint of a nod, but Ava could hear the steel edge in his voice. "Now, if you don't mind, I'll be off to bed."

"Running away to hide beneath the skirts of yer girl?" one of the drunk men asked. "She's a bit young to be yer wife, eh?"

"I bet she ain't his wife, Bert," another one said. "I bet she's his familiar."

"You mean the young girl is how he commands his monsters to do his bidding?"

"And his bedding."

The sound of steel leaving its sheath rang clearly through the room. The buzz of conversation was silenced as all eyes and ears turned toward the confrontation. The drunk man stumbled back a step and Ava's father pressed the blade of his knife against his throat. "I'll suffer none of that sort of talk," her father said. He was a breath away from killing the lot of them for their foolish words.

"And I'll suffer no bloodshed under my roof," the owner barged in as he crossed the room. He was holding the cudgel in his hands and Ava noticed that it had big dents in it from previous use. "I told you, I didn't want any trouble from you, hunter. I advise you to retire to your room if you aim to stay. I can handle this lot just fine if they don't get provoked by the likes of your sort."

Ava could tell that her father was struggling to keep his tongue still. Ava could hardly believe what she saw and heard. She always imagined that being a monster hunter would be a glorious job, that they would be hailed as heroes and protectors wherever they went. Now she understood why her father hadn't taken her along when she was younger but she still couldn't understand why they would distrust monster hunters so much.

Her father turned to leave without another word, disappearing up the stairs. Ava scrambled to replace the board and rushed over to the table where her stew sat untouched. She shoveled down a few spoonfuls, nearly choking on the cold food. Her father came in with a deep sigh as he folded his cloak. He smiled at her and then climbed into his bed, rolling over to face the wall. Ava was dying to know what he found out tonight before the excitement began, but she knew from experience that he wouldn't say a word until he was ready to. She turned out the lamp and climbed into her own bed, unable to fall asleep. Her mind was too busy replaying the scene she saw below.

Gradually, her mind began to wander as she heard the soft snores coming from across the room. She felt the urge to look at the crossbow bolt every night since she had found her father but never had a chance while camping outdoors in the woods because clouds obscured the moon and the stars. Tonight, on the other hand, was the perfect opportunity with a thick aura of silver light flowing in through the window near her bed. She sat up, the sheets falling in a crumpled heap upon the ground. The floorboards chilled her bare legs as she knelt to remove her pack from beneath her bed. The bundle holding the bolt fell into her hands and she gasped at the pulse of fear that rippled through her. The mattress on the other side of the room creaked and Ava held her breath. She held it until the burning was too much and she sucked in a deep breath. Her father was still asleep. The cloth fell away and she took the black shaft in one hand.

A scream pierced the air as the sun descended in the sky, a misty haze hovering over the ground. The jolt of the galloping horse rattled her jaw and she clung tight to the waist of a tall figure. A small house, blanketed in darkness, stood in the distance wedged between two steep hills. The dark figure in front of her stiffened as a second scream echoed after the first. Her vision flashed a bright white, followed by darkness.

When her vision returned she was standing in a small room, her eyes burning and cheeks wet. The floor beneath her feet was warm with a thick, sticky liquid. Red filled the room around her, contrasting starkly against the black and white backdrop. A pair of figures were on the ground in front of her, one sitting while holding the other in his lap. One crying, the other bleeding. Ava gasped when the man lifted his head, as she knew him. He was younger than she knew, with fewer scars and a different way of dressing, but she would know her father anywhere.

She looked closer at the other figure, clutched in his arms. Her vision blurred and she lifted tiny fingers to wipe away the moisture. Crimson hair blended with the crimson liquid flowing from open wounds. She let out a cry as recognition set in and her vision flashed a bright white, followed by darkness.

Ava jumped at the touch on her shoulder. She looked down at her hands through blurred vision and saw they were empty. She turned to see her father kneeling beside her, eyebrows raised and a frown on his face. Ava shook her head and wiped a tear away.

"It was nothing," she said after taking a deep breath, "I just had a nightmare and must have fallen out of the bed."

"Are you sure, Avalina? I could--" he trailed off as she shook her head. "If you need anything, I am here."

Ava nodded and gave him a hug. His embrace reminded her of the vision she saw and Ava fought back the wave of emotions surging through her. She would cry for her mother, the woman who died when she was three, but not in front of her father. He wouldn't be able to handle hearing that she just dreamed about that night. She was sure he'd probably been plagued by that very dream for many years. She crawled back into bed, facing the wall and trying to put the images out of her mind. Yet when her eyes closed, all she could see was crimson.

CHAPTER EIGHT
Following the First Trail

Ava opened her eyes the next morning to find her father already awake and dressed, idly chewing a hard biscuit while poring over a map. She sat up in the bed and tossed the sheets aside while trying to suppress a massive yawn. He looked over at her and smiled with a warmth that made Ava feel at home and forget about the nightmares of the previous night. She clambered across the room, rubbed one eye with a curled fist, and smiled back at him.

"How much did you hear?" he asked her. His attention was already turned back to the map in front of him. Ava froze, biscuit halfway to her mouth, uncertain how to respond and avoid trouble. "I know you spy on my meetings, Avalina. You've been doing it for years and have gotten quite good but not good enough to get past your father. Now, tell me, what did you learn?"

He wasn't mad and that surprised her. If nothing else, there seemed to be a hint of pride in his voice when he confessed his knowledge of her spying habits. "Not a whole lot," she answered, "at least not about what we're doing or where we're going. You were too far away." Her father nodded so she continued. "But I did catch the commotion near the end with those four men."

Silence. Ava watched as her father drew a line with practiced skill, straight as an arrow, between two points on the map without the aid of any tools. She wanted to study the map but the question burning in her mind burst from her lips before she could stop it. "Why don't they like us? Monster hunters, I mean. Don't they know we keep them safe?"

Her father stopped. The quill hovered over the map, suspended from the mark it was about to make. He turned toward her and set the ink-tipped feather down next to the map and pulled her close. She could smell the bitter tang of tea leaves on his breath and his rough stubble scratched her skin but she didn't complain. After a few more moments of silence, broken by a heavy sigh from her father, he began to explain.

"Fear makes people say and do stupid things. They will believe ridiculous lies when they are afraid. And monsters, rightfully, frighten many people because they are seen as savage and vicious and uncontrollable. The Order of Light vilifies them and cautions against reckless interaction with monsters but that only serves to feed the frenzied emotions of distrust and fear. And many monsters in this world are exactly what they fear: wild beasts that slaughter without mercy and invade civilizations. History has proven that the monster population, if unchecked in a kingdom, will eventually lead to the destruction of people in that area. There used to be 13 kingdoms, each territory ruled by its own monarch with various dukes, barons, lords, and elders running the towns and villages in the kingdoms. Tirgoth is such a village, located in the kingdom of Hárborg.

"In the deep south was a kingdom, bigger than all the others, called Drexlan. While all of the other kingdoms flourished by focusing on advances in weaponry and alchemy and magic, that kingdom sought to establish a peaceful equilibrium with the monster population. Instead of heroes and warriors and wizards, their populace filled with scholars and scientists and merchants. This is where the Order of Unity was founded many years ago before The Uprising occurred. And for a while the kingdom of Drexlan flourished in its own manner.

"But eventually the monsters invaded, paying no heed to the unsanctioned truce proclaimed by the Order of Unity. It started with the smaller towns and villages, picking off the farming communities with their vast pastures. The trade routes that were vital to their success were slowly cut off by droves of monsters, all working together as though they were an army controlled by a great leader with an uncanny, strategic mind; goblins fought and died alongside gigans, wargs, rockmen and many other great and terrible monsters that would usually fight each other for territory."

"Different types of monsters fought together?" Ava asked. She shook her head, not willing to believe such a thing could be possible. The idea of a united army of monsters was terrible indeed. An army of goblins had managed to wreak enough havoc. What if there had been a frostwyrm or two working together with them, or even just a few berserking gigans? Tirgoth might not have survived such an attack even if her father had planned for weeks.

"They did, many years ago," her father answered, "and slowly but surely they conquered each portion of the kingdom of Drexlan while pressing the survivors south toward the coast."

"But why didn't they send for help? At least someone in that kingdom must have had enough sense to fight against the monsters."

"I'm sure they tried once they realized their mistake. But by then the roads to all other kingdoms were overrun with monsters. Messengers never got through. Reinforcements probably wouldn't have made it, even if the requests had gone through. The kingdom of Drexlan crumbled under the invasion and it seemed as though the monsters were poised to press their advantage into neighboring kingdoms." Her father stopped.

Ava's eyes were wide with excitement, rapt with attention to hear the rest of the story. She wondered which great hero stormed the lost kingdom, vanquishing the threat. Maybe it was the first monster hunter of legend, Tyrion Stormcloak. "Well, who fought them off?" Ava asked, unable to wait any longer.

"That is the curious thing," her father answered, "because no one fought them off, at least as far as the official historical records show. The monsters just stopped all of a sudden and scattered. Some of the monsters are there, in Drexlan, which is why it is still in ruins even to this day. But many of the monsters have since spread back into the other kingdoms, living independently. Although," he whispered, leaning close to her ear, "some believe there was a monster king or queen controlling that army. And that one day it will return to finish its conquest of all the 13 kingdoms."

Ava gasped, falling back in her chair. That had to be the reason behind the goblin attack, why they had started to accumulate again in such vast numbers. The master monster was back, and Ava vowed in her heart to kill it. She would be the one to track it down in the heart of Draxlan. She would lop off its head with *Seraphina* and bring peace back to the 13 kingdoms. That would make her father proud.

The pair of monster hunters left shortly after Ava finished her breakfast. The enormity of the task ahead of them was still fresh in Ava's mind. The sun crept up on the horizon, rays of the morning light splashing amidst the dark shadows ahead, locked in a struggle of dominance. The light would win, of course, as soon as the sun rose high enough in the sky. Hadn't the Order of Light taught her that the light always banished the shadows of the night? But it was always certain that darkness would return in time.

Monsters must be like the darkness, Ava thought to herself as she saddled her horse, *because even if they leave for a while, they are bound to return eventually. I will never let my guard down until I rid the world of the master monster.*

They rode for hours over rolling hills and through plains that were thick with wildflowers. Bees buzzed as they gathered pollen and a flight of butterflies fluttered in the air. The breeze was cool on her face and she relished the feel of the wind in her hair as they rode. Her father led the way, silent yet sure as he navigated the terrain. Ava couldn't see tracks anywhere along the ground, nor signs that anything had passed this way, but it didn't seem to deter her father.

"Father, what are we tracking?" she asked.

"Monsters," he answered, not looking up.

"I knew that, but what kind of monsters?" He didn't answer, so she tried asking something else. "I can't see any tracks. What am I missing?"

"The tracks are here. They have to be," he responded.

She had never seen her father like this before and it frightened her a bit. Was it determination to run down the failed hunt from the past, to finally cross it off the list? What could the monster be? It was devious enough to escape her father at least once and that meant it was bound to be clever and dangerous. But it was something her father never wanted to talk about. At least not yet. Which meant she could only guess, to piece enough together from the tidbits of information she had learned over the years. But she knew almost nothing about what it was or what it could do and that worried her.

He finally came to a halt near a stream and swung out of the saddle. They worked together to prepare their lunch; Ava dipped their steel flasks into the stream while her father pulled out hard biscuits and strips of dried meat. It was the same as the last meal they had before arriving at the Storming Stallion. Which meant it was the same as the meal before that and too similar to the meal before that one. Ava was certain she'd either grow sick of biscuits or else turn into one by the end of their journey. But she was hungry, so she ate without vocalizing a complaint. She tried to get her father to talk but he was busy poring over a map, marking and measuring over and over. Her mind returned home to Tirgoth and Edgar. She wondered what he was doing, if he had healed, and if he hated or missed her.

Her father folded up his map, breaking Ava from her thoughts. She moved to mount again, but her father stopped her.

"Not yet," he said, his hand on her shoulder. "I realize I have been neglecting the training part of your apprenticeship. That neglect ends today." Ava beamed but then she saw he wasn't smiling back. "It will not be easy, my Avalina. There may be days where you are bruised and sore and will hate me with every fiber of your being. But you will be stronger for it by the end. It will sharpen your body and mind for all that lies before you on this journey and those to come after it."

He pulled two long wooden rods from a bag and tossed one of them to Ava. It was shaped and weighted like a real sword, perhaps a bit heavier, and Ava knew that it would hurt if it struck her. Perhaps even break bones when used by a master, although perhaps a master would also know how to strike so as not to break bones. She was thankful for the years of practice with Edgar. She was beginning to imagine that she would be able to surprise her father and avoid many of the painful lessons he hinted at. Perhaps he would even be the one getting bruised and lumpy today by underestimating her skill. She was ready, but was he?

"I understand that most of your time was spent with swords," her father said. He held the rod like a sword and Ava could see the threat clouding in his eyes. "Let's see how you measure up in a real duel." He was a swordmaster, he was one with the blade. She often admired his fluid grace and deadly accuracy when she watched him train with the men of Tirgoth on straw dummies. She tried many times to imitate it, spending long days out practicing until the sun had set. And now that deadly precision and skill was being directed at her. A flurry of blows rained down.

She brought her own rod up to block them. Left. Right. Left. Left. Parry. Thrust. Ow! The rod had rapped her knuckles, not hard enough to break bone but hard enough that she could feel the pain pulsing. She hadn't even seen the blow coming. She swore to be more watchful the next time.

"Your form is excellent," he said. A small smile appeared on his face to mirror hers.

He pressed in again. She deftly dodged a strike and ducked under a swing. Ava stabbed and jabbed with the rod. Yet she caught nothing but air every time. He came back at her and perspiration trickled down her forehead. Her cloak was interfering with the timing of her strikes and blocks; she should have taken it off. His rod connected once, twice, three times on her ribs before she could move away or strike back. The pain pulsed through the fibers of her body.

"Is that your best?" he asked her. His voice was devoid of emotion. Ava tossed the cloak aside, grit her teeth, and tightened her grip on the rod. She slashed but he was gone. He moved so fast without all that heavy armor on. It was like chasing her shadow, a frustrating and futile task she often attempted as a child. She mirrored every thrust and slash she had practiced and he met them all with his rod. She invented a few impromptu maneuvers in her desperation to land a blow on her father. By the end of an hour her skin carried several indigo and violet welts where he struck her and he was still untouched. He called for them to stop.

"Good," Ava's father said with a smile. "You have learned much from observing and managed to perfect many of them. I'm proud of you."

"But I didn't hit you," Ava said.

"There were times when you nearly did," he answered honestly. "You threw a few surprises my way."

"I did?"

"Aye, you did. It will take years to perfect the speed and precision of the weapon, but you are off to a much better start than I had. Now, let me see your wounds." He inspected each bruise, poking and prodding with gentle fingers. Even his most tender touch felt like needles lancing through her skin. He rubbed some sort of paste on a few of them and an icy rush tingled in its wake. She was still sore, and would be for some time, but she felt better by the time he was done. And then it was time to ride some more.

"How much further?" Ava asked, climbing into the saddle.

"We'll be there in a few hours and then you can rest while I search around."

She didn't want to rest by the time they reached the circle of jagged rocks. This was the place where the monster was sighted last, according to the stories at the tavern. He dismounted and circled the area on foot. Ava followed behind him, careful to avoid making any sudden noises. She held her breath every time he stopped and stooped down, observing the ground with an experienced eye. Once he even tasted a clump of dirt. She watched him chew the gritty earth and spit it back out in a gooey glob. She didn't understand it but she said nothing. She knew he would explain eventually. Hopefully he'd even teach her a few things about what he was doing or the monster he was tracking. Was he trailing this monster king or were they hunting something else along the way? She still had no idea how her father approached the task, but she knew she needed to be patient and trust him.

The light of the sun faded fast and her father still scoured through the area. He was busy making his eighth round through the terrain. He barely said a word since they arrived and Ava stopped shadowing him after the fifth circle. She was weary and sore from the riding and the training. The travel rations weren't keeping her full. She was ready to make camp, set down for a supper, and drift off to sleep, but it appeared those things were far from her father's mind at the moment. She wondered if she should say something. If she didn't, would he keep circling all night long? Whatever he was hunting, he was very desperate to find it. It had to be a monster that he was desperate to find.

She decided to walk back over to the horses and sit down for a cold meal. She watched her father while chewing on another dry biscuit. After her stomach was content, she pitched her tent and then sat, polishing and sharpening *Seraphina* and her knives. Her father was still circling, although he had taken the time to light a torch from his pack so that he could see. She didn't know when he lit the torch but it didn't matter. What could he hope to find now that he didn't see in the sunlight? Were some tracks only visible in the dark, or under moonlight? She hadn't heard about that but she supposed it could be possible. Maybe that was why he was still skulking around, looking for moon runes that were only visible in a certain light. But what if they only glowed on a certain day and they missed it? Her mind whirled trying to think of the impossibilities.

He finally gave up when Ava put her weapons away. She had to force her eyes to stay open, but she could tell her father was in worse shape than she was. He sat down, shoulders slumped and head in his hands. When she brought him some meat and a biscuit to eat, he took it without looking up at her or saying thanks. When his gray eyes finally met hers, she could see the humiliation. He found nothing but emptiness.

"False trail," he announced, as though she hadn't guessed that hours ago. "I reckon the folks back in town only imagined they saw something." He paused. The silence was awkward, as though he didn't know how to explain it to Ava. But she understood.

CHAPTER NINE
A Royal Reception

It didn't take long for Ava to realize that being a monster hunter was not quite as fun as she imagined. She rode for countless hours on a horse every day and her father spent most of the time in silence. They would stop at random intervals for some sparring sessions with wooden weapons representing swords, maces, axes, staves, warhammers and other weapons that she didn't even know existed. And every time they stopped for one of these sessions, the next part of their journey was inevitably more painful due to new tender spots on her body. She had more bumps and bruises than she cared to count from the beatings she took, but she could tell that she was improving each week with a variety of weapons. Most nights were spent in flimsy tents in the countryside, although occasionally they would stay in run-down inns. On those nights her father would spend the evening sitting in a corner to eavesdrop on conversations. He usually made her stay in their room where she would routinely eavesdrop and then report to him what she saw and heard. But she was allowed to join him on occasion, which delighted her.

They followed two other leads, both of them cold within three days. Her father scrawled every lead and rumor in a small journal that he carried. He bent over it late into the night, drawing sketches and scribbling notes on every inch of each page. Ava was curious about what it contained. She asked to see it once, but he scowled and told her that she would see it when she was ready. He didn't seem to think it important to let her know when that would be, so she dropped the matter for the moment. But he couldn't prevent her mind from imagining what secrets his journal might contain.

Every bump in the saddle sent sharp pain coursing through Ava's body and she fought to keep her eyes open. She had not slept well the past two nights, ever since her father told her they would be staying as guests at the castle in the kingdom of Hárborg. She was too excited to sleep. She didn't know what she was looking forward to the most: hot baths, a lavish feast, or the comfortable beds. Not to mention getting to see a castle in person after growing up hearing dozens of stories about them. She would encounter knights and real wizards and hear bards strumming fantastic stories about the heroes of old. If she was lucky she might even see a real live Hero at the castle! She knew that her first stay at a castle would be a memorable one no matter what happened, and all of that excitement bubbled up in the form of insomnia. How her father could sleep peacefully, knowing what awaited them, was beyond her understanding.

All of her pain and discomfort were forgotten as soon as she saw the crenelated stone walls of the castle breach the horizon ahead. Twin battlements towered over either side of an iron portcullis. A black banner with a silver trout danced in the wind atop each battlement. Archers patrolled the wall dressed in black tunics embroidered with silver threadwork. The rooftops of houses poked up above the wall with brick chimneys puffing thick smoke into the air. A pair of knights armored in full plate mail stood in front of the gate with large spears in their hands. Ava could see the towers of the Hárborg Castle in the distance, its massive towers looming over the city. It was everything she anticipated a castle would be. She couldn't wait to get inside the walls and begin exploring its depths. Perhaps she would find an adventure or two awaiting her inside the kingdom.

Then the knights crossed their weapons in front of them, armor creaking as the men moved. Ava and her father reined in their mounts, coming to a stop a few feet from the knights. Ava could see the stubble on their chins, smell the stench of their sweat. She looked to her father, waiting for him to do something amazing like draw his sword and strike the men down. Instead, he straightened in the saddle and spoke to them.

"What is the meaning of this?" he asked.

"None shall pass by order of the king." one responded. He shifted his grip up on his massive axe.

"Since when have the gates of Hárborg been barred to weary travelers?"

"The castle is not accepting new immigrants at this time. There are perils in the kingdom and the king is restricting travel into or out of here until they are resolved."

"What sort of perils? Plague?"

"Nothing so dreadful as that. Just a monster menace."

"Oh, so there is a monster inside and the king is keeping us safe by containing it within the walls?"

"Perhaps, but the monster may also be out beyond somewhere. Roaming the wilderness of the kingdom."

"Then would it not be dangerous to turn away helpless travelers?"

The two knights looked at each other, frowning. "I hadn't thought of that," one said.

Her father led his horse forward a few steps and slipped a purse into the hands of a guard. His words were too soft for Ava to hear, but they had the desired effect. The guards smiled and stepped aside. Her father winked at her as he mounted his horse and rode into the city without hesitation. Even the Tirgoth elders, with their magical powers, couldn't have impressed her more at that moment. Her father managed to get them inside the walls of a real castle! She shivered and her arms tingled with excitement as she crossed the threshold and entered the walls of the castle.

Buildings stretched in all directions as far as Ava could see, clustered together so tight that Ava wondered how they could feel a breeze blowing into a window or see the sun set. Some buildings were made of brick and some of clay, though most were formed from treated lumber. The rooftops of the houses varied equally, ranging from thatched grass to baked clay tiles skillfully layered. The variety in this castle town was overwhelming. It seemed that no two houses would be the same. Thousands of people swarmed through the streets or stood in doorways, many of them dressed in torn and dirty clothing. She could hardly believe that here, inside the walls of this city, there were people living much like she had back in Tirgoth. She always imagined the city to be full of prim and proper lords and ladies but there were very few of them in sight. The people that she observed were mostly farmers and gardeners, stable hands and cobblers. Many of the trades were familiar to her and it made her feel more comfortable with being in Hárborg in spite of the varied buildings. Maybe it wasn't so different after all.

The swarms of people thinned out as they navigated the labyrinthine twists and turns of the outer city. She could smell fresh fruits and meats and the aroma of burning coals from the furnaces of blacksmiths. Peddlers were stationed alongside wooden carts, holding up their wares to try to attract customers. Vibrant colors and smooth layers of cloth replaced the dirty and torn clothing of the outer city. This part of town felt more alive to Ava even though there were fewer people crowding the streets. This was a wealthier part of Hárborg and Ava recognized that fact even though she couldn't attach a name to it. She was still able to recognize some of the trades being advertised although there were some that she had never heard of. They didn't needed a hat maker or a dressmaker back in Tirgoth and she wondered what exactly the men wandering in white hooded robes were doing. They appeared to be begging money from people, waving their hands in a complicated pattern and speaking in an odd language every time someone donated.

The farther they traveled into the city the more open space they encountered. Houses and other buildings were scarce, replaced by flowering trees and flowing fountains. Thick tufts of green grass lined the sides of the paved road as they rode toward the castle itself. Ava stared up at the building that towered far above any other, her heart fluttering in anticipation of getting to see the inside. Her wildest imagination had failed to do justice to the enormity of the structure. It was nearly as tall as it was wide and there were dozens of chiseled statues carved into the stone spires. She spotted gargoyles, goblins, fairies, and elves among the statues towering overhead. Gleaming suits of armor stood on display on either side of the gate, so lifelike and perfect in their presentation. Ava never imagined a knight could stand so still. Would he move if he had to sneeze? If he got an itch could he scratch it? Her imagination swirled in a wild flight of fancy and excitement. She could hardly wait to get inside and explore the hundreds of rooms and corridors that must be found in such a large building.

Ava's senses were assaulted as she stepped inside the castle, drinking in the sights of red runners and vibrant tapestries and more decorative suits of armor all around. She could smell the dinner cooking in the kitchen and the delicate aroma of beef and spices made her stomach remind her how hungry she was. It seemed like ages since her last proper meal. The chords of a lute rang through the chamber and was accompanied by a honeyed voice. She wished she was close enough to make out the words but even the blend of sounds itself was a pleasant delight. A dozen maids, wearing black dresses lined with silver lace, curtseyed and bid them welcome. A bald man stepped forward, his earth-toned robe dragging along the ground behind him.

"Welcome to Hárborg," the man said. He flashed a withered smile at them that Ava didn't quite trust. Ava noticed that his gold-tinged beard was so long that the man had it tucked into the belt of his robe. "The king has been expecting you for some time now."

Ava's father furrowed his eyebrows in response. "I didn't realize he had been made to expect our presence."

"He has been waiting for weeks for a bounty hunter to come and heed his call for help. He is eager to, ah, eliminate the present problem. I'm sure you understand his concern, given your profession," the man said with a polite bow of his head. Ava noticed that there was a drawing of something on the top of the man's head. Was that a triangle? How odd!

"Then he will be pleased that we have come," Ava said, stepping forward. The man studied her with a scrutinizing stare. "We are good at getting rid of monsters. Hunting and killing monsters is what we do."

"The king will be pleased to hear that," he said, clapping his hands. The maids split into two groups, forming a line in front of her and her father. "You will be dining with him tonight in the great hall. These handmaidens will assist you in becoming presentable for the banquet. If you are in need of anything, simply ask and they will see to it."

"His grace is most kind to dine with us," her father said, bowing stiffly. Ava thought the words sounded forced, a rigid formality that went together about as well as a wild bear in a glass maker's shop.

The odd man left the room, his robe still dragging along the ground behind him. The group of maids surrounded her and ushered her up the stairs with polite words. They giggled constantly as they surrounded her. Ava tried to look back and find her father but he had already been led out of the room by his team of maids. She had no choice but to follow them to her room.

Ava bit her lip as the maids worked on three different things at once. Two of them scrubbed her skin, lifting limbs free from the dirt-stained water that had lost most of its warmth ten minutes prior. Another two tugged ivory combs through her tangled hair. The rigid teeth of the comb ripped through every knot they found with ruthless efficiency. It hurt like mad, far worse than any bruise from training with her father. Ava kept touching her scalp to make sure they weren't tearing it all out or making her bleed but there was no sign of blood. Yet.

The last two maids paraded an assortment of dresses and jewelry in front of her, praising the style of each and how grand she would look before the king if she wore them. Ava had no interest in looking grand for anyone, not even a king, but they refused to consider letting her wear her old tunic no matter how much she complained. In their opinion, she needed to look the part of a proper lady. Ava thought they were too much like her old neighbor, Hazel, in that regard, which only made her think of home. She'd much rather be off running through the desert sand with Edgar, getting as dirty as she pleased, than dressing up for some fancy meal with a bunch of stuffy nobles.

She admitted to herself that she enjoyed being dried off with the soft cotton towels but any pleasure was immediately revoked when they started powdering and painting her face. Ava tried to close her eyes and hold her breath during the torture but eventually she needed air. She took a deep breath, planning to hold it in again, but got a lungful of the powder instead. She doubled over in a fit of coughing. The maids responded by tsking and one of them cleared her throat, stepping in front of Ava.

"If you don't mind, Miss, we'd appreciate it if you didn't move so much."

"The powder," Ava said and the maid shook her head.

"You'll adjust to it eventually, Miss. We all do. But now stand still or you'll make a bigger mess of things and we'll have to start over."

"Anything but that!" Ava said. The maids giggled and went back to work on her. The one in front of her dropped into a small curtsey.

"I'm Reina, Miss. We'll get you finished in no time so long as you don't resist anymore." Ava wondered why anyone would choose to suffer through this madness every day.

But Ava drew the line with the shoes. After suffering through her hair getting primped and curled, her face being disguised under paint and powder to the point of being unrecognizable, and wearing a dress so large and poofy that she could hardly sit down, she was at her wits' end.

"Reina, I am not wearing those," she snapped as the maidens tried to cram her feet into tiny pointed shoes.

"Ah, miss, but these are fashionable." Reina answered with a curtsey.

"I don't care. I will either wear leather boots or go barefoot." There was no way she would wear those uncomfortable shoes.

The maids looked at each other and Ava could feel the weight of their displeasure. The Reina turned back to her, a smile on her face.

"Of course, Miss. Your feet are pretty just as they are. No need to wear these tonight. Perhaps another time."

Ava was surprised that they listened, allowing her to go downstairs in her bare feet. Suddenly this one small victory made her feel a bit better about the entire experience. These women weren't completely heartless. But she still memorized each of their faces in case the chance ever arose where she could repay them for that torture. Except for Reina. She seemed to understand.

When Ava stepped into the grand hall, everyone was already seated around a long wooden table. Platters of roasted fowl and assorted nuts and fruits were scattered across the table along with large flagons of wine. A bowl of steamed vegetables, glazed with honey and seasoned with a spice she had never smelt sat in the center of the table next to a massive bowl of crisp green lettuce. The assortment of food made her stomach rumble so loud that she suspected the king could hear. Her father choked on his wine when he saw her step in. She assumed it was because she looked so ridiculous in all of this clothing. A young man in a red jacket rose from the table and came over to greet her. He took her hand and raised it to his lips, an act which Ava thought ridiculous, bowing as he introduced himself.

"M'lady, allow me to escort you to your seat," he said, his voice pleasant and deep. "My name is Flynn, the heir of Hárborg."

"Thank you," Ava mumbled, blushing when she realized everyone was watching them. Flynn led her to a seat across from her father and slid into the spot next to her. The delicious smells of the food were making her hungry in spite of her discomfort. She reached for a turkey leg but the prince grabbed her hand, shaking his head.

"Allow me, m'lady." He carved off a dainty piece of the turkey with his knife, placing it on her plate. He piled on some leafy green vegetables until her plate was overrun and filled her goblet with a light red wine, smiling at her the entire time. Ava sat there, her hands in her lap, not knowing what to do with herself while being served. She was thankful, for the moment, for all the powder on her face because it might hide the color rushing to her cheeks. She could hear hushed whispers from the other end of the table and wondered what they were saying about her. Was it obvious to everyone else that she didn't belong here? Why was the prince giving her so much attention when there were dozens of girls in this room who were older and prettier and richer than her? Was it simply because they were a guest or was there some ulterior motive behind it all?

"Your timing is perfect since we just had a monster invade our domain," the king said. His mouth was full as he spoke and crumbs of bread came flying out of his mouth, "Naturally, you'll want to know the reward in store?"

"I'd prefer to know more about the beast, your grace," her father answered, setting down his empty goblet on the table. "Has the creature been identified?"

"A bounty hunter who wants to hear about the job before he hears about the reward?" the king asked, slamming his fist down on the table and laughing heartily. "I like this new you, even though your presence has been sorely missed at our celebrations."

"Back to the monster, your grace?" her father asked.

"Ah, yes, Tristan. The monster invaded a few weeks back, taking up residence in a cavern in a ravine to the northeast. The one eyewitness I have interviewed said it was a large lizard that breathes fire and swears it was some type of dragon."

"That is one possibility," Tristan answered. "Has it left the cave since it arrived?"

"Not to my knowledge," the king said, tearing a roast chicken in two with his ring-adorned fingers. Ava wondered why someone would need to wear a ring on every finger, much less two or three like the king. "But I can't really afford to monitor the bloody thing. I find it is much cheaper and easier to hire someone to kill it."

"You will supply me with a map of where this cavern is?" her father asked.

Ava lost interest in the conversation, picking at her food while her mind wandered. She imagined her father and her finding the biggest red dragon ever seen. They would work together as a monster hunting team to slay the fierce beast and their exploits would be sung about in mead halls for centuries. She knew there was no power in the world that could stop them so long as they were together. Her thoughts were interrupted by the prince, who nudged her ribs with his elbow.

"Do you not like the food," he asked, gesturing toward her half-eaten meal. Ava smiled at him, lowering her eyes. She wasn't sure if that was right or not but she had seen another lady do so earlier and therefore decided to imitate the action.

"It is delicious but I find I have little appetite tonight."

"Are you unwell?" Flynn said.

"I am fine, just not in a feasting frame of mind," Ava answered. She wished he would let her return to her thoughts or, better yet, just go away completely.

Flynn clapped his hands once and a tall, silver-haired gentleman strode toward them. "I know just the thing to bring you cheer," Flynn said. He turned toward the man as he arrived. "Simeon, play a tune for m'lady."

"I know just the one, your lordship," the man said with a flourishing bow. He strummed his lute, accompanying it with his rich voice. Under different circumstances Ava probably would have enjoyed the song but her mind was distracted by the prospect of hunting a dragon. She took a few more bites of her food as the song ended, hoping that the prince would be content to see her eat some more. She listened in on her father's conversation for a few moments but they were negotiating the price of the hunt and she had no interest in that. It wasn't until the king cleared his throat, silencing the entire room, that Ava truly paid heed to what was going on. Apparently they finally agreed on some sort of terms.

"For the retrieval of the monster in the cave, dead or alive, I offer the following to Tristan: a sum of sixty gold crowns, five hundred silver marks, and his choice of stallion from the royal stable." The whole table nodded in agreement except her father. Those were clearly not the terms he hoped for. "And to his daughter, young Avalina, I offer a betrothal to my son, Flynn."

Five minutes ago, Ava thought this night couldn't possibly get any worse but she was wrong. She was going to have to marry this prince, who she hardly knew and who already annoyed her far more than Edgar ever could have? Her father would certainly refuse the offer and renegotiate for some alternative deal that didn't involve a marriage proposal to a stranger. She was his apprentice now, a monster hunter in training, not some royal lady. She hated being dressed up and waited upon. She had never spent a day at court in her life and that clearly meant she didn't belong here. Surely he would realize that.

"Your grace is too kind," her father replied.

"But father," Ava started.

"Avalina, leave us."

Her face blazed, although she doubted anyone could see it under all the paint. Her father raised a hand to silence her protest and she stormed off. Right now she did not care if it was proper or expected. She thought that being forced to marry a stupid prince wasn't proper so why should she worry about being ladylike?

Her tears warmed her pillow as she cried in the bed they had prepared for her. Even though it was a lot more comfortable than any bed she had ever slept in it wasn't home for her. It wasn't what she wanted. If she was going to be forced to marry a boy, couldn't she at least have a say in which boy? Just when she thought she was setting out on an adventure with her father, everything had to be ruined by a boy. They always seemed to ruin everything.

CHAPTER TEN
Imprisonment

Ava woke up to smeared colors upon her pillowcase. The sight sparked her memory of the previous day's events, which made her feel like crying. Or sleeping more. Or perhaps just hiding under the bed for the rest of her life. Anything sounded better than going downstairs to face the nightmare of last night, especially the boy she was being forced to marry. She wanted her father to come and reassure her that it wouldn't happen, but instead she had the six maids invading her privacy. She scowled at them as they flurried about, flinging open curtains and dragging her out of the bed.

"Isn't is just so exciting," one said as she removed the pillowcases from Ava's bed.

"I know," another one answered. "Who would have thought; the prince, engaged!"

"It's because of that dress," the first answered. "As soon as I saw it, I knew something magical was going to happen."

"The dress is a curse, then," Ava snapped. She yanked it over her head and tossed it aside. Six pairs of eyes watched her without blinking for a moment. Then they all burst into giggles.

"I know it seems like a lot to take in, Miss," Reina said as the maids went about fixing her hair, nails, skin and other features.

"No, I don't want to be betrothed." Ava said, crossing her arms.

"Nonsense," the maid said. "Every woman in Hárborg would love to be in your place."

"Hush, Anjelica," Reina said. "Can't you see the young miss is overcome with emotion?"

"Overcome with love," a maid named Edina said. She was shorter than the rest with a brown mole on the side of her chin. Ava mentally vowed to exact revenge.

"Stop it," Ava shouted, stamping a foot on the floor. A numb, tingling sensation was her reward. "I'm not engaged to anyone, especially not some prince I just met."

Although she couldn't prove it, Ava thought that it felt like the women tugged the brush harder and scrubbed fiercer in response to her vocalized complaints. It was a silent message, a warning to her that they could make things a lot worse each morning if she failed to cooperate. And she was going to be forced to suffer a lifetime of this. Eventually she succumbed to the torture in silence, but once again she memorized the features of each face so that she could get them back if the opportunity ever arose.

Ava saw her father waiting outside her door. He was seated in a rickety wooden chair that appeared moments away from falling apart. The expression on his face was unsettling. He wouldn't look into her eyes and kept touching the hilt of his sheathed sword. His feet, enclosed in thick hide boots, tapped the ground in an irregular rhythm. Ava had never seen him in such a state and she didn't know how to react to this. "Father?" she asked. He didn't answer, taking a deep breath instead. Why was he acting this way? Even though it felt like he betrayed her last night, she still loved him. He had to know that.

"I'm sorry, Avalina," he said. He was staring at the ground by her feet. Ava noticed the dark shade around his eyes. Had he been up all night? "I've tried to talk some sense into the king but he is set on his announcement."

Her heart caught in her throat but Ava sensed she needed to be strong for her father. "It's okay; we'll figure something out after we kill that monster. I know we will come up with a way to get out of it. When do we leave?"

"That's the other thing," her father said. "He is adamant that you remain here while I search for its lair. It could take days if I'm lucky and months if I'm not. The cave where it was spotted may no longer be where it resides, and I am obligated to seek until I can find the monster no matter how long it takes. But he said I would be going alone, until I returned with its head or else firm news of its lair."

"But we're a team," Ava said. She clutched his arm but he didn't look over. "We have to go together. How else am I supposed to train as a monster hunter?" She stamped her foot in response to his silence. She dug her nails into the skin of his arm, needing an answer. To hear something, even if not the answer she wanted. "I am still going to train as a monster hunter, aren't I?"

"I don't know," he answered. His gray eyes met hers, cloudy and bloodshot and distant. He rested a hand on her shoulder and continued. "Most people find it... unnatural for a woman to fill the role of a hunter. In time, perhaps."

"I don't want to be a proper lady," Ava snarled. She slammed a closed fist into the breastplate of his armor. She fought hard to ignore the dull ache that throbbed up her arm, but she couldn't prevent the tears from welling. "I just want to be me. Isn't that good enough?"

"It always has been and will be for me. But until I return, you'll have no choice but to go along with their expectations. Things will be far worse for you, if you rebel. I knew the king many years ago and he is not a bad man. You'll be safe here and may even come to find a thing or two that you can like about the castle life." He got to his feet and his eyes darted down the hall. His tone changed, hardening. His eyes burned with a fierce determination. The father, the protector Ava knew and loved and idolized, was standing in front of her again. She smiled and he looked down at her. "I'll be back as soon as I am able to take you with me. Even if I have to flip over every stone in the ravine and search through every inch of thick prairie, I will discover the monster's lair and return for you. I will come and take you on your first real hunt. I promise."

Never for a moment did she doubt those words. She watched him disappear down the hall, his black cloak billowing behind him as he turned the corner and was gone.

Her first days of imprisonment, for that is what she equated this forced stay to, were miserable. She spent most of her time sulking in her room and refused to let anyone in or to come out except when it was time to eat. Even during those meal times, she only lingered in the great hall long enough to devour her food in a most unladylike fashion before departing.

After three days the king himself came to visit her. She could hardly refuse him, of course, without the risk of getting beheaded or worse, so she let him in and hoped he was willing to overlook her tangled mess of fiery hair or her wrinkled blouse. It was easy for her to ignore him when she was in the crowded, busy great hall but here in this room she was subject to his scrutinizing stare. He was portly and the years had claimed most of the hair from his head. Ava knew he was a sloppy eater because he was often drowning in drink but his clothing was crisp and tidy. Perhaps he had handmaidens to dress him and make him proper as well. To make him look like something he was not, just like they did to her.

"I remember, years ago, when your father first came to my court," the king said. He sat down in a chair across from her, a wistful smile on his lips. "He was my diplomatic expert, mingling with foreign dignitaries and easing their suspicions prior to critical negotiations. Trade boomed in the kingdom while your father served on my court, and he was suited for the life. Did you know this, child, that he wasn't always a hunter?"

Ava nodded her head. She knew her mother had been the huntress when she was younger, but she knew so little about her father's life during those years.

"When your mother died, he departed from that life at court. We've never been as prosperous as the time when he was here. He loved that life. I imagine that he'd still be living that life, had things gone differently. It suited him, far better than I imagined, the title of hunter would. He's grown into that, over time, because he was forced into that role. But you, Avalina-"

"Ava."

"Excuse me?"

"My name is Ava. You can't call me Avalina." Ava insisted.

The king stumbled over his words for a moment. "Apologies, Ava. I simply assumed since your father..."

"No one else can call me Avalina."

"Ah, I understand. As I was saying, your father loved being at court and the life that entailed. I know your heart is set on being like your father, but this life is like him as well. Perhaps you'll come to love it, as he once did."

She scoffed at that in her mind but didn't give word to her doubts. Let him believe what he wanted. She couldn't change her current situation of being here, but she could try and change her level of comfort.

"Maybe I will," Ava lied, "but I want to explore. There is a whole world to explore outside of the kingdom. I bet there are exciting adventures to be found."

"A proper lady shouldn't go gallivanting across wilderness."

"I'm not a proper lady."

"Not yet," the king replied thoughtfully. "But that could change."

"I do not want to be locked inside these walls." Ava said.

"Would it help if you were allowed to explore outside the castle itself?"

"You mean explore the crowded streets crammed full of people and merchants? No, thank you."

The king pulled out a small scroll and spread it out across a table. Ava stood up to see what was on there. A map of Hárborg, with dull browns and grays showing the streets and buildings. But also with lush greens and yellows for plant life and fields and dense clusters of trees. She had no idea those would be inside the walls of the city, but she wanted to go explore them.

"I can see from your expression that there are places on here you'd be willing to explore."

"Yes, your grace."

"Please, when we are alone you are welcome to call me Quinn."

"As you wish, your grace. I mean, Quinn."

"Do you see the thick, black lines running along the outskirts here?"

"I do," Ava said, leaning in closer.

"You are free to explore anywhere within there on your own during your personal hours. If you wish to explore anything beyond there, you must notify me and I will provide you with an armed escort of guards."

"Seriously?"

"Seriously. On two conditions."

Ava's heart sank down to her toes. Now would come the things that would end all of her dreams of fun and adventure that had sprouted in her mind.

"First, you will go to the castle library every morning after breaking your fast. The master scribe here will provide you with lessons in reading and writing. Those are skills that every proper lady must learn."

Ava's mind jumped to the journal her father kept hidden away. She'd learn to read and understand the words inside of there! She had a rudimentary education in that area already, but it had never been formal or focused.

"Second, you must attend a formal dinner every evening. You must come dressed in the style your maids select for you. You must interact with those in attendance, at the very least those seated around you. And you must remain until dismissed. If you can do this, then you are free to dress as you desire during the other hours of the day."

Ava considered this condition and what it entailed. She would need to be tortured each night by Reina and her flock of maids. That undoubtedly meant daily baths, vigorous brushings of her hair, and paint on her face. It would mean uncomfortable and impractical clothing and sitting next to Flynn. Could she endure a few hours of that each day if it meant the rest of the time was her own?

"I have a condition of my own, your grace."

"And that would be?"

"I choose my own shoes. I will never wear those pointed things they wanted me to wear on that first night."

The king laughed. He wiped a tear from his eyes and smiled at her. "Very well," he said, "your shoes are your own to pick."

Ava wasted no time. She shed her dress and the uncomfortable shoes that were forced on her as soon as the king left her room. She wriggled her toes on the cold floor and felt the blood rushing back into her feet. She wandered over to her wardrobe and pulled out a black and silver tunic along with charcoal breeches. She was happy to slip her feet into polished black leather boots, grateful to have the comfort of proper shoes on her feet. Her old scabbard for *Seraphina* had been replaced with a black one as well, trimmed with silver. She realized that they were already trying to dress her in the house colors but at this point she didn't mind so much. These clothes were a lot more comfortable than what she was wearing last night. These clothes were proper for doing, while dresses were for being looked at. And Ava was a girl who preferred to do things: useful, fun, and adventurous things.

Her first destination was the castle courtyards. A dozen shouts and grunts echoed in the air as men practiced with weapons, sparring with each other or stationary dummies. Since her father was gone, she needed to find someone to train with if she wanted to get better. In a castle like this, there were bound to be masters in axes, staves, bows, spears, and more. Plus dozens of masters with the sword and the shield. Ava pictured the look on her father's face when he returned and found she was better with a sword than him. The thought made her genuinely smile for the first time since he had left and she envisioned the moment when her practice sword would strike his chest and he would laugh and wrap her in his warm embrace.

It didn't take long, though, for that dream to be shattered. She walked out to the courtyard where the sound of steel clashing on steel rang through the air. A commander in a red coat shouted orders to the combatants.

"Tien, strengthen the grip on your hilt. You aren't holding a blasted fish! Gormund, your strikes are sloppy. You won't be able to hit a practice dummy."

The courtyard stank worse than the stables back at home, but Ava needed to be trained. As the two sparring soldiers broke apart, Ava stepped up and drew her sword. The welcome reception she imagined she would receive didn't happen. The soldiers burst into laughter, nudging one another with sharp elbows.

"Oi, little girlie, get back to the kitchens where you belong," said one.

"You better give that back before some soldier notices their blade has been swiped and comes for vengeance," called out another.

"These courtesans keep on getting younger and younger. Little girl, you aren't needed until after we're done here. Go wait in the barracks."

Ava's face burned from their remarks, her cheeks blending with her crimson hair. She didn't understand half of their remarks, but she knew none were good. One thing was certain: she couldn't train in the courtyard with the soldiers. They would never accept her as a warrior or a peer, even if she bested them, and would never willingly spar with her. She would have to find someone else, or some way else, to get her training while stuck in Hárborg. The realization crushed her and she spent the remainder of the day wandering through the sparse forest, skirting along the boundary set by the king. She climbed to the top of the tallest trees and peered out into the distance to see if she could see her father. She never did.

She knew that her day of climbing and traversing across trails would earn her a rough reception with the handmaidens that evening so she waited until the last possible moment to head back to her bedchamber. They were in her room, waiting with the empty basin for her bath and clothes piled upon her bed.

"Oh my, how dreadful!" the tallest one exclaimed. The others all gasped and nodded and their chatter, for a few moments, blended into an indecipherable babble. Ava blinked at them, mouth hanging open as she tried to follow their preening comments. Finally Reina grabbed her hand and dragged her forward. Ava stood mute as they stripped the tunic off her while two of them rushed to fill the washbasin with hot water.

"Who did this to you?" Edina, a short girl with plump, rosy cheeks asked her.

"Did what to me?" Ava asked, hoping to shake the question.

"Your clothes are dirty and torn," she answered, "so did one of the commoners push you into a bramble bush?"

"Not exactly."

"I bet some of the boys in town chased her through the streets and into the woods," Anjelica said. She ignored Ava's frown and continued. "That must have been how she got in such a state." The chatter erupted once more and Ava sighed. Trying to follow their conversation was making her head throb.

"I climbed trees," she burst out at last. The silence that followed was deafening, broken only when the two girls came panting back into the room with more water. The splashing of the water being poured snapped the girls out of their daze and they went on chattering as though Ava weren't there.

"How dreadful it must be to grow up learning to climb trees instead of learning to sew," one of them commented.

"I hear that the village folk are only half civilized, practically savages." said Anjelica.

Every time Ava opened her mouth to interject, they pulled some clothing over her head or spoke louder and faster to cut her off. And soon they thrust her into the steaming bathwater. They showed no sympathy when she cried out from the scalding heat. Nor did they heed when she complained that their scrubbing and brushing and primping was painful. They were merciless in their attack on her appearance. When they were finished a stranger peered back at her from the mirror. Could that really be her? For the first time in her life she felt like more than just a plain little girl, someone undeserving of notice. But even though she might look the part she knew that her heart and spirit did not belong in this life.

But she couldn't stop herself from wondering what Edgar would say if he could see her now.

Dinner was the one event that Ava was dreading that day. She stepped into the dining hall only because she cherished the freedom to explore. A few people turned to look at her, but most kept focused on their feasting and conversation. In spite of the noise, she could hear every thump of her heart and every stomp of her shoes on the hard floor. She took her seat beside the prince. Flynn was garbed in a silver jacket, trimmed with black. He bowed and held a chair out for her. Ava blushed as Flynn shared samples of food with her. The roasted potatoes were especially delightful, although she ate more things than she imagined possible. Her belly ached and still the prince insisted she try everything that was set upon the table.

"When I was a young child, I used to cram my plate full of everything that passed by. My mother used to chide me for the waste, as I would hardly touch more than a few bites. Yet I desired to have my fill of everything, a trait that lingers still."

"There are so many things to try. Are all meals so large?" Ava asked.

"Sometimes. Father likes to hold lavish feasts. While I enjoy them, I find it to be a waste of the treasury's funds."

"Why does he do it, then?"

"Something about entertaining the nobles, and letting the common folk find a seat in the palace. Some of them are down at the other end of the hall, although I would never go near there. Father always does. And he distributes the leftovers among the peasants."

"Sounds like a generous thing to do."

"They should be paying the crown for the privilege of living here, not the other way around. He's a fool for throwing these things away, spending my inheritance without a second thought."

Ava bit her lip, considering the things she just heard. The prince stabbed at a piece of poultry, his anger reflected in his tight grip on the fork. She needed to change the subject before this turned into a long night of hearing him rage and sulk.

"What about the castle? I bet you explored in here all the time as a child."

"There isn't much special about it. Dusty corridors. Stuffy rooms full of books and maps. Knights patrolling at all hours."

"Are there secret chambers hidden within the castle?"

"A few," Flynn said, shrugging. "I found one that went to the center of the whole world once. I was down there for days, and my parents had the entire kingdom searching for me. It was closed off after that."

"Oh," Ava said. She wished he would have told a proper story, one filled with adventure and excitement. Monsters to slay. Traps to avoid. The heroic sort of thing you heard in a bard's tales. But Flynn didn't appear to have the desire to embellish his stories beyond those simple details.

The prince fell silent, picking at his food. She could pick out the baritone voice of the bard singing a tune and playing a flute to accompany the story. There was so much noise in the hall that she could barely make out the words, but she leaned forward and strained to make them out. He ended his tune and a light applause followed.

"This next tale will be about the rise and fall of Drexlan," the bard said. He lifted the flute to his lips and played a lilting melody. Ava scooted onto the edge of the bench, leaning forward to hear the words.

"What does your mother think about you chasing after monsters?" Flynn asked. Ava frowned. He chose now to want to engage her in conversation?

"She died when I was three," Ava answered. A long silence pierced the air between them. Flynn stared down at his plate of food, a slight pink coloring his cheeks.

"I'm sorry, I didn't know."

"You wouldn't."

"Mine died when I was seven."

"Oh," Ava whispered.

"I miss her a lot. She was always there for me. Pushing me to learn, to enjoy life. Father just wants me to be ready to rule one day. But mother, she wanted me to be me."

"I don't really remember my mother," Ava said. "But she was a huntress, too. Before my father was. I hope she would be proud of me."

She never did hear much of the Drexlan epic, as they spent time talking about their parents. Ava found herself actually enjoying parts of the conversation, getting a chance to know a little more about the prince. Ava curtseyed deeply as she left the great hall. It felt like ages had passed them by while she had been in there and she couldn't wait to change into something far more comfortable. And perhaps she would even try to explore the underground depths of the castle tonight after everyone else was in their beds. She allowed the maids to change her into bed clothes and, as soon as they left, she wriggled out of those and slipped on her adventuring tunic. At least that was what she was calling it now. She snuffed out the candle by her bed and lay on top of the covers, waiting in the darkness for the sounds in the halls to subside. She had no idea that Hárborg rarely slept; there was always some sort of activity taking place within its extensive series of chambers, and the silence she waited for never came. But sleep did.

CHAPTER ELEVEN
The Order

The door to her room opened and the handmaidens filed in like a swarm of ants. They smiled and chatted among themselves, clearly unfazed by the lack of sunlight at such an early hour. Ava groaned and rolled over, tugging the blankets high over her head. She wanted another ten minutes of sleep, but an army of hands tugged the blanket free from her grip and pulled it off her bed. Half a dozen gasps rang through her room and the silence that followed made Ava's heart sink. She knew they must already be scheming how to torture her as repayment for her disheveled appearance.

"Mistress Ava," Reina chimed in a voice she rarely heard her father use, "what in the 13 kingdoms happened to you last night?"

"What do you mean?" Ava asked, uncertain what was wrong. She knew that they'd likely scold her for wearing her tunic to bed, but that was hardly good cause for a proclamation.

"Just look at you," she answered, dragging Ava out of the bed and over toward the full-length mirror in the corner. They loved to stand her in front of that thing but Ava could hardly understand the reason why. She looked how she looked, and that was that. Why obsess over something so trivial as her appearance? She looked at her reflection now and, admittedly, she looked a bit messier than normal. But she was no painting to be kept on display. She had a right to dirtiness and disorder when she desired. Her shoulders lifted in a shrug and she turned away from the mirror.

"You slept in your tunic and breeches," Anjelica muttered.

"And not this comfortable, silk nightgown. I worked so hard to press so that it would be nice and comfortable for your ladyship," added Edina.

"And the boots!" Milena said. "How dreadful it must have been to fall asleep wearing those boots. I'm just glad they weren't covered in mud or any other dreadful filth. Could you imagine how long it would take to get a stain like that out of the bedding? Well, we simply cannot allow you to go about your morning looking like that. Come on, we'll get you right and proper in no time. After all, you cannot expect to attend the service at the Order's temple while looking like that."

"Looking like what?" Ava asked. They ignored her question and pulled her tunic over her head and slipped her breeches off as two handmaidens rushed to fill a copper washbasin. Ava shivered as she stood in her undergarments waiting for the water to arrive. She folded her arms across her chest and rubbed her hands along her arms but it didn't have much effect. The handmaidens who undressed her were too busy debating what clothes she should wear for the service today to notice her discomfort. The first buckets of water splashed into the basin, steam radiating into the air. The steam had vanished by the time the second set of buckets arrived. It was a long process to fill the basin, and so far the water would barely reach above her ankles if she stood in there. The chatter of the maidens around her clothing options became a dull buzz that Ava shut out, focusing instead upon wondering what adventures her father might be having right now. Had he found the dragon yet? Was he riding back, at this moment, with its head or a wing strapped to his saddle? Three bucketfuls. Four. Five.

Ava finished undressing and slipped into the water. Too much of her skin remained exposed, but she no longer cared. Her legs were submerged in heated bliss and she sighed as a smile crossed her face and she closed her eyes. Each bucketful that rained down upon her was a blessing from Eodran and soon the basin was full and the handmaidens returned their attention to her. It had been nice to be forgotten by them and she had cherished it while it lasted. But now they circled around her, equipped with their tools of torture.

One maiden tugged a brush through her hair, the boar bristles scratching her scalp with every stroke. A pair of them took thick cakes of yellow soap and scrubbed Ava's skin until it was raw. A fourth maiden plucked her eyebrows, one hair at a time, and was less delicate in her approach every time Ava complained about the pain. They were ruining the essence of the bath, which was supposed to be a soothing and relaxing experience. Not an opportunity to break someone under torture. Ava would have given up any secret she knew by the time they pulled out the scratchy towels to dry her off. Not a single face showed a spark of sympathy for her plight, and they all talked around her repeated complaints about their treatment. They must have formed an unspoken alliance against her, possibly to try and break her so as to leave the prince a bachelor. If this was what she had to look forward to every day, she was certain she would lose her mind. Ava tried to ignore the tangle of crimson hair being swept up and the stinging she felt on her red knees and elbows, but it was impossible. They were impossible.

Ava stuck her tongue out at the maidens' backs as they left her room. The door shut behind them and she sighed and sank to her knees on the floor. The tears she had fought to hold in burst forth now and a sob wracked her body with convulsions. She allowed herself a few minutes there, alone in the room, to unleash the well of emotions inside of her. Then she rose to her feet, wiped her eyes until they were dry, and strode over to the mirror. A few moments were all she needed to touch-up her appearance, hoping that no one would be able to see signs of her weakness. Today was an important day and she needed to make the right impression if she was going to be stuck in this forsaken castle until her father returned. The Order of Light had been almost equal in power to the Circle of Elders back home. Maybe they could find a way to get her free from the threat of betrothal and bestow a hunter's blessing upon her. Besides, she would need to pray for her father. She had almost gaped at the prince when he asked if she would want to attend their weekly service at the Order's temple. Did he think she was a faithless, monster-loving fool?

Her thoughts were disturbed by three raps at her door. A voice like dried parchment called out, "Prince Flynn to provide escort to Lady

Ava" and Ava cursed under her breath. She knew that it would be impossible to avoid the prince today, but she still wanted no part of his company so long as it could be avoided. She had prayed for a carriage ride and nothing more, but it seemed he was going to impose his presence upon her regardless what she desired.

"One moment," Ava said. She bit her bottom lip and looked once more in the mirror. Not that she wanted to impress the stupid prince, but because she needed to make a good impression with the Order of Light. It would hardly do to appear before them disheveled and all a mess. She wasn't about to let a boy ruin today's plans. Satisfied, Ava spun toward the door and strode across the room. Flynn stood outside, leaning against a marble pillar that stretched so far over her head that Ava was sure she would be able see her village from the top of it had it been a tree outside.

"Allow me to provide you with some company," Flynn said with a slight bow. He was attempting to be civil, but at the moment Ava had no desire to be civil. Her morning had been ruined by the maidens and now this prince was going to impose his presence upon her first trip to the Order of Light. Yet she checked her emotions and smiled at the prince, flashing her teeth as she uttered thanks and took his proffered arm. They strode through corridor after corridor in silence apart from the servants who would stop, bow or curtsy, and greet Flynn as the pair of them passed by. Flynn never answered them, nor did he even glance in their direction, yet Ava offered each servant a small smile. She wouldn't be callous and ignore the staff in the castle. It could hardly be their fault that they were not born into wealth and power. It had been only a few days ago that she was no more important than they were, and she vowed she would never forget that no matter what might happen.

The butterflies pounded against the walls of her stomach as soon as the red-domed spires of the Order's temple came into view. Flynn still hadn't said a word since they left her room, and now she almost wished he would break the silence. Anything to divert her attention from the experience of entering this place for the first time. She had ideas of what they would encounter in there, but this temple was large enough to fit nearly her entire village inside. It made the Temple of Light at home seem like a stable. The stone exterior had a reddish-pink tint to it that reminded Ava of a summer sunset. The stone arch surrounding massive oak doors had words chiseled into the surface, although Ava couldn't read the words. A stream of men and women, all dressed in fine clothing, swarmed in through the doors. On the side of the building there must have been a second entrance, because Ava could see a line of dirty, bedraggled men and women lined up over there. She tried to pause to get a better look but Flynn kept walking and she stumbled to catch back up to him.

When they stepped inside the building, she understood why the temple was so large. A second and third level spanned around the entire chamber with those she assumed were not nobles filling in the space. The bottom section in front of the priest was reserved for those of wealth and privilege. There was no seating in the temple, but rather padded benches where people knelt. Ava guessed that the padding was only present down on this level, assuming that the poorer people wouldn't get that addition. Flynn led her to the front and he knelt next to his father, leaving Ava to kneel along the outside of the aisle. The padding eased some of the discomfort of kneeling, but she imagined that it wouldn't be long before it made little difference. Unless the preaching of the priest were short, her legs would undoubtedly fall asleep before the end.

The king cleared his throat and stood up. The cacophony of a thousand voices were silenced within moments and then a priest in red robes strode out from behind crimson curtains. He knelt before the king, kissing the king's ring. Then the king knelt and the priest chanted a blessing on the king and his household. Not a person stirred in the temple, and Ava struggled to keep from shifting herself. Already, these stupid benches were making her uncomfortable. She prayed that this would be kept short. The priest took up his place, standing behind a marble altar, and locked eyes with Ava. Her heart skipped a beat and the fluttering in her stomach doubled. She bit her lip to keep from squirming beneath that cold, iron gaze. At last, he shifted his focus to the gathered assembly and began to speak.

"Your majesty, royal nobles, and our honored guests, today is Saint Aspen's Day. We must remember the history of this glorious Saint and the deeds he accomplished during his lifetime before his untimely death. It will be a day marked with remembrance, but also one of feasting and celebration, for that is what the departed saint would desire from this collection of followers. In honor of Saint Aspen's Day, the king has generously offered to provide a sacrifice from his herd of cattle and has made a decree that all in the kingdom shall do the same, in order to provide the meat so that all may join in the feasting regardless of wealth or station."

Cheers drowned out the next words from the priest, as the upper levels tossed hats into the air and pumped their fists in celebration. Feasting on meats was clearly a rare experience for them, and their gratitude brought a smile to Ava's face. But the faces of the nobles that she could see were darkened into scowls. Clearly they did not desire to share even one animal from their herd for the poor. Ava glanced at the king to find him watching her, wearing a smile. She had misjudged the king. Perhaps, in time, even Flynn might be able to become a good ruler like his father. The noise settled down and then the priest continued.

"History teaches us that Saint Aspen was one of the first to cling to the three tenets of the order. His life demonstrated them over and over again, leading to his place in our history and, more importantly, securing his sainthood within the Order. I cannot express enough how important those tenets are, nor how rare it is to discover someone who truly puts them into practice as well as Saint Aspen did. Only our beloved king, here among us today, comes close to achieving perfection when employing these tenets."

The priest continued rattling on but Ava looked toward the king. Her eyebrows climbed toward her scalp and she blinked. The king was a close follower of the tenets? Even her father fell short from time to time with one of the three. She made a mental note to ask the king, next time they were alone, how he managed to accomplish such perfection in following the ways of the Order of Light.

"The first time that Saint Aspen encountered a monster, he reacted in the appropriate manner: he submitted to the greater power that the monster possessed. He subjected himself, placing his person in service to the monster."

Ava couldn't stop the gasp that escaped her lips. The priest droned on, but Flynn elbowed her hard in the ribs and a few glares were shot in her direction. She was confused: didn't the Order believe in the extermination of monsters rather than subjection?

"And so you can see how Saint Aspen demonstrated our first tenet: The mighty shall inherit the entirety of Aralin. Whether it is the might gained through wealth, or the might demonstrated with brute force, the strong are destined to rule. Yet later in life, Saint Aspen also demonstrated the second tenet: Possession of might shall be demonstrated through challenge. When he was commanded to follow the instructions of a lesser monster, Saint Aspen challenged that monster's authority and, through cunning and power, defeated that monster and claimed command of that unit for himself. He ruled for several months, until a newcomer was transferred to his unit and challenged his power to rule. It was then that Saint Aspen demonstrated the third of the tenets: the subjected shall labor and obey without question toward the mighty. When he was defeated in combat, his life was spared and he became an obedient soldier beneath that commander. We would all do well to follow the example of Saint Aspen, knowing our place in the hierarchy of power and accepting it without question or complaint."

Ava wanted to run far away from the temple. She had heard enough of this drivel to know that their tenets were unfair and impossible. Flynn grabbed her arm and yanked her back down when she tried to rise to leave, commanding her to remain until the priest dismissed them. Ava sat there, the words of the priest buzzing past her unheard as he droned on about Saint Aspen and the importance of might as a gauge for influence and command. Tears streamed down her cheek and her body wracked with silent sobs as she prayed to Eodran for her father's safety and his speedy return. She needed to leave this place, and fast.

She spent the day in her rooms, remaining apart from the feasting and the celebrating going on outside and in the castle. Three times the prince had come to her door, demanding she join in with the activities. Three times she told him what she thought of his idea and of their Order's teachings. She expected the king to come after the final time, when she told Flynn that he couldn't command her, based on his Order's tenets, because she was stronger than him. She vowed to never attend a service at that temple again, no matter how long she was forced to stay in Hárborg.

Ultimately, her body spoiled her convictions to remain locked up. Hunger drew her out that evening, yet she was in no mood for idle chatter nor merriment. Flynn sat between two young noblewomen who fawned openly over him, and Ava stuck her tongue out at him the one time he looked her way. He thought to try and make her jealous, but she only hated him more for it. She didn't understand how she could have such a strong hatred for the prince after such a short time, but she simply couldn't stand him. That night she prayed again to Eodran to bring her father back safely, and fast, before she lost all hope of escaping Hárborg. Her sleep was restless, and she tossed and turned in bed yet sleep refused to come. The celebration went on outside the castle walls and the orange and red lights of fires danced on her wall. Eventually sleep found her.

CHAPTER TWELVE
A Monster in Hárborg

The handmaidens were shocked when they woke her the next morning. They chided her for her bloodshot eyes and the chain of yawns that Ava failed to suppress. They assumed she had been up late, celebrating like so many of the others in the kingdom, and Ava chose not to correct them. Their task of preparing her for the events of the day was swiftly finished in spite of their disapproving comments and they departed from her room in record time. Ava could already tell it was going to be a good day.

The massive library took her breath away. Row upon row upon row of books filled the walls in every direction. The shelves spanned nearly to the ceiling, each one crammed with dusty volumes. Lanterns hung on poles everywhere, casting light throughout the room. There were still many patches of shadows where the circles of light didn't overlap, but far more of the room was covered in light. Table upon table filled the floor space, most of them containing dozens of books stacked in unruly piles. Few people could be seen seated at those tables, with small, shielded candles burning as they pored over documents and maps. A frail man with thick spectacles came up to her and grabbed her by the arm. His grip was far stronger than she expected. He appeared to be a little older than her father, with a lot more gray than brown in his hair.

"You must be the future princess, Ava. I am Heimdal. Come, this way."

"I'm not a princess yet," Ava replied.

"A detail, princess, that will soon be remedied." He led her through the library, past rows of tables and stacks of books lining the floors and walls.

"What if I don't want to be a princess?"

"Nonsense, child. Who wouldn't want to have access to all these priceless treasures found in the library here? As princess, and someday as queen, even the most restricted volumes would be yours to enjoy. The prince's late mother used to spend a lot of her time in here, too, you know."

"Books? I want adventure."

"Every tome in this place contains an adventure of some sort."

"Adventures of exploring and battling dangerous monsters?"

"Some of them, yes. There is even a collection of the annals of famous monster hunters in here."

"What's an annal?"

"A record of events in history. Sometimes recorded by the hunter themselves, other times written posthumously by a scribe. I knew a few hunters who carried their own journals where they chronicled the events, preparing things for the time when an annal would be constructed."

Ava gasped. She suddenly understood what was in her father's prized journal. Could there possibly be one of these annals for her mother? Had her mother kept a journal? "What are we waiting for," Ava asked, "let's start reading." Heimdal laughed, although it sounded more like the ragged gasps of a man about to die.

She relished every moment of her first lesson in letters. Heimdal was quite patient with her. She made many more mistakes than successes that morning as she attempted to read and copy down letters and simple words and he was never harsh with her. But she could tell when she was making big mistakes because Heimdal would wring his hands and tug on the sleeves of his onyx doublet. It amused her and occasionally she would intentionally make a mistake just to see his fidget.

She noticed Flynn, who was studying at an adjacent table in the library, was staring at her with a smirk on his face as she studied. His scrutiny made Ava shift in her chair and, eventually, she turned her chair so that her back was to the prince. She prayed that her lessons would end quickly so she could get far away from the prince and his gaze. It was unnerving her today. When Heimdal released her, she rushed out of the library and back to her rooms so she could bathe, scrubbing away the feeling of his stares.

Flynn caught up to her later that day as Ava was out wandering through the fields within the city. He was wearing red and orange robes that looked like flames dancing on a campfire as he walked toward her. In his hand he carried a staff of rowan wood that was a full head taller than him, carved and painted with ornate images. As he grew close enough she noticed they all had one theme in common: fire. It would seem her betrothed had a small obsession with burning things.

"You should be more grateful," Flynn said as he waded through thick grass to catch up to her. "You will have a handsome and powerful husband when your father returns. A husband who will someday be the king of Hárborg."

"I am a better fighter than you," Ava challenged, knowing he was armed with only a stick, "and I am willing to prove that my steel is better than your staff."

Flynn laughed. The prince shook his head, saying, "I don't doubt your prowess with that sword of yours, but you would be no match for me. I'm the youngest in the history of the kingdom to be elevated to the rank of Second Sorcerer and this autumn I will be raised to the rank of First Sorcerer."

"Well I'm an apprentice monster hunter," Ava spat, "just like my father. And there is no monster that we can't handle together."

"I'm pledged as a Pyromancer, the first in the history of Hárborg," Flynn said as he twirled his staff, "and there is no monster I can't handle alone."

"You're lying," Ava said.

"Watch this." Flynn stopped walking and placed both hands on his staff, chanting in a foreign tongue. Ava thought he sounded ridiculous and noted how easy it would be to slip a dagger between his ribs right now. As he chanted she counted the number of imaginary stabs she could land and knew that he would have been dead several times before he ever finished casting a spell. What good was using magic if it left you weak and vulnerable like this? A good sword and shield were far more dependable companions in a battle. Then a pale red glow surrounded Flynn's staff and he pointed it at a field of wheat in front of them. Flynn unleashed a torrent of fire that swept through the air. The heads of wheat were scorched under the intense inferno, charring and disintegrating rather than catching fire. Flynn stopped his spell by slamming the butt of his staff in the ground. He turned to Ava, the smirk on his face bigger than before. "See, I'm stronger than you," he said. "I bet you couldn't do that in a thousand years."

She was going to reply but someone beside the field had caught Flynn's attention. It was a small, mousy boy garbed in a green tunic with brown breeches and thick boots. He had a satchel slung over his shoulder and he rushed across the open ground. The people around him ignored the boy as he wove through crowds but Flynn watched him like a hawk circling its prey. Ava admired the agile way the boy moved, seeming to know the right place to step at the right time to miss being trampled and to avoid notice. At least to avoid the notice of anyone else in the crowd.

"Mouser," Flynn called out and then the prince walked through the scorched wheat toward him. The small boy froze in place and a palace guard rammed into him. The boy hit the ground hard, groaning and clutching his arm. Flynn laughed as the soldier berated the boy, rapping his head with a gauntleted hand before rushing off again. Ava felt sorry for the boy and sped to catch up to Flynn and this newcomer.

"So... sorry your lordship," Mouser said with a stiff bow. "I didn't see you there. No letters today, s... sir."

"I'm not interested in that," Flynn said. The prince cracked his knuckles as he spoke. "It's you I wanted."

"I'm not sure I follow, sir. Did you need a letter delivered to someone, sir?"

"Of course you don't," Flynn sneered, "since you're just a simple messenger boy. You're too stupid to understand anything." Flynn took a step toward Mouser and the boy's brown eyes widened as the color leached from his face.

"What are you doing?" Ava asked. She took a step toward the prince. "He's done nothing."

"He annoys me," Flynn answered. The tall prince pushed Mouser to the ground. The boy landed with a solid thud and his eyes were wide and his mouth hung open. Flynn laughed and lifted his staff overhead. "I'll teach him to cross my path."

Before she could consider the magnitude of her actions Ava reacted to the scene. *Seraphina* flashed out of its sheath and cut through the air. Ava shifted and braced herself to catch the force of the blow on the flat of her blade. Their weapons crashed together, locked in a struggle of force. The look in Flynn's eyes was fierce and hateful. Ava clenched the hilt with all her might and pressed back against his staff. Mouser scrambled back, moving away from the scene unfolding in front of him. Flynn let up first and Ava's muscles ached in complaint from the strain. The prince was a lot stronger than he looked. Ava and Flynn stood apart, staring at each other with weapons ready to strike again. Ava counted her heartbeats, waiting for the prince to make his next move. After a long silence, the prince looked away from her and lowered his staff.

"You're lucky," he snapped at the boy, "that a girl was here to save you, Mouser. Next time you won't be so lucky." Mouser scrambled around a corner and quickly disappeared from sight. Ava didn't blame him for wanting to put as much distance between himself and the temper of the prince as he could manage. If she was smart, she would have been right on Mouser's heels and far away from the prince by now. But she stood her ground, sheathing her sword and waiting for the wrath to be redirected toward her. Flynn spun back toward Ava, his eyes smoldering with ire. "What did you think you were doing?"

"You had no right to attack him," Ava said, crossing her arms across her chest.

"Who asked you to be the judge of what is right in my kingdom? I am the prince, the next in line to be the king. Someday soon I will be the one ruling here, and my word will be law. Any who defies me will be publicly flogged as an example. You're just lucky that you are my father's guest in Hárborg. Next time I won't let you stop me, even if it means I must face my father's wrath later. I won't let a girl interfere with my plans."

"And you'll lose the next time as well because you didn't let me do anything. I stopped you and you know it," Ava said. She hoped her voice carried a confidence that her mind lacked. She wasn't sure that it was the right thing to do. She had just attacked and threatened the prince of this kingdom, and apparently her future husband. Her father would disapprove. He would remind her that the way of Eodran is to love those who hate you, to refuse to let the words of the opposition affect your actions.

Flynn didn't respond to her claims. He spun on his heels, robe whirling in the breeze, and stormed back into the castle. Ava was pretty sure the king would be visiting her tonight once he heard about this scene. Would she be moved to the dungeon? At least that might end her betrothal and get her out of this unwanted marriage. Her father would break her out of the dungeon and then they could ride off into a different kingdom and go on living as monster hunters. A few days in a cell were certainly bearable for that and there were twelve other kingdoms to visit and make a living. Well, eleven feasible ones because no one would consider settling in Drexlan.

Ava was right about one thing: the king did visit her room that night. But not to punish or threaten her. She had expected her bedroom door to swing open and crash into the wall, but he rapped with a gentle knock before entering. He shut the door behind him and sedately crossed the room.

"May I?" he asked, gesturing to a chair opposite her. Ava blinked at him and then nodded. The king sat down in the chair, a soft sigh emerging as he lowered himself onto the soft cushion. "I hear that there was a bit of a commotion today. Care to share your side of the incident?"

"Lord king, uhm, I mean, your Quinn," Ava stammered. She could feel the heat radiating from her skin. "It isn't how it sounds."

"And how does it sound?" he asked, white eyebrows raising high enough to nearly touch the bottom of his crown.

"Like I attacked the prince," Ava said, looking into the king's eyes, "but it isn't true. I used the flat of my blade and never swung at him. I was only defending Mouser, who didn't do anything to deserve being attacked by the prince."

"I see. And this Mouser asked you to help protect him from my son?"

"Well, not exactly. But Flynn should not be able to just strike someone because he doesn't like them."

"He is the prince. When he is king, who would be able to tell him not to? Or that it was wrong to do that?"

"I don't know," Ava confessed, "but it isn't right. He shouldn't be able to do those things. Not without a good reason, at least."

The king rose from the chair and Ava looked down at her feet. She knew what was coming next: a reprimand and then her punishment. Instead, a cold hand lifted her head to look up at the king. He smiled at her while shaking his head. "Ava, I want to thank you for standing up to Flynn like that. I wish more people would do that, but everyone walks delicately around him because he is going to be the next king. They are afraid of offending him and seeing that wrath come down upon them once he ascends to the throne.

"Which is why you are exactly the sort of woman he needs in his life. You can be that voice of reason, the force to fight for what is good and just and right for the kingdom and its people. Someone who is not afraid to stand up against him and tell him when he is being a..."

"A wool-brained lout of a fool?" Ava chimed in helpfully.

The king laughed and agreed with her. He stayed for only a few minutes more, extolling her virtues and how they were exactly what his son needed. It seemed he was even more adamant than before about the proposed marriage. Ava shuddered with dread when she thought about her fate and wished with all her heart that she could change her stars. But she began to wonder if even her father would be able to untangle her from this terrible mess.

Ava ran into Mouser again after three days of searching through the kingdom. His immediate reaction was to turn and flee. She understood. He was afraid that Flynn was stalking around a corner. Mouser didn't realize the prince hadn't so much as said a word to her since the incident, not even during meals when he was forced to sit beside her. She gave him chase, her arms pumping as she sprinted down the street. Mouser slipped between the people traveling down the street, weaving through the crowd without issues. Ava bumped into more people than she could count, shouting a hasty "Sorry" as she scrambled to catch back up to Mouser. He wasn't as fast as she, but he knew the streets and how to move through a crowd. Their chase led her down winding streets and through dark alleyways. After a while, though, she caught up to him.

"Mouser," Ava called out. She stopped and doubled over, panting. He didn't seem to be nearly as tired by the chase as she felt. "We need to talk."

"I'm not going to apologize," Mouser said.

"For running away from me?"

"No, for making you fight with the prince."

"You didn't make me do anything. He had no right to treat you like that."

"He's the prince."

"So? You're a person, too."

"Then you aren't mad at me?" Mouser asked in awe.

"Mad at you? Never! I was actually hoping you'd be willing to do me a favor."

"Anything you wish, princess."

"I'm not a princess!" Ava said, stamping a foot for emphasis.

"Not yet, but you will be."

"Call me Ava. And no, I might not be. But it doesn't matter. What does matter is that I need you to help me learn the city better."

"Why me?"

"Because you know this city. You know where to go, how to navigate through the crowds. Could you show me around?"

"I have to deliver some things," Mouser said, patting his pouch.

"Perfect! I'll come with you!"

She accompanied him on his deliveries around the kingdom, marveling at his mastery of all the roads and routes. Mouser let her in on secrets, like how Baen the Blacksmith was fond of fresh pastries and Alera the Dressmaker loved the purple flowers that grew on the other side of town. By the end of the day Ava was ready to believe that Mouser knew everything about everyone. But there was one thing he didn't know: how to defend himself. And that was something she knew quite a bit about.

"Thank you, Mouser, for showing me around today."

"You didn't slow me down as much as I expected." Mouser grinned.

"I'm faster than you," Ava retorted.

"Not in a crowded street," Mouser replied with another smile.

"I want you to show me around again. I need to learn this place better. If I am stuck here for now, I might as well make good use of my time."

"Well, I don't know," Mouser said.

"I'll make it worth your time. When you aren't delivering, I will teach you how to use a sword and defend yourself."

"I'm not strong enough to use a sword."

"It isn't about being stronger than the other person. There are many styles of fighting, and some of them use speed rather than strength."

"And can you teach me that?"

"Absolutely. Deal?"

"Deal," Mouser said. Ava extended her hand out and Mouser shook it. His hand was neither smooth nor rough, with enough callouses to show he worked hard.

"Again," Ava said, wiping sweat from her eyes. Mouser was getting better with the sword. She could tell, because she was having to work hard to defend his attacks.

Mouser slid forward with the grace of a swan. His slender practice sword slashed and stabbed. Ava cursed under her breath and backed away from the onslaught. The boy was far faster than she first believed. Maybe as fast as she was. She dropped her own practice sword to parry a strike and the wooden blades clashed with a loud crack. She countered with a swing of her own. Clack! Mouser pivoted around her. His weapon flashed high, then low, then low again. Ava blocked each stroke but it was getting close.

Mouser grit his teeth and pressed in with increased fervor. Ava gave up ground with every defensive move. Her back hit the wall of a house. She could feel the rough edges of the stone through her tunic. She saw Mouser grin and grip the hilt in both hands. He brought the weapon up for an overhead strike. Ava ducked.

The wooden sword splintered as it cracked against the stone house and Ava jabbed her practice sword into Mouser's ribs.

"Dead, again," Ava said. They both looked at the remnant of a sword in Mouser's hands and burst into laughter.

"I thought for sure I had you," Mouser said between giggles.

"You nearly did," Ava confessed. Which made her realize that he really had gotten a lot better. He was taking to the lessons with an intensity that matched her own. While Mouser was making huge strides forward, she could tell that she was getting better as well. They weren't really evenly matched yet, as she often remained on the defensive, but he was close to breaking her defenses. A few months ago, with another boy, she would have been angered by that close call. Today she celebrated all of Mouser's progress.

"What did I do wrong?" he asked. Ava smiled. That was the right question.

"You changed your style. You had me against the wall and, instead of continuing what was working, you tried for a power stroke."

"It's how the soldiers do it," Mouser said.

"But it's not how we do it. It is easy to forget in the heat of battle, but you need to stick to your style at all times. That shift cost you today."

"I'll never be good enough to beat you." Mouser looked down at the broken sword in his hand.

"You almost did today," Ava said. "You did really well."

"Truly?"

"Aye, keep this up and you'll be the one dishing out the lessons to those soldiers. Now, let's get to your deliveries before it gets too late."

They ran off together, laughing as they raced into the heart of the city. That night, Ava realized she was better equipped to be a hunter than ever before. Her days were consumed with learning to read and write, training with the sword, and navigating the city. She spent the nights poring through some of the old books in the library. They had tomes on various monsters, the legendary deeds of heroes and knights and even a few on monster hunters. She pored over the monster hunter tales in search of record of her mother, reading anything that looked relevant and skipping over the parts that were too old or unrelated.

Another month passed with no word from her father. Hárborg was not a large kingdom but it was still full of hundreds of places that a dragon could hide. Ava knew he was out there, searching relentlessly for the monster. And she believed he was also thinking of a way to get her out of this marriage. Perhaps he already came up with a plan and was simply trying to get everything he would need to free her from that commitment. So while she felt anxious to hear word of his return, she didn't worry herself too much. After all, as he reassured her following a hrundtboar battle, no monster was a match for him. Especially not one cowardly enough to hide from him like this dragon was.

Ava and Mouser wandered through the streets of the town on a sunny Solsday afternoon. He had no more deliveries to make and they had already spent hours crossing swords. He was getting so much better at dueling and was starting to be able to hold his own against her. She could tell that the training was helping her to sharpen her reflexes and technique as well. She learned new things almost daily through taking the time to teach Mouser. She could hardly wait to practice against her father when he returned. But Ava and Mouser weren't up for more sparring just yet; nor was Ava interested in winding through the town. She wanted to go somewhere that neither of them had been yet and so she and Mouser made their way to the massive forest.

Ava knew that a small portion of the woods was free for her to explore and they travelled to the boundary a few times but had neither found adventure nor excitement in the trees apart from the thrill of climbing to the top of the tallest trees. Today she was determined to test her limits, to press on beyond those restrictions placed on her by the king and go deeper into the forest to where the really tall trees towered overhead. They strayed from the trimmed path of grass and wandered deeper into the shady recesses of the forest. She could smell fresh, vibrant berries that were heavy with thick juices. She heard colorful songbirds fluttering from branch to branch as they sang sweet melodies. They felt the leftover morning dew rolling along blades of grass and dripping down verdant leaves. It was a wonderful fusion of sensations that delighted Ava as they explored this new territory.

"I think we should turn back now," Mouser whispered after an hour passed. The newness and excitement wore off for him. His smile was gone and his skin looked pale in the shadows of the forest. He stared at her with wide eyes. "What if we get caught by the king's guards and thrown into the dungeons and have to live off blackened bread crust and water for the rest of our lives?"

"No one knows we're here," Ava said. She flicked her hand dismissively. "Where's your sense of adventure? I bet there's hidden treasure or something in here. That's why it's out-of-bounds."

"Maybe," Mouser admitted, "but I'd prefer the cobbled streets of Hárborg to this gloomy old forest."

"Gloomy?" Ava asked, skipping along in front of him, "how could you think of this as gloomy? It is so full of life!" A chorus of songbirds took up a new song as if taking her side in the argument. Mouser frowned and looked down at his feet.

"I miss the sunshine and the bustle of people around me," he admitted. Ava came back and slung an arm under his.

"Come on," she said as she pulled him with her. "I see a clearing full of sunshine up ahead. That'll lift your spirits!"

They ran ahead, one eager and the other reluctant. There was a clearing up ahead and sunlight filled the place. His hesitation faded and they both laughed as they ran and leapt over roots and sprung off smooth rocks along the way. The trees and bushes thinned out around them and were replaced by tall wildflowers and thick grass. A small lake, its water so clear that the children could see the bottom, was full of water that sent delightful shivers down their spines. They splashed each other and drank deeply to satisfy their thirst. For a few moments all fears and responsibilities were forgotten. Ava and Mouser frolicked and played, laughing and chasing and making merry sounds. Birds perched on their hands and shoulders and wild game came and licked their hands. It was turning out to be the best day either one had had in a long time.

Mouser spotted them first: butterflies. A whole flight of them lighting around the wildflowers. Ava and Mouser crept toward them. For a moment all other things were forgotten as they snuck up on the butterflies. Each small step brought them closer and they crept with the utmost care, not wanting to scare away such a rare sight. But the creatures had a keen sense of their surroundings and took flight before either one reached them. Yet to their surprise two butterflies flew toward them. Mouser's butterfly had green and gold wings that fluttered in the air and it landed on his shoulder. He gasped but Ava was already mesmerized by her own approaching butterfly.

Blue and pink wings, smooth as silk, beat the air as her butterfly came closer. Ava gasped when she realized it was not a butterfly, as she had thought. A tiny figure, ice blue skin wrapped in leaves and flower petals, was flying toward her. Numinites. She'd heard very little about them, as her father had never seen one. But she had heard tales of men who spent their whole lives chasing after the beautiful creatures without ever catching a glimpse. Here they were, presumably a whole flight of them, and one chose to approach her. She hesitated. She was a monster hunter and this was a monster. Was she supposed to catch it? Kill it? All monsters were bad, weren't they? That was what the Order of Light had preached week after week back in Tirgoth. But she decided, as the numinite landed on her outstretched hand, that monsters were like people: some were good, others were bad. These numinites had to be good. At least she knew intuitively that this one was.

The numinite opened her mouth to speak and a tinkling of bells filled the clearing. Both numinites were chattering away but neither Mouser nor Ava could understand a word. She smiled at the creature, so small even in her tiny hand. She didn't know what it was saying and she wished she could understand it. And in a moment it was done talking, flapping its wings to take flight again, and Ava was sad to see her go. She came closer, flying at her face, and hovered before her. The numinite leaned in and graced Ava's cheek with the lightest of kisses that sent radiant sparks shooting through the girl's body.

It was odd. She felt as though she could single-handedly find and slay a dragon. Or that she could read any book, climb any tower, learn any secret. It was a lucky day, she knew, thanks to the numinite's kiss. She watched it fly away and saw Mouser's numinite join her own. They both disappeared. Ava turned to Mouser. His face was aglow, shining with joy. Ava suspected her own face mirrored that look and a wordless glance shared between them spoke volumes. They headed back to Hárborg, each filled with a sense that something magical would happen for them both today and eager to learn what it could be.

CHAPTER THIRTEEN
The Annals

They parted ways when they reached the outskirts of Hárborg. It grew quite late in the day and Ava knew she had only a handful of hours before she must suffer through dinner in the main hall. She navigated through the streets and alleys of the marketplace, rushing past rickety carts and tanned canvas tents. Merchants and peddlers shouted out their wares, the voices blending together in an indecipherable cacophony of sound. She knew this part of town quite well, thanks to Mouser, and knew the fastest way to reach the castle. She sensed that something important was there, waiting for her to find it. Ignoring the glances that the castle guards gave her, Ava rushed up into her room. That was not her final destination but she knew it needed to be the first stop.

She caught her reflection in the mirror when she entered her room and instantly understood the strange looks the guards were giving her: she was very dirty from her trip into the woods. Thorns ripped open small tears in her tunic and brambles clung to her breeches. Smears of grass stains and a layer of light brown dust clung to her clothes. She hated to admit it but she would need to change before wandering through the castle to whatever her destination was. Her appearance would raise far too many questions if she didn't clean up and change, and she was not wanting to answer questions nor raise suspicion. Not that what she was doing would be against the king's law, certainly, but it would still be best to blend in as much as she could and avoid notice. She rang a bell that was beside her bed, the first time in her entire stay that she rang it. A high peal echoed throughout the room and the handmaidens came in shortly after the sound stopped echoing in her chamber. They masked their expressions but Ava could see the hints of raised eyebrows and widened eyes. She speculated that, when the bell rang, they looked at each other with mouths hanging open. Ava broke precedent and, when they saw the state of her, they understood why without needing to be told.

With much tsking and whisking about the room, the maids poured a warm bath and laid out proper clothes. For once Ava didn't argue because she realized she'd have to change into them for supper soon anyway. They scrubbed her skin and combed the tangles out of her hair and even washed her tunic. Ava could tell they wanted to ask her a thousand questions and, for some odd reason, she found herself telling them about her adventures. The expressions on their face were priceless. They murmured and sighed and all wished they had been there to see the numinites, too. They asked if she had seen many other magical creatures, namely unicorns, aqualocs, and other numinites. Ava hadn't seen any of them, of course, but she read about them this past month so she retold those tales. The maids hung on every word.

Ava felt refreshed and relaxed and enjoyed the attention of her handmaidens for the first time. One of the girls even offered to patch up the tears in her clothes, an offer which Ava instantly agreed to. Ava had no skill with a needle, nor any desire to learn to use one. Her swordplay was her needlework, and a far more important skill than sitting in a room making clothing. As soon as the maids left, she stepped before the mirror to look at herself. The rose-colored dress was far too poofy and the matching shoes already made her feet ache but there was no denying that the maids knew how to make her look pretty. She had rarely felt feminine or beautiful in all her years growing up at Tirgoth, and even now she couldn't imagine herself in a palace life. It took so much work, all of that paint and pampering to make her look like more than just a plain tomboy. She'd never steal the attention of an entire room when she entered it. But that girl in the mirror right now, looking back at her with that small smile, she could do all of that. Could that truly be her own reflection in the mirror?

Ava spun away from the mirror and walked into the halls. Her feet led her down spiraling staircases and across landings on a familiar path. She didn't know she was going to spend time in the library tonight, but that was where instinct drove her and she followed it without question. A few candles were still burning down in the room and cast just enough light to see by. She wandered along the shelves that covered every part of the walls, her fingers dancing along the spines of the old books. Some of them were covered with too much dust to read their titles and she dragged her finger over those, parting the dust. But she didn't try to read the titles as she went along--that would have taken far too long. The library was massive. She thought half of Tirgoth could have fit inside this one room and there were more books here than grains of sand in the desert beside Tirgoth. She only found a few volumes of interest in her month at Hárborg but those were all on the other side of the room. She followed her feet, led by instinct, to a rather ordinary bookshelf on the eastern wall. Her eyes flitted along the titles: *The Long History of Hárborg, A Horse Breeder's Handbook, Seven Sauces for Every Banquet*. They may have interested others but none of them were what she was looking for. She could feel that this was the right shelf, so the book she came for must be higher up.

She kicked off her shoes and hoped her dress would cooperate for a change. She placed a bare foot on the second shelf and eased her weight onto it. The structure felt like it would hold her weight. Satisfied with this result, she scurried up the bookshelf. Her eyes lingered on the occasional book but none of them felt like the right one. But she went even higher to the point where even she was afraid to look down. She never understood why they built the shelves in this room so high. Twice she had to force herself to hold in a sneeze, as clouds of dust circulated in the air. And then she saw it, tucked away on a shelf that was only three shelves away from the domed ceiling.

The book was unremarkable in every way. It was black leather with gilded writing on the spine, similar to others around it. It was neither short nor tall, neither thick nor thin. It was extremely average to the point where it could never be picked out in a crowd of books. But Ava could sense, even before reading the title, that this was the book she came in here for. It was the book that the numinite charm helped her find. She sounded out the words on the spine, carefully brushing away the grime so she could read it clearly. She gasped in amazement, eager to pluck it free and retire to her room. She whispered the full title: *The Annals of the Monster Hunters, Volume VII.* Something important was in this book; she could sense it even though she didn't know why this volume was the proper one and not one of the previous six. It didn't matter. This was the book.

She wriggled it free from the shelf and tucked it under her arm. It was going to be a long climb down but that didn't matter anymore. The book she came for was in her possession. She eased a foot down to the shelf below, and then another. The wood of the shelves creaked from the strain as she descended. She was moving with greater speed than when she came up because she was eager to reach the bottom. Her hands were slick with perspiration from the climb, making it difficult to get a good grip on each shelf. And then it happened.

The dust swirled in her face in just the right way, at the most inopportune time, and she couldn't stop the sneeze. She reeled backward from the force, and another sneeze followed immediately after. The book fell from her arm. She reached for it, all caution forgotten in a moment, and her other hand slipped off the dusty shelf. Ava fell to the ground. Time seemed to slow as she fell and she could count the shelves passing by. One, two, three. The fall was giving her a queasy sensation in her gut. Four, five, six. She landed hard on the stone floor. The wind departed from her lungs but it didn't feel like any bones were broken. Thankfully she had been most of the way down before her fall. The book lay on the ground beside her, pages flipped open to a spot near the middle. She sat up and looked at the title on the page. She cried, tears of happiness bursting free. It didn't matter who saw her weeping now. Flynn could come in and taunt her all he wanted. The story was about her mother, Kenna.

She tucked the book under her arm and rushed across the library, heading back toward the exit. She had nearly reached the doors when she realized her shoes were still beside the bookshelf. She ran as best she could in the dress which, as she learned, was not very well at all. Why would anyone think this was a practical thing to wear? It was terrible for climbing and running, and she could only imagine how dreadful it would be to swordfight in this dress. But soon enough she recovered her shoes and returned to her room, her shoes in one hand and the book in the other. The shoes clattered onto the floor beside her bed and she flopped onto the down-filled mattress. Ava knew dinner time would arrive soon but she needed to at least flip through the pages to see if there were any more stories about her mother besides the one she noticed when the book fell open. And it turned out that there were a dozen different tales, along with a few transcripts of songs written about her. She also noticed a brief biography of her mother. Ava tried to remember the names of the songs so that she could request them at dinner. Hopefully one of the bards in Hárborg was familiar with them. She slammed the book shut and hugged it to her chest. Surely no one would ever notice if this book stayed with her forever. Ava slipped it under her mattress and reluctantly went to dinner.

The dinner dragged on forever. Two hours felt like six to Ava and the whole time she wanted nothing more than to rush back into her room and read every tale about her parents a hundred times by candlelight. She was largely disappointed with the bard because he knew only one of the songs she requested. But Ava asked him to sing it twice during the dinner and some of the verses echoed in her mind as she headed back to her room after dinner. The first thing she did after the maids had dressed her for bed was to open the book to those pages and go over a few of the verses. It was a long tale, and she was too excited to read everything else, so she only read a few of the long verses.

> *A dark figure towers over the lines*
> *of enemy soldiers, covering ground*
> *swiftly with his great strides. Armor entwines*
> *his large body. His melon-head is crowned*
> *with plated steel encircling its round*
> *face. One red eye, bigger than a man's fist,*
> *scans through the crowd of men gathered around.*
> *A more fearsome cyclops does not exist,*
> *wearing white bones of men he has slain on his wrist.*

> *His massive maw opens, a vast bellow*
> *bursts forth, "Is there no man here who is bold*
> *enough to accept my charge, no fellow*
> *who thinks their might meets mine? I hold*
> *no tricks, no deceitful lies have I told,*
> *only seeking a soul who will wager*
> *his life against mine. Come forward, uphold*
> *your glorious kingdom against nature.*
> *Grapple and spar with me, come forth into danger."*

Stepping forward is she, monster huntress by trade,
red curls emblazoned by morning sun rays.
A hushed silence ensues. She draws her blade
and calls back to her foe, "Go! Run away
if you value your head or I shall slay
you where you stand. Your words may strike terror
into the hearts of these men, but today
you face a stronger soul. I am bearer
of truth. Facing me would be a fatal error."

Ava smiled at the boldness, envisioning an older version of herself taking up the challenge of the massive cyclops. She flipped back to the first pages on her mother and began reading through the biography. It said that her mother died in 3107 C.E., which was three years after Ava had been born. Just like her father told her. But it didn't mention what killed her, only that it was the result of a hunt gone wrong. And it mentioned Ava in the biography, too! She could hardly believe she was seeing her own name written there. Ava read on through all twelve stories, switching the candle out twice. She didn't feel tired at all, even though she knew she should try to sleep. When she came to the end of her mother's information, she was disappointed that she had reached the end. She desired to read more about her mother, or to find out about her father. But there was no more she could discover in this book. She blew out the candle and lay down to try and capture some restful sleep.

Ava's eyes flickered open. Her mind refused to shut down enough for her to fall into a slumber. She sat up in the bed and stretched her arms out as far as they would go. She considered grabbing the annals again and spending more time poring over their pages, but a different object tugged at her awareness. Her bare feet padded along the floor and she crossed over to her pack and pulled out a bundled cloth. She peeled back the layers like the peel of an orange and stared down at the black crossbow bolt. One hand reached for it and paused, inches from the surface, as she remembered the traumatic experience she had the last time she grabbed the bolt. Yet, somehow, she felt like she needed to revisit that again tonight. Her hand closed around the smooth shaft and the taint of the object flooded up her arm. Her stomach heaved violently and her eyes clenched shut, yet she kept her hold on the bolt.

She stood inside a small house, in a small room partitioned off by a shelf of books and a small round table. A small woolen doll was in her hand but her eyes were not upon the doll. Her father stood in the doorway of the house, wobbling with slurred speech. A woman, a handful of years older than him, stood inside the house sharpening a small dagger. Their mouths moved yet no sound could be heard. The woman looked over at her and smiled, but a frown reappeared when she looked back at her father. He took a step into the house, raising an arm overhead and then gesturing toward something outside the house. A sob caught in Ava's throat and the doll dropped from her fingers. Hot tears trickled down her cheeks yet neither of them turned toward her. Rage oozed from them both, enveloping her in a shroud of heated emotion. Her vision flashed a bright white, followed by darkness.

Darkness descended upon the landscape around them. Tiny arms clutched tight around his waist as the horse beneath them trotted away from the small cottage. The shadow of the beast and its riders led the way along the winding road. Her hands slipped time and again, slick from his sweat bleeding through his tunic, yet she held on with all her might. Terror hovered in the air like a mist, filled her lungs like vapor. A scream rang through the air. The silence that followed rang in her ears and she squirmed closer to her father and tightened her grip around him. The horse continued forward as if oblivious to the danger closing in upon them. A second scream brought them to a halt and her father turned the horse back toward the house standing between two hills. Her vision flashed a bright white, followed by darkness.

When her vision returned she was standing in the small room once more, her eyes burning and cheeks wet. The floor beneath her feet was warm with a thick, sticky liquid. Red filled the room around her, contrasting starkly against the black and white backdrop. A pair of figures were on the ground in front of her, one sitting while holding the other in his lap. One crying, the other bleeding. Her father clutched her mother in his arms and she could feel the life ebbing away from the woman. Her vision blurred and she lifted tiny fingers to wipe away the moisture. Crimson hair blended with the crimson liquid flowing from open wounds. Pain lanced her heart and the sobs flowed freely from her throat. Her father howled in anguish and Ava sensed the final moments descending upon her mother. Laughter, cold and harsh, flooded her mind and she clutched her hands to her ears to drown it out. Yet it grew louder, rising in intensity like an orchestral crescendo. She screamed but no sound came out. She wept but no tears fell. She ran but the scene of her mother's final, painful moments remained etched before her. Her vision flashed a bright white, followed by darkness.

CHAPTER FOURTEEN
An Unwelcome Companion

It felt as though she finally closed her eyes to catch some sleep when the handmaidens came in to wake her that next morning. She fought to stifle the barrage of yawns that threatened to unhinge her jaw as the handmaidens went about their task. The maids could have tried to rip her hair from her scalp and she wouldn't have noticed. Thankfully they were kind to her that morning, although they were likely disappointed by the lack of interesting stories being told. Ava would have found it impossible to get them out of her room if they suspected she had a whole book of stories under her bed.

She went straight to the library after breaking her fast on some warm biscuits with fresh honey and a small bowl of creamy porridge. Normally she delayed this visit as long as possible but today she was eager to get to the library and ask the master scribe a handful of the million different questions that swirled in her mind.

Ava knew that Heimdal carried around a leather pouch filled with assorted quills and inks and a bag full of books, some of them containing only empty pages. He often said you never knew when you might need an empty book to write in, and right now Ava felt as though she needed one.

"You look rather excited this morning," Heimdal observed. Ava slid into her chair and smiled up at him.

"I suppose I am," Ava said. She kicked her feet back and forth in the air and her fingers drummed on the table. Heimdal raised an eyebrow and she blushed, forcing her limbs to stop moving.

"What's on your mind, Ava? I can see we will get nowhere on your lessons until you let it all out."

"I was wondering how I might go about getting a book," Ava said.

"There are thousands in here. You must simply ask and you can take them with you to your room."

"Not one of these books. A book of my own. To write in."

Heimdal blinked, his brows furrowing. Then a grin split his face. "Ah, yes, of course! I had hoped you'd want that someday, but I assumed it would be years before the scholar in you might surface." He dug a hand into the satchel at his side and pulled out a small book, a quill, and an ink well. He set them down on the table and Ava leapt from her chair and wrapped him in a hug.

"Thank you," she whispered and his arms slowly reached out to return the embrace.

"Of course, child. If I had known how eager you were to record your studies, I would have done this weeks ago."

"No, the timing is perfect. What do I owe you for these?"

"Your excitement is payment enough. Now then, is there anything you wanted to place first in your book?"

"A map!" Ava shouted. She hunched down as a dozen pairs of eyes turned toward her. Sitting back down at the table, she repeated herself in a quieter voice

"A map of every kingdom, or just on of Alexandria?"

"I think all of the kingdoms. Can I draw them all in one large map or do I need to do each one by itself?"

"Whichever way you wish."

"Both," Ava said. She bit her bottom lip to hold in the excitement. Heimdal strode off, grabbing rolls of parchment off some of the lower shelves in the library. His arms were full as he returned and he set them down on the table.

"You may take these back to your room, if you wish. Copy them carefully into your book and then return them here, in the library."

"Seriously?"

"Seriously. Now go, off with you!"

"Wait, what about my lessons today?"

"Consider map-making your lesson for the week. I expect this task will take you longer than you anticipate." Ava hugged him again and looked at the collection of maps on the table. She frowned, trying to consider how to get them all to her room in one trip.

"Allow me to help you carry some of those," Heimdal said.

"Thank you," she answered, gathering up an armful of maps. She couldn't wait to get to her room and begin copying them into her very own book.

That day she spent hour after hour meticulously copying the maps into her journal. It was difficult and exhausting work. The next day was spent in similar seclusion, and she was able to finish the largest map at last. After the second day Mouser came to see her. He wore a grin that split his face and one of his eyes was swollen shut.

"Do you remember when we saw the numinites?" he asked her, shutting the door.

"Of course. It was a wonderful day!"

"Yep. After you left, I ran into one of the soldier trainees, Xanth. He tried picking on me and I stood up to him, so he challenged me to face him in the practice ring."

"And that is where you got the black eye?"

"No, that happened yesterday. I fought him with a practice sword, just like you taught me. And I bested him!"

"That's great, Mouser. But what exactly happened yesterday?"

"Apparently Xanth has had it rough from his commander since I bested him. He brought some friends and attacked me in an alley."

"Oh, no!"

"It's okay, Ava. That just proves he knows he needs a group of people to win. His commander happened to walk by during their attack and Xanth is being reassigned."

"He deserves worse than that."

"Nah," Mouser said, shaking his head. His smile grew even bigger. "The commander is arranging for me to join his army next month. He needs some messengers, and I've proven I can wield a sword now."

"Oh," Ava said. She tried to hold back a frown. "So I guess you won't need me to train you anymore?"

"Are you kidding me?" Mouser said. "Of course I still want to train with you. The way you use a blade is so different than a normal soldier. I won't learn half as many useful things from them."

"So we still have a deal, then, until my father returns?"

"Definitely."

Ava was putting the finishing touches on her final map when her father finally returned to Hárborg. She was so excited to see him again and wanted to visit him immediately. She rushed through the halls only to find him being led into the throne room.

"Father!" she cried out. He said something to the guards and they stopped. He spun around and gave her a special smile.

"Avalina, dear one." Ava darted toward him, eager to feel his embrace. The guards stepped between them and Ava slid to a stop.

"Father?" she asked.

"It's okay, Avalina. They have been instructed to take me to the throne room right away."

"But Father," she said, stepping closer. One guard held out his arm to hold her back.

"Don't worry, this shouldn't take too long."

"You've been gone for so long!"

"I know, and I'm sorry for that," he said with a sigh. "But be ready to leave when I am done."

The guards turned around, grabbing him by the arm and leading him into the throne room. The double doors slammed shut behind them and Ava shed a small tear. Her mind buzzed with questions. She wanted to know if they were leaving to kill the monster or if that had been accomplished. Maybe she was going to depart on some other adventure with him. But she was still destined to be married to Flynn, wasn't she? Unless he was negotiating a new deal with the king right now. She sat down on a bench and let her mind wander, not wanting to miss the chance to see her father when his meeting was finished.

"Avalina," her father called out as he opened the door and exited the throne room. He was covered in dried mud and had dark circles under his eyes. He was leaner than before, and his face was worn thin beneath his gritty beard. The beard had grown long in his absence, as had his hair, and he smelled like an unkempt stable that also housed a pack of wet hounds. Ava didn't care. She rushed into his arms, wrapping him in a massive hug. Tears streaked into his beard. Whether they were his or hers she didn't know, perhaps both. She was just glad he was back at last.

"Did you kill it?" Ava asked him.

"Not yet," he answered, "and we don't have time for the tale just yet. We must be on our way. It is close, I've chased it to a waterfall cavern near Hárborg, and you are coming with me to kill it."

"Truly?" she asked. She could hardly believe her ears.

"Truly. You don't think I'd let you miss out on this adventure, did you?"

"But the king?" Ava started to ask.

"Has no choice but to let you come with me. It cost me half of my reward but in the end he gave in."

Ava grabbed her things and followed him out of the castle. Her father didn't head toward the stables like she expected. Instead he cut through a field and onto a rocky path winding out to the east. Ava followed along, relishing the sunlight, the breeze, and her father's presence. Everything was right in the world once again, and she had things to show and tell her father later! Especially her journal, which she had tucked away securely in her room with the maps. She wondered if her father kept a journal with him at all times, or if it was something he worked on in the quiet days between hunts.

Along the way he filled her in on his travels. He had trekked all across the kingdom of Hárborg in search for news of the monster. The trail led him in a giant, winding circle back toward the castle. He searched this cavern before, when he left, but it was long deserted. That was no longer the case. But he didn't know for certain whether the monster was truly a dragon or something else. Most of the stories whispered dragon but it seemed, based on other accounts and descriptions, to be too small for a dragon unless it was just a hatchling. He was going to withhold judgment until he could know for certain.

Ava was about to recount her tale when her father missed a step. It was the slightest of reflexes but Ava knew it meant he sensed something. The monster? He brought a finger to his lips and they continued forward at a slightly slower pace. It would be easy for something to hide in the tall grass surrounding the sides of the path. But it was about to learn that it wasn't easy, or a good idea, to try and sneak up on her father. Tristan edged closer to the long grass as they walked. His left hand disappeared in a small pouch in his belt and came back out with a small, smooth beige stone. He threw the stone at a specific spot and Ava knew he was certain something was hiding there even if she couldn't see it.

"Ow," came a familiar voice from the tall grass. "How dare you assault the prince of Hárborg." Flynn rose up, rubbing his temple. He was carrying his staff and wearing robes that matched the color of the grass. No wonder he had been hidden.

"If his royal highness wishes to avoid assault," her father answered with a small, stiff bow, "then he would be wise not to sneak around like a bandit."

"I'm just following father's orders to ensure you don't run away," Flynn said. The prince stepped out onto the path and bowed to Ava. Ava rolled her eyes and shook her head.

"We're not going to flee," she told him. Her blood was already boiling. How could he dare to insinuate such things? They were no cowards. She and her father were hunters, fierce devotees to the Order of Light, not some pampered royalty who basked in the privileges that the Order of Might's teachings allowed.

"All the same," answered Flynn, "he wishes to be certain. Besides, you might need my help in taking on the dragon." Before her father could answer Flynn formed several balls of fire in his hand. The flames burned bright and Ava felt their heat. And then Flynn did the strangest thing with them--he started juggling. The flames leapt high into the air, weaving into irregular patterns and Flynn grinned as he manipulated their flow.

"You need to go back to the castle. It isn't safe, especially if you refuse to take the matter of hunting monsters seriously."

"If she can come, I can come." Flynn glared at Ava and the flames died in the air. His voice was flat and his stare could cleave a stone in two. "No girl is more capable at chasing down monsters than I am, not that I'm even certain these monsters exist. Besides, if I return without you, I'll make sure my father sends a regiment of guards to arrest you both and you'll both spend your lives rotting in a cell."

"I hate him," Ava said later, when Flynn was far enough ahead of them.

Her father smiled and shook his head slowly. "He has given you little reason to like him," her father answered, "but I cannot overrule a king's judgment any more than I can fly like a dragon or knock down walls like a hrundtboar."

"Couldn't we just disappear and not kill the monster?" Ava asked. She was desperate to find a solution that would not bind her to Flynn and no longer cared if her father knew it. She wanted to be as far away from him as possible.

Tonight.

"We would have a hard time finding jobs after that. The king would publicly denounce us and all men would believe us craven. The king isn't very popular in hunter's circles but even a black mark from him would make life very difficult in the future. It would likely force us north into the fringe kingdoms up there, or else east to the island kingdoms. But even then, word might find us. Things like that tend to find the worst of times to resurface." He paused and placed a large hand on Ava's shoulder. "But know that if I am presented with a path that does not make you marry that prince, I will take it. Even if it means doing this job, and any future jobs for this king, for free."

"You would forfeit payment?"

"Your happiness is payment enough, Avalina." She fell into his arms and hugged her father tight. Tears streamed down her cheeks and, for once, she did not try to hide them. After a long moment she let go and took a step back, brushing the bodice of her tunic with her hands. "Let us rejoin our braggart guide," her father said, "so we can kill this monster and be rid of him sooner."

The trio traveled in silence for an hour as they walked across fields and climbed up steep hills. Ava was the first to hear the sound of rushing water. They all took that as a sign that they were close to their destination. She ran ahead of Flynn, eager to reach the waterfall, but was disappointed to find that it was not within sight. She wished they could reach their destination, partly to have an adventure at last with her father and partly to be rid of the prince sooner. She wondered which she wanted more right now.

"How far to the waterfall?" she asked as she waded across a shallow spot in the river.

"Not far," Ava's father said. "The sun will be about another hand lower in the sky by the time we get there. We just need to follow the river north for a while and we'll be at the cavern in no time."

"Getting tired?" Flynn asked her. "We won't be stopping so that a weak girl can rest, you know."

Ava clenched her fists until her knuckles turned white as she spun toward the arrogant prince. Her father spoke up before she could yell at Flynn, saying, "She was curious is all. My daughter is the strongest woman you'll ever meet." Flynn dismissed the comment with a slight shrug, marching onward. "I wouldn't be surprised if she ends up having to carry you home, your lordship." Ava and her father shared a smile that Flynn didn't see.

"I won't be having a girl carry me," Flynn said, placing a drawling emphasis on the word girl. Ava wondered what happened to the prince who had shown some hint of manners when they first arrived for dinner. Or the one that surfaced while talking about his mother. Clearly the polite Flynn had all been an act, put on for the king's benefit in order to maintain his position as future heir to the throne. Ava guessed that this was really what Flynn was like. She wished her father would stop chiming in so that she could put Flynn in his place. He wouldn't make fun of her when she had him writhing in pain. She was certain a dagger could draw some blood from him without causing any serious injury.

"Then I suggest you pick up the pace, your lordship," her father urged.

Flynn ran to catch up with Ava and took back the lead along the river. She thought about tripping him as he passed. She could probably even make it seem like he had stumbled over his fancy stick. But she knew her father would disapprove.

They reached the waterfall within an hour, just as Ava's father promised. Clear water cascaded down from the cliffs above and crashed into the rocks below in a white mist. Half a dozen rainbows danced within the splashing current, clothed in radiant colors as they shimmered in the air. Sparrows and finches flocked upon the branches of a nearby tree, mesmerized by the rapids while they sang melodious songs. All of the plants were alive and vibrant in color. She could probably sit here for hours, just watching the beasts and the water and enjoy every moment of it.

But they had a job to do, so she followed her father and Flynn as they stepped across a few large stones and disappeared behind the waterfall, appearing to walk into the wall of stone itself. Ava put her arms out in front of her as she stepped toward the water. She was expecting to find a wall of stone and nearly fell on her face as she entered into the mouth of the cave. It was only her fast reflexes that kept her on her feet as she joined her father and Flynn, water from the falls dripping down her shoulders. The water sent chills down her spine and made her tunic stick to her back. Laughter filled Flynn's eyes as though he knew what happened. She wanted to punch him in that large nose of his but he turned away before she could. She was stronger than him and better than him and she didn't need to stoop to his level to prove it. Even if he deserved it.

CHAPTER FIFTEEN
Not Quite a Dragon

The light behind them was fading fast as Ava, Flynn, and her father navigated deeper into the depths of the waterfall cavern. She couldn't see the gray-green flecks of color in the stone walls anymore, nor could she see the stones sticking up from the ground. Three times one of them stumbled, snagging a toe or clipping a calf on some unseen obstruction, before her father called for them to stop and pulled a torch out of his bag.

"No way," Flynn said, "we don't need that old-fashioned thing to see. Watch this." He twirled his staff, its tip narrowly missing the walls around him. A pale yellow glow surrounded the end of the staff and he uttered some words in an unrecognizable language. Ava noticed her father put his torch back in his pack and was waiting for the young prince to complete his spell. Ava didn't blame him; why spend our resources when this arrogant boy was willing to do it for free? The staff stopped twirling, the butt slamming into the ground, and the glow around the tip intensified until it cast bright light in all directions. Ava shook her head, marveling at how bright the light of the spell was. It was almost as though the sun was shining directly from his staff and every feature of the cavern was illuminated. There would be no shadows for anything sinister to lurk or hide in. For once, Flynn was proving useful to have along. She wondered how long that would last and, if she had to guess, it would last about twenty more seconds.

The tunnels of the cave twisted and turned as the three of them strode along the path. Several times they reached a crossroads, each time her father calling for them to stop while he studied the ground around both tunnels. He called her over each time after he observed something and pointed out the minor traces of the creature's path. Sometimes it was as obvious as the broken tip of a stalagmite. Other times it was a subtle scent of smoke or sulfur lingering in the air. One time it was even the sound of a flowing stream that led them down one path instead of the other. But every time after her father chose a path he never questioned the decision he had arrived at. He was certain they were on the right trail, even if Flynn still had doubts.

Early on in the cave they were able to speak, although it was usually Flynn voicing his concern about their path or complaining about the damp air or threatening to give his father a poor report due to their treatment of him. After a while her father urged them to speak softly but still allowed their occasional comments and conversations to be voiced. But now he demanded absolute silence, motioning for them to be quiet every time Flynn or Ava kicked a pebble or stubbed a toe. Ava could sense they were getting close even though she had never been on a hunt with her father. She wished he would allow himself to talk, to explain how he knew they were near the dragon. Was it some sound he heard when she wasn't paying enough attention? Could it have been some subtle shift in the smell, such as the disappearance of the musty scent? Her mind was left to wander and wonder as they moved in silence and she hoped that she would remember to ask him those questions later.

Ava knew they had finally neared its lair when her father motioned for them to stop. Sweat beaded on her forehead from the heat radiating around the corner and a faint orange glow emanated from the tunnel ahead. Her father signaled for Flynn to cease his light spell and Ava could see that the prince wanted to argue the point. After thinking it over he went ahead and let his light flicker out without so much as a complaint. The prince had at least a marginal amount of sense in that thick skull of his. Her father crept forward, keeping low to the ground as he disappeared from their sight. He was only gone for a matter of seconds, but to Ava it seemed like an hour. Sharp aches lanced through her legs and butterflies were dancing in her midsection by the time he reappeared.

He pressed in close to them. "It is sleeping," he whispered, "so if we are smart about it we will be able to slay it without a challenge."

"Where is the sport in that?" Flynn whispered. Ava noticed his features were alight with excitement. It was almost as though he had fire dancing in his eyes.

"Survival," her father answered. "It is worth far more than a famed battle that the bards will sing about."

"You might not want any songs," Flynn said, "but Simeon the Silver-Tongue already has composed two about me and I intend this encounter to be the third." Her father grabbed Flynn's arm but the young prince jerked it free and stepped around the corner. Ava heard his staff slam on the ground before he called out, "What sort of pathetic excuse for a dragon are you? You aren't even half my size!"

Ava rounded the corner and saw that Flynn was right. The monster didn't look like any dragon she had ever heard about. It didn't even have any sign of wings on its back. She noted that it had smooth, orange skin that glowed brighter with every exhale. Two massive nostrils sat atop a short, round snout and a black forked tongue flicked out with the occasional breath. Its short, stubby legs were sprawled alongside its long body and a short, club-like tail was curled around it protectively.

"It isn't a dragon," Ava's father whispered, "it's a pyreken and very dangerous if not dispatched properly."

"It is no match for my flames," Flynn said and then he started chanting a spell. The pyreken's red eyes snapped open and it scrambled to its feet. Tiny sparks sprayed from its mouth as it hissed at the intruders.

"Stop it!" her father shouted. "The monster feeds on fire."

"Let's see it feast on this," Flynn said. And then he unleashed a torrent of flames. A spiral of orange and red and blue flames danced across the cave, engulfing the monster. Flynn focused his power on that spot until sweat dripped down his forehead and his limbs quaked from the effort. The heat radiating from the area made her break out in a light sweat. Ava could hear the cavern rocks bubbling and melting from the heat but she never heard the pyreken cry out in pain. When Flynn slumped to his knees, ending the spell, the pyreken had swollen to three times its original size and was glowing brighter than Flynn's staff had earlier.

It hissed in delight before unleashing its own stream of flames at them.

"Get down!" her father yelled. He yanked Ava around the corner. Flynn cried out in pain as the fire flashed across his face, burning his hair and roasting his flesh. The air stank of charcoal and of seared meat. Ava retched on the rocks. Her father darted back out into the tunnel and grabbed the prince under his arms, dragging him back to safety. Ava could hear the pyreken's stubby legs clambering over the rocks as it headed toward them. She expected her father to tell her to leave but instead he looked at her and nodded. It was time for her to earn the title of apprentice and help slay the monster.

Ava drew *Seraphina* from its sheath and stood firm while brandishing the sword in her hand. She held her breath as she watched her father get into position. He notched an arrow in his bow. His plan was simple, but Ava was having a hard time focusing on the task at hand. It probably had to do with Flynn shrieking every five seconds while writhing in pain on the ground. Her father reassured her that the burn should not be fatal, but he figured it would be enough to make Flynn pass out from the pain. Her father clearly hadn't told Flynn about the passing out part yet, because the prince seemed to be in no hurry to do it. Why were boys so stubborn? If he would hurry up and pass out, she could focus better on dealing with this pyreken so they could all get to safety.

Her father pulled back the string of his bow. He held it taut and waited for the pyreken's approach. The stupid monster was impossibly slow as it advanced, making Ava wonder how it eluded her father for all those weeks. The heat was getting stronger, the hairs on her father's beard were starting to singe, so she knew it was still approaching. Her father glanced at her and she raised *Seraphina* overhead. She had to be ready to bring it down in a deadly arc when she saw the monster's exposed neck.

A stream of flames spewed from the monster's mouth, scorching the wall beside her father. Ava was roasting under her leather armor even though the fire wasn't touching her. She thought about jumping out early, taking on the monster head-on to spare her father, but she knew he'd reprimand her for the thought. He would want her to stick to the plan even if it cost him his life. But if she saw an opening to dispatch it earlier, she was determined to take it, plan or not. Not for glory, but for survival. Every moment this monster remained alive was another moment in which one of them might die, and she couldn't allow that to happen.

She saw the orange snout poke into her line of sight. Any moment now, she'd be able to strike the monster with her sword and bring its miserable life to an end. She took a deep breath that filled her lungs. Her father loosed an arrow and the shaft spun as it raced toward its mark. The feather fletching of the arrow burned before it could strike and the shaft turned enough mid-flight to bounce harmlessly off the pyreken's forehead. Her father cursed and notched another arrow. The monster, in this overheated state caused by Flynn, was too hot for the shaft to get close. But at least it kept the pyreken's focus away from the real threat looming around the corner. *Seraphina* was far more deadly than any old arrow being shot from a bow, having been forged from pure steel in the hottest of fires.

Its red eyes came into view and the monster spewed more fire at her father. He dove aside to avoid the flames and rolled to his feet, loosing another arrow that would have found its mark on any other monster. The pyreken let out a low growl as it turned its head to follow her father. The plan was going mostly as expected. It was almost her time to strike. But striking too soon could almost be as costly as striking too late. She had to wait for the right moment.

Ava had been surprised when her father wanted to give her the job of killing the monster. She wasn't as good with a bow as her father, but she figured she could have kept it distracted just fine. Her father trusted her to finish the job and she wouldn't let him down. The pyreken's neck came into view and Ava brought her sword down. The air whistled as the steel tip of *Seraphina* raced in a deadly arc. She felt the resistance of the blade cutting into the flesh and muscle of the monster's neck, heard its groan of pain that echoed off the walls. And then the sword stopped. It was embedded in the pyreken and now its groans shifted into growls of rage. Those red eyes rolled around, desperately seeking to find the source of its pain.

Ava pressed down with all her might, trying to behead the monster, but her sword wouldn't budge. The pyreken was still moving and now it unleashed blasts of fire in every direction it could, to try and kill its unseen assailant. Her father shouted at her to get away and she shifted her grip on the hilt. Ava pulled up but the sword was lodged into its neck. It wouldn't move in either direction. Ava turned and ran away. She backed farther into the tunnel and her father followed close behind. Ava noticed he was dragging the unconscious Flynn with him. The pyreken tried to turn its head toward them but the sword caught on the rock. At least they were safe from its flames until it finished rounding the corner. And its slow pace would buy them precious time to regroup and rethink how to face the beast.

Her father shoved his bow and quiver in her hands. "Shoot as many arrows at it as you can. Keep it focused on you but stay out of its range. Can you drag the prince with you, if needed?" Ava nodded and slung the quiver over her shoulder and then grabbed Flynn under his arms, dragging him backward. He was surprisingly light, since he was wearing no armor beneath his cloak. His staff was lost back where he collapsed but there had been no time to rescue it. The wooden weapon was likely reduced to ash by now.

Ava dropped the prince and notched an arrow. She watched her father draw a spear and a small axe, both weapons made completely from steel. The pyreken was finally able to start turning the corner so Ava shot her first arrow at it. The shot went high and sailed over its head. The arrow crashed harmlessly into the wall. She hurried to notch another arrow. She knew that she needed to get its attention before it decided to roast her father. This time, their plan hinged on her ability to keep it distracted. The second arrow was a little better than the first. The arrowhead bounced off the monster's back. Its head swung toward her, vermillion eyes blazing with fury. She flinched when it shot fire at her, but the orange and red flames only came halfway to her even though waves of heat rippled into her. There was plenty of time before it got too close, but she knew she couldn't let up with the arrows.

Ava lost track of her father. She was too busy firing another arrow. This one managed to hit its eye, making the pyreken cry in pain. It scrambled forward at a faster pace and glared at her with its one good eye. A second belch of fire came just inches short of the unconscious prince but she stood her ground and shot another arrow. She tucked the bow under her arm then bent down to get a grip on Flynn. She dragged him back, stumbling on an unseen stone. The pyreken inhaled deeply, readying another round of flames that would certainly torch her this time. They were out of time and now they would both die together under the inferno from the pyreken.

Her father thrust the spear into the pyreken's side. The sharp steel head pierced the monster's hide between its ribs. Its fire sputtered and fell short as the monster let out a bellow of pain. Her father drove the spear in deeper, slamming the monster into the wall. Her father's clothing was smoking and small holes were burning through the cloth from the heat radiating off the pyreken, but he ignored the discomfort. He dropped the spear and swung the axe in an underhand blow. The crescent blade tore through the throat of the beast. Its limbs flailed in desperation, scrambling backward, but her father had grabbed the spear again and pressed it against the wall as steaming blood bubbled out from its wound. The pale orange glow dimmed as the life left their foe and her father released the shaft of the spear, slumping to his knees.

Ava ran to him and wrapped her arms around her father. He managed to laugh around a mouthful of red curls as he returned the embrace. In that moment, Ava thought he was the bravest man alive. He did not escape the close proximity without his share of burns, and his armor was still warm to the touch, but Ava didn't mind. They did it. They killed a monster together. This was the best day ever. Not because her father killed a monster to save her life, but because they faced it together.

He pulled the weapons free from its carcass and handed *Seraphina* back to her. She grabbed its hilt, blushing because she hadn't been able to kill the monster in one strike. Her father would have taken its head off with that blow, sparing them from the danger of the extended battle. She saw him drop to his knees, clasping his hands in prayer, and she followed suit. Together they prayed to Eodran and thanked Him for protection, strength, and victory against the evil of the monster. And even though she detested the prince, they prayed for the life of Flynn to be spared.

"Claim your trophy, Avalina," her father said in a soft voice as he rose to his feet. He looked at her and nodded with a reassuring smile. She walked around to its back and sliced off the end of its tail. The skin still retained a slight glow, enough to be able to light their way back out of the cave. She reached down to pick it up and released the tail as soon as her fingers closed around it. Her father gave her a thick leather glove from his belt and she put it on. Her hand was tiny in comparison to his, two of her fingers fitting into each one of the finger slots, but it worked well enough for her to pick up the tail without getting burned further. They looked at the unconscious Flynn and then at each other, each thinking the same thing. They could be free from obligation to the king if they left now. No one would be able to follow them. But Ava admitted that taking Flynn back home was the right thing to do even if it was very inconvenient.

"Let's get the prince back to Hárborg before he regains consciousness," her father said as he picked up the young man in his arms. She led the way back through the cave, relying on her memory to guide them in the right direction at each crossroad. Even though the prince was light and her father was strong, she noticed his labored breathing as they navigated through the caves. But he never showed any other sign of struggle or discomfort. They both let out a small sigh of relief when they heard the rushing sound of the waterfall, even though it meant returning with the injured prince and facing whatever consequences awaited them.

CHAPTER SIXTEEN
Outlaws

The citizens of Hárborg looked on in silence as Ava and her father passed through the town burdened with the unconscious prince. Ava could hear the rush of whispers behind them, threads of gossip woven in their wake. Her father warned her that it was likely to happen and told her to not allow it to bother her. But the hushed words did bother her, because they didn't bother to ask what happened. Would they be portrayed as monsters in the retelling? Ava would hardly be surprised to find out that was the case.

The unfairness of it all made her want to stop and shout the truth to all of them. Her father told her they would go on believing the whispered rumors and her attempts to protest would only make them confident the rumors were true. Ava trusted her father, yet a small part of her proclaimed she couldn't be certain that he was right.

Flynn caused his injury by being such a stupid boy and now they were the ones paying the price for it. Nothing would likely change. Ava wondered if these boys were getting hurt intentionally to win her sympathy somehow. Perhaps they were only getting hurt to make her look bad.

The flow of whispers moved ahead of them, rushing like a river toward the castle. The king would hear the gossip long before he heard the truth and would likely form his own opinion prior to hearing their account. Her father warned her of that as well. Ava was stuck with the negative stigma unless she wanted to go into another line of work, and doing something with her life other than hunting monsters was unthinkable.

A trio of knights rode out to meet them halfway to the castle and relieved them of the unconscious prince. They made better time after that because they were able to cut through the crowd. Ava saw familiar faces, people she exchanged kind words with previously, but there were no smiles nor kind words for her today.

The guard at the castle gate frowned at them as they crossed the bridge, his knuckles white as he gripped the hilt of his sword. Ava hadn't realized the arrogant prince was such a beloved person in the kingdom. Perhaps the tension of the moment, seeing the heir injured, had everyone on edge. She saw his true character on their hunt, and had seen glimpses of it even before that, and she hated him even more than she already had. She wished with all her might that the prince might die so that she wouldn't have to marry him. Well, maybe not die, she conceded. But at least be wounded badly enough that the king would release her from the betrothal. She would rather go home and tend a farm with Edgar than live in this castle with Flynn. It was not the first time she contrasted the two boys. At least Ava knew the real Edgar, even if he was clumsy and slow and a poor hunter.

The king wore an expressionless face as they set foot in the throne room. The silver carpet that was normally rolled across the stone floor had been replaced by a black one and he wore a plain black robe instead of the one trimmed in silver. The back of the silver throne towered above his head. A dozen onyx stones were placed in a circle around the throne. Most gemstones reflected torchlight but Ava noticed that these seemed to suck the light from the room, casting shadows in unusual places. A chill traced down her spine as she sensed an evil presence. She wondered if her father could sense it as well, but if he could he said nothing.

A man, bent with age, shuffled along the back of the room. He raised himself on his toes to whisper in the ear of the king who responded with a curt nod and a flick of his hand to dismiss the man. Ava watched the stooped elder disappear behind a silver curtain. Her father stopped walking and dropped down to kneel before the king. Ava hurried to do the same and found herself staring at a small stain on the floor as they waited for the king to speak. A long silence pierced the chamber as they knelt there, no one speaking or moving. Ava's legs were stiff by the time the king broke the silence.

"Rise," the king said, his voice flat. His gaze passed over them as he spoke. "What truth is there in these words about the prince?"

"If your grace would be so kind as to enlighten us to the words spoken," her father answered as he rose to his feet, "we can vouch for their accuracy, if there is any."

The king scowled, his gaze dropping down to them at last. "There is talk that you tried to sacrifice my son to appease the dragon, to try and claim its power for your own."

"Lies!" Ava shouted. Her father shot her a look and its message was clear: he was warning her to keep quiet.

"What my daughter means, your grace, is that there is no truth to that statement. It is merely the fabrication of overly-inventive imaginations and baseless accusations."

"How do you explain his condition, then? I told you to face the monster alone, but that didn't suit your purpose. My son was forcibly taken from his room in the castle, dragged along on your conquest, and when he tried to resist you bound him." Ava's father started to speak but the king cut him off. "I have concrete evidence to support those facts so don't bother trying to argue. Then you took things a step further by trying to sacrifice him when you found the monster. Count yourself lucky that you failed in those dark tasks."

"I told Flynn to stay back when we reached the monster."

"Clearly you did not make an effort to enforce that, if what you say is true," the king said, slamming a fist on the arm of his throne. The rings on his finger clanged against the metal of the arm, the sound echoing throughout the room. "Would you not have made a greater effort to restrain your own daughter from such danger? My son is on the brink of death because of your failure to obey my orders. Your prince, and future king. You should have showed him the proper fealty due to his rank and, given our history together, you should have kept him far from harm's reach."

"He refused to heed my orders," her father answered calmly.

"You claim to be able to slay monsters yet you cannot control a child of fifteen?"

"I never said that I could not," her father started.

"So you admit you could have controlled him?" the king shouted, his round face bright like a cherry. "Then why is he dead?"

"He is not dead," Ava said.

"He might as well be," the king answered. "Even if he survives this injury he will have a hideous scar where the burn was. People will not follow him when he becomes king, whispering that he has been marked by monster hunters and fearing that he will transform into the dragons you fly on."

"We don't fly on dragons," her father said.

"Convince the people of that."

"We did you a favor, your grace," her father said through gritted teeth.

"By ridding me of my only son?"

"No, by ridding your realm of a pyreken."

"It wasn't even a dragon that did this to him?" the king asked, a purple vein throbbing in the center of his forehead.

"I never said it was, your grace."

"You expect my gratitude when you allowed my son to get injured?"

"We had a bargain," her father said. He looked at her and nodded. Ava pulled the pyreken tail free from her pack and held it up for the king to see.

"Put that useless thing away," he answered. "I am a man of my word, although you are clearly not a man of yours."

"Your grace is kind," her father answered politely although Ava could see in his eyes that he had a different opinion of the king.

"The bargain has changed, in light of the circumstances. I am certain you will find the new arrangement to be satisfactory. The reward of gold and the horse will be withheld to recompense the crown for the expense of tending to the prince's wounds. Furthermore, the betrothal will no longer take place between our children." Those words were music to Ava's ears. Although she stopped herself from smiling, her eyes shone with delight at the news.

"Because my son still lives, and in honor of our previous relationship," the king continued, "I will show mercy and spare your lives. You have until sundown to depart from my kingdom." Ava expected her father to claim that as unfair, knowing that sundown was nearly upon them, but he said nothing. "If you are still within these walls at that time, the gallows shall become your reward instead. Is that understood?"

"Perfectly, your grace," her father answered with a bow. The king dismissed them and they turned to leave.

"One more thing," the king called as they reached the door. "If the prince dies from his wounds, there's no place you can hide in the 13 kingdoms where I will not find you. Pray that he lives, if not for his sake then for your daughter's sake."

CHAPTER SEVENTEEN
Escape

They rode through the night, urging their horses along at a steady pace. Ava could tell by his sour mood that her father didn't like risking the horses by riding them so late. He had always taught her that night riding was a sure way to break your horse's leg in a hole or over a fallen log, but he felt a need to distance themselves from Hárborg. She didn't trust the king to stay true to his word any more than her father did, so she wasn't against the idea but she kept having to raise an arm to rub her eyes or to stifle a yawn. Twice she shook her head violently to stay alert. Sleep threatened to overpower her with every passing minute and it was still hours before dawn.

Dark clouds rolled across the moon, obstructing their only source of light. Her father eased his horse to a slow canter and Ava followed suit and pulled up beside him. He looked over at her and studied her face. He must have seen something, the circles under her eyes or the drooping lids, because he sighed and stopped his horse, dismounting. She felt grateful and did the same. Ava fell into her father's arms as she failed to dismount with dignity or grace. Tristan set her down against a fallen log and she watched him grab their sleeping packs from the horses. He had to be at least as exhausted as she was, the circles under his eyes were even darker than before, but he kept moving for her sake. She was grateful, because she couldn't have set up her own sleeping roll even if she wanted to. Crawling under the cool covers, her eyes crept closed as sleep consumed her.

✗

The next thing Ava knew she was being shaken awake by her father. The sun was starting to creep into the sky, casting vibrant pinks and oranges and yellows upon the sheet of blue. She rose to her feet, rubbing the sleep from her eyes and yawning. It was going to be another long day of riding. She wasn't ready for it but it seemed like they didn't have much choice in the matter. They had barely crossed the border last night before her father decided to stop. Her limbs were stiff and her bottom ached and another day in the saddle would only amplify those, but she assumed her father wanted to ride farther into Alexandria before he would slow down. It was her first time being in a new kingdom, and so far the experience was fatigue and soreness. Hardly the excitement Ava had expected.

"Avalina," her father said, his voice soft yet firm. He tossed a long wooden shaft toward her and it landed on the ground at her feet. It was nearly the length of the spear her father used against the pyreken, the shaft smooth and the ends rounded. Black leather was wrapped around two feet of the shaft on one end, signifying the end she should hold. She looked up at her father, waiting to hear what he intended.

"Pick it up," he told her as he drew a similar shaft from the bags on his horse. "It is time I taught you to fight with a new weapon. Today we learn the spear."

"What about the king?"

"We're out of his jurisdiction now. He has no power in Alexandria."

Ava bent down to pick up the weapon, red ringlets of hair dangling in her face. She gripped it with both hands and squeezed the leather until her knuckles turned white. At first she wielded it like a sword, the tip of the weapon pointed upward, but she noticed her father used a different stance. She shifted her body to imitate his, turning to the side and holding the weapon parallel with her hips.

"Very good," he said with a curt nod. "Like all other weapons, the spear is merely a tool. Think of it as an extension of your body. In expert hands it becomes downright deadly, capable of slipping between ribs or scales and piercing vital organs with a quick strike. It has enough power to pin an enemy against a wall or tree when wielded properly. It has a long reach which will allow you to keep far from harm while harassing the enemy with sharp strikes. You remember seeing some of this in the cave?"

Ava nodded as she thought back to the pyreken getting pinned against the wall of the cave. The attack slowed it enough to allow her father to finish it off.

"Good," he said, "now attack me with the spear."

Ava strode forward and thrust the weapon at her father, bending forward to extend the attack further. He easily deflected the attack by whirling his own spear around to smack her wrist. She dropped the shaft and rubbed her arm to ease the pain.

"Again, Avalina," her father said without waiting for her pain to subside. She picked the spear up and repeated her attack. This time she pulled back quickly to avoid his counter. He sidestepped her next thrust then slammed the round shaft of his weapon into her exposed shoulder. Ava cried out in pain and took a few steps back.

"The best use of a spear, as you can see, is in defense. There are exceptions to that rule, of course, such as when you need to keep an opponent beyond arm's length. Now try to defend my attacks."

Her father stepped forward and imitated her first attack. She turned and slammed his spear with her own but it didn't get knocked off course like hers. His thrust grazed her side and Ava scowled in response.

"Keep your body sideways," he said. "It gives your enemy less of a target to aim for." When she had turned again he nodded. "Now shift your weight, planting your back foot firmly in the ground. That will strengthen your defensive maneuvers and help give your strikes more power."

She readied her stance and he thrust his spear again. This time she knocked his strike aside, slamming her spear into his ribs with a strong counter-attack. He smiled at her and opened his mouth to say something when the sound of horses stopped him. They both rushed back to their own mounts. Ava started to get into the saddle but her father stopped her. He leaned in to whisper in her ear. "When I give you the signal I want you to mount up and head south, deeper into the kingdom of Alexandria.

You should only need to ride hard for a few hours and then you can slow down. I will meet you in Albrooke as soon as I can shake these guards." She started to argue but he cut her off with a shake of his head, raising a hand to his lips.

A dozen men came into view as their horses crested a hill. They were riding toward them at a breakneck pace. Their horses were slathered in sweat from the hard run. Most of the men looked to be in a similar state of exhaustion, sweat beading their foreheads and their hair disheveled. They must have left in a hurry because most of them were without much protective armor. Their captain wheeled to a stop in front of Ava and her father and glared down at them before dismounting.

"By royal decree, you are under arrest," the captain said. Ava's eyes widened but her father remained unaffected by this news.

"What is our crime, captain?" her father asked in a low voice.

"Besides being in league with monsters and demons?" one of the men chimed in. The captain glared at the man and then turned his attention back to Ava and her father.

"For the death of the royal heir of Hárborg," the captain answered.

"Flynn is dead?" Ava asked. She looked at her father and wondered what to make of this news.

"You confess you knew him?" the captain said. He licked his lips and watched them with a small smile.

"He can't be dead," her father said, staring at the captain.

"That's what I said, isn't it?" the captain replied. "The prince is dead and now the king wants vengeance. You can either come quietly or we can do this the hard way. Your choice." It was quite clear, from the expression on his face, which option he would prefer. Ava sensed that the hard way would happen even if they chose to come quietly.

"You have no jurisdiction here. This is outside your king's realm."

"What are you going to do, petition to the king of this territory when you're a corpse?" The men all snickered at the captain's reply but when he raised a hand they all grew serious. The sound of eleven swords being drawn echoed through the air. "Last chance. Surrender or we kill your little familiar first."

"Over my dead body," her father answered. He placed himself between Ava and the men and pulled his own sword free from its sheath. Ava followed suit and took comfort from the familiar weight of her sword.

"Now you've got the right idea," the captain said, drawing his own sword. "Whoever captures the man alive gets the girl as his reward." The men crept forward, eyeing Ava with grins that made her skin crawl. She felt naked beneath their stares and clutched *Seraphina* even tighter in her hands.

"Remember all that I told you," her father whispered as the men advanced. "Get on your horse and ride as far and as fast as you can."

The men leapt into action before she could answer him. Her father raised his sword fast as a lightning strike and blocked two blows at once as the battle began.

Ava knew he would have better odds in the battle if she stayed to help him. Even though they were outnumbered, they could win. Her father's sword came alive in his hand, dancing through their defenses. Nothing could defeat her father. Especially not some stupid guards in the service of a deranged king.

But she didn't have time to watch him attack the guards for long. As soon as she was in her saddle she urged the horse into a gallop and reined it away from her father and the fight. Three of the men abandoned the battle and came after her. That was three less men her father had to deal with, which she was thankful for, but she knew she couldn't let them catch up to her. She was weary from the hard ride yesterday but she and her horse were in better condition than their pursuers. Unlike them, she had managed to rest for a few hours. And that seemed to make all the difference as her steed increased its lead over the guards.

The three men were relentless in their pursuit. Ava had to let her horse trot for a while but by the time it was necessary, she had already pulled ahead by enough to be safe from any arrows that they could fire. They gained ground for a few minutes as they urged their horses to expend themselves. Soon their own horses threatened to drop from exhaustion and they had to match her trot. Time passed by in this fashion with the four of them urging their horses into gallops whenever they sensed their mounts had the energy to do so. But Ava knew that her horse needed water soon. And to be walked and groomed. Something needed to change, because this chase couldn't last much longer. Sooner or later the horses would give out, and she didn't want her own mount to suffer that fate if it could be avoided.

Ava leaned close to the horse's head and whispered reassurances and encouragement. She promised to reward it with a few sweet apples and lots of water if it could pull through long enough for her. She pressed it into a gallop and cut west toward a small rocky valley. If she could manage to get a big enough lead, she thought she could lose them in the cover of the large rocks and, perhaps, ambush them.

She moved quickly behind the cover. She knew she didn't have long before the three riders would reach her and she knew where they'd expect to find her. She dropped from the saddle and grabbed her bow and three arrows. She checked to make sure her sword was still in its sheath, and ducked low as she ran back a few rocks. She stuck two arrows in the ground at her feet and knelt, pulling the last one taut on the string of her bow. She could hear the pounding of hooves getting closer. The first raced past in a blur. Ava corrected her aim to where the other two riders would be heightwise. The second came in, just a little slower than the first. She heard shouts from the first. They had seen her horse. The third man stopped and was just barely in view. Ava loosed the arrow. The steel head sunk into his neck and the man fell to the ground with a garbled cry of alarm.

She didn't have time to watch him to be sure he was dead. She shot a second arrow toward the men rushing her but they sidestepped right as she released the shot. The string of her bow was still vibrating as she dropped it to the ground. She drew her sword and stood ready. They both rushed at her. She was prepared and parried the first thrust that came her way. She dodged the second swing. *Seraphina* became an extension of her arm as it lashed out at the vulnerable spots in the guards' defenses. Her strikes did not have enough force to be lethal, but she knew the flurry of wounds would help distract her opponents at a crucial moment and the wounds would wear them down over time. Ava had been taught that one small mistake in battle can bring about the end. She was determined to make sure these guards were the ones who made the mistake.

The sound of clashing steel filled the air over and over and the coppery scent of blood filled her nostrils. Sweat dripped down her face as she fought off the two men. She lost ground with every strike. She dodged behind rocks, ducked under sword swings, and skirted around the slower guards. She was weary and her arm ached with every clash of their blades, but she took comfort in knowing that they had to be tiring too. She was a monster huntress and that meant she was stronger than any old palace guard. Yet it was all she could do to keep up with defending their attacks.

She ducked under a strike, grabbing a handful of dirt in the process. She popped back up and hurled the dirt into the man's eyes with one hand while swinging her sword with the other. His initial reaction was to rub his eyes and that proved to be his fatal mistake. Ava drove *Seraphina* into his chest and wrenched the blade. The man dropped to his knees, gasping in pain. She struggled momentarily to remove her sword and just managed to pull the sword free in time to deflect an attack from the other man. He lashed out in a fury, calling her a coward and a sneak with every strike. His anger fueled him, adding power to each blow, but it also made his attacks predictable. Ava was able to dodge or parry each thrust and slash with ease while the man wore himself out.

His swings grew slower, the force behind them dwindling. His technique was sloppy as he thrust his sword. She had no trouble avoiding his attack and her instincts kicked in before she even saw the opportunity she needed. Ava grabbed the sleeve of his tunic and tugged him off-balance. Ava took advantage of his disorientation and darted around him, thrusting a dagger deep into his back. The guard arched his back and Ava ran him through with her sword. He slumped to the ground, bereft of life.

The battle was over and she dropped to her knees in prayer. Eodran had kept her alive and safe in the face of danger and she needed to give Him thanks for that. "Thank you, Eodran, for the shelter of your protection. I pray you cared for my father, as well, and that he would meet up with me soon. Amen." Then she took an oiled cloth from a pouch in her belt and wiped the blood off *Seraphina* before sheathing her weapon. She stumbled back over to her horse and paused long enough to pull out her journal and look at the map of Alexandria she copied. She guessed at her location and saw there was supposed to be a river just a little farther west. She grabbed the reins and led the horse along the rocky terrain. She realized he never really told her what they were going to do once they arrived in Albrooke. He only said to meet him there. But what if he never showed up? What was she supposed to do then?

CHAPTER EIGHTEEN
Fading Hope

Ava was ready to sleep in a bed by the time she finally reached Albrooke. She managed to get lost twice along the way, though she didn't miss the village by much either time. She expected a large city would be her destination but this place was even smaller than Tirgoth. She could have shot an arrow from one side of the town and had it land cleanly on the other side, missing all of the run-down and rotting houses that lined the muddy streets. She marveled that this place appeared on maps, although she figured a small village like this might serve for a good place to lie low for a while.

Ava suffered with restless nights since her escape, each spent half-awake worrying about her father. She had expected him to catch up to her long before Albrooke, especially given her difficulties in locating the small village, and now her last hope was that he made it here before her. He had to be here by now; she certainly took long enough in arriving for him to cover any lost ground and then some. She walked her horse through the town three times while looking for a place to stay. She didn't trust the look of the first place she saw, The Speckled Duck, but it didn't take long for her to realize this was the only inn to be found in Albrooke.

The inn was nicer looking on the outside than The Storming Stallion, but there was something about it that made Ava's skin crawl. The red exterior was freshly painted and a crisp sign, in the shape of a duck, hung over the door proclaiming the name of the establishment. But there were no windows to be seen on any side. Ava found this small detail to be both unusual and unsettling because inns from the stories were warm and inviting. So she did the sensible thing and spent an afternoon watching the place. The people she observed stumbling out of the building were hideous and scarred, slurring their strangely-accented words and lumbering with an uneasy gait onto the path. But Ava had no choice; she had to go in and see if her father stopped here.

The owner of The Speckled Duck was a stout man with thick red hair pulled back in a ponytail that reached down to his waist. His face was hidden beneath an unkempt jungle of hair that was supposed to pass for a beard. He was passing out drinks to a table of drunk men playing dice. The owner looked up, saw her, and flinched.

"We don't serve your kind here," he said while crossing the room. That statement had the unfortunate effect of turning everyone's gaze toward her. Ava was thankful that her cloak was large and heavy and capable of deflecting the weight of the roaming eyes that wandered over her in those fleeting moments. What did he mean? Was this place hostile toward monster hunters? Then there was no hope of finding her father here. When he was closer Ava could see his blue eyes with more clarity and could read his expression: concern. "You are too young for this place, lass," he said so that no one else could hear. He motioned for her to step outside and she followed. Ava couldn't suppress a shudder as she felt dozens of eyes watching her every move.

They circled around the building and he stopped in front of a hidden door. "What can I do for you, lass?" he asked, his voice still quiet. She wondered how much she could tell him. She didn't trust the look of the establishment but she felt she had nothing to fear from this man. She decided to not reveal everything at once, in case he was fooling her, but she still needed a place to stay and thought to start with bargaining for that.

"I need a room for the night," Ava answered, "as well as food. I can pay." She fished out two silver coins and placed them in his hand. He stared at her for a long time without responding. Ava shifted from one foot to the other while waiting for his verdict. She had no idea what she would do if he turned her away, but she knew securing a room was at least as important as finding out if her father had been here recently.

"You see this here door? This is the servant's entrance and no one uses it except those who are employed here. There are a few rooms at the top where my family and my staff sleep. I could rent you one of those." He paused and frowned. He studied her and Ava twirled a strand of her hair around her finger. Had the king sent a bounty ahead of them? "You look familiar," he said at last. "Been here before?"

"No, sir," Ava said and her heart flooded with hope. She decided to gamble and hint at her reason for being here. "But I am supposed to meet my father here."

The man said nothing for a moment, appraising her gear and her appearance. A slow smile came on his face. "You're Tristan's daughter, ain't ya?"

"Yes! Is he here already?"

"I ain't seen Tristan 'round these parts in, oh, nearly three years. Always did enjoy our roast duck. I should like to have him 'round here again soon. Is he coming?"

Ava didn't know how to answer and in the silence the man touched her shoulder and comforted her. He must have guessed what happened, at least that they were forced to separate. He slid the coins back into her hand and told her to hang onto them since he still owed her father a small debt. He promised he'd send one of his servants, Marlene, around to show her to her room.

Ava spent the next three days sitting quietly in her room eating duck while poring over maps in her journal. Every night she would listen carefully with the hope of hearing word of her father. But day after day passed by and still she heard nothing. Not even a word was mentioned about any monsters terrorizing the land nearby. Her stay in Albrooke promised to be disappointing in every way. Her father should have been here by now, or at the very least he should have sent word to her. She was terrified by the possibility that he had been captured or killed by the guards. He was invincible, right? Hrundtboars and other monsters couldn't kill him, so how could some ordinary guards manage the feat? He had to be alive and simply couldn't get to her just now. Or there was a reason he needed to delay in coming to her. She would give him some more time before setting out to try and track him down herself.

Late that afternoon, Marlene brought her an extra treat between lunch and supper. Ava eyed the sweet bread that was dripping with honey and she smiled, eager to dive into the delicious food in front of her. But Marlene wasn't ready to leave. The young lady shifted uncomfortably from one foot to the other, her fingers toying with her white apron while staring at the floor as Ava bit into the bread. It was the best thing she tasted since leaving the castle and she smiled at Marlene. Then she noticed the girl was standing off to the side, tapping her foot on the ground. She was staring at the floor and biting her bottom lip. Ava took a few steps toward her, still smiling at the girl, and Marlene suddenly looked up and spoke in a hushed whisper.

"You must leave tonight," Marlene said as she leaned close to Ava's ear. "And never come back. This place is not what it seems and you are being detained for a purpose. You would do well to trust no one until you are far from here."

"What reason would they have to keep me here?" Ava whispered back.

"I can't tell, I'm not privy to that information, but I know that what you are seeking is not here. You are being tricked into staying until the shadow conquers. It is always watching. Its eye has been upon this place constantly since you arrived."

"What shadow? Conquers what?"

"Please," Marlene begged her, grabbing her hand. Ava yearned to believe her but how could she leave without knowing about her father's whereabouts unless it was to hunt a monster? She was not a trained hunter yet. What was she supposed to do out here in a different kingdom without her father's guidance and companionship? "You must go, before they learn I have been here and told you this," Marlene said and looked over her shoulder. Her skin was drained of blood and felt like she had just plunged into the river in the dead of winter.

"They won't know you've said anything," Ava whispered. "I promise not to tell."

"They will know. The shadow always knows and always sees. They have the weardstán in their possession."

"The what?" Ava asked.

"The weardstán, a seeing stone. Many of the shadow's minions carry a fragment of the stone."

"I still don't understand. What minions, what stone? Is the master of monsters controlling them?"

"Marlene," came a voice from down below. The maid jumped, her eyes pleading for Ava to listen and do as she asked.

"Come with me," Ava whispered. Marlene smiled at her and shook her head.

"It is already too late for me to flee. Please, leave here before it is too late for you. Don't let my sacrifice be for nothing." And then Marlene was gone without another word.

Ava mulled Marlene's words over in her mind. What did she mean? What sacrifice? Who was she worried would find out? Certainly not the owner of The Speckled Duck. Ava trusted him more than anyone else here and, if she was in danger, certainly either he would have told her. Or else Marlene would have mentioned the name of the person threatening her life. No, she decided, she was going to stay here and see what turned up tonight. If there was no news of her father or of a monster, she would move on and head back up to the kingdom of Hárborg to see what she could learn there about his possible whereabouts

A different girl brought her dinner that night. This girl was taller and thinner than Marlene. When she asked the new girl about Marlene, Ava was simply told that Marlene was taking the night off. So Ava brushed her unease aside and listened to the conversations below through a hole she made in the floor.

Ava was excited to hear news of a monster nearby. Ava leaned down low, pressing her ear to the floor to hear better. It was hard to make out with all the competing noise, but it sounded like the guy was mentioning a four-armed gripmaug as the fearsome monster. Ava frowned with uncertainty. Was that a real monster? She hadn't heard of it before, but she also hadn't heard of a black-tailed warg until her father brought home its pelt. There had to be hundreds of monsters she had never heard of. Ava listened to the sound as coins changed hands and peeped down through the hole in time to see a hooded man wander away from the table right below her. A smile flashed across her face and she sat up. She finally had a clear lead to go off of. No more feeling useless while waiting around for her father to return.

She thought about replacing the floorboard and writing what she heard in her journal, but something kept her there. The man wasn't very sure of the monster's location, speaking only in vague terms of some riverbank around here. Ava wanted to see if anyone else brought news of a monster tonight, perhaps with better directions. It didn't take long before another hooded figure, this one dressed in a blue cloak, approached the person at the table below her. Ava wondered about the man seated below her room, receiving this information. She couldn't see him clearly but he had enough weapons strapped to him to be a monster hunter. The room was open and receptive of the hunter, something that wasn't the case at The Storming Stallion with her father. But if the innkeeper here knew her father, it made sense that the locals were accepting of hunters. She wondered if her path would cross this monster hunter's path. She had never met a monster hunter other than her father and considered how that meeting would transpire.

This newcomer repeated the same information about a four-armed gripmaug off to the southeast. But this one gave a few landmarks to help guide Ava there. She pulled open her journal and looked at the map. Sure enough that particular statue was marked and was right next to the bank of a major river. She had a monster and a destination. She considered staying for the night but she wanted to get a start on the hunter below, which meant she needed to leave tonight or risk being too late.

She shoved her few belongings into her pack and left a few coins on the table. It was only right since the innkeeper refused to take her money, claiming every day that it was still less than he owed her father. She hoped that Marlene, not the new girl, would find the coins in the morning and that it would bring a smile to her face. After all, she wanted Ava to leave, right? And that was exactly what she was going to do. It was time to hunt again.

Her adrenaline surged as Ava dashed down the secret stairs and over to the stable. Her horse was groomed and already saddled but she didn't think anything of it as she mounted up. The only thing on her mind was killing a monster. This time there would be no help from Edgar or her father. There would be no townspeople waging war around her against goblins. This time it would be her skill as a monster huntress against the skill of the monster and she couldn't wait to face it and write all about it in her journal.

CHAPTER NINETEEN
Hunting Alone

Ava followed the directions from the man at The Speckled Duck and arrived at the landmark in under five hours. It was a rather easy ride, traversing mostly flat grassland along the way, and that raised her spirits. Fortune was on her side so far, guiding her path so that she could accomplish her first solo hunt before her father would catch up to her. She imagined the proud look on his face, the same one he wore when she informed him of the coming attack on Tirgoth. While she didn't prefer hunting without her father, tonight the monsters of the 13 kingdoms would be served notice: Ava is a huntress that no monster will want to tangle with.

The landmark of her journey, a tall statue made from an aquamarine granite, loomed just ahead. Its features were smooth and worn from the weather, their individual faces were indistinguishable, but she could still make out the original image carved by the sculptor. It was depicting a trio of men and one woman, a party of unnamed individuals that performed heroic deeds long ago during the Wizard Wars. When Ava was close enough she could read the short inscription at the base of the statue which read: "These four warriors fought to maintain the balance in the world. They fought bravely and their sacrifice for the side of the Light will forever be remembered." The rest of the words had been worn down to the point where they were no longer legible.

Ava sat in her saddle and contemplated the deeds of these bold warriors from the past. Had they not acted, perhaps the world would be radically different than the world she was living in now. It was clear, from the inscription that remained, that these four were important in shaping history. She bowed her head and spoke to Eodran:

"Almighty Eodran, I thank you for these four nameless warriors who died defending the world from the darkness. I pray that they would be rejoicing in your glory today in the 14th kingdom. Grant me the courage to continue the fight against the darkness, to press it back in Your mighty name. Amen." As she was closing her prayer she heard a quiet splash downstream. Could her fortune be so good as to lead her directly to her target so soon? She dismounted and secured her horse's lead around a small tree before heading off to investigate.

It didn't take long for her to locate the source of the sound. It strode on two legs like a human but there were far more differences than similarities, even if Ava overlooked its two extra arms. Its arms, neck, and face were a dark green color but around its midsection the color was a lighter shade. Its muscles rippled beneath the thick hide-like skin. Its long, slender fingers had sharp talons that could tear through flesh with ease. In its left arms it gripped a long metal pole that was as tall as it was and the end of it branched into three sharp points. She had never seen a trident before, but she heard enough about them to recognize it upon sight.

She would be at a disadvantage because it had more arms, a longer weapon, and it stood nearly a foot taller than her. It was heavier and had natural armor for its skin. Ava considered, for a long moment, turning back and returning to Albrooke. Her father confessed to ending a hunt when he recognized a distinct set of disadvantages. But she was also a monster huntress and ought to be willing to step in and take on foes that ordinary men would retreat from. Fleeing now might place her on a path that would not lead to her becoming a huntress. She would rather die than live a life that didn't involve hunting monsters.

She was still uncertain about what to do when she heard a plea for help. Both her and the gripmaug looked over at the source of the sound. Tied to a tree was a young woman, hardly older than Ava herself. The bonds looked to be a mix of seaweed and some sort of silk-like fiber woven together into a makeshift rope. The girl struggled against the bindings and wept. The gripmaug hissed and said something in a language Ava didn't understand but the message was clear enough. It was telling its captive to be silent or else. Before she could consider the ramifications of her actions, *Seraphina* was in her hands. This girl would die tonight if Ava turned and fled from the monster. She would be the main course for this gripmaug's dinner unless someone intervened, and at the moment there was no one but Ava who could do so. Perhaps this night would be the first step toward fixing people's attitudes toward monster hunters.

Ava caught the girl's gaze and raised a finger over her lips. So far the monster had no idea she was here. It had turned back to the water and was chanting in its language. Did monsters have magic? She hoped never to find the answer to that question! She moved with practiced care, crossing the distance between them. Surprise was going to be her greatest asset right now and the gripmaug might be preoccupied long enough for her to free the girl and get away herself. She drew a dagger in her offhand and sawed at the seaweed ropes. She had to give the girl credit, at least she was keeping her cool enough to not draw its attention. As the final strand broke free the girl fell to her knees. The monster's head snapped around and its eyes locked onto the newcomer. It rose to its full height, thrusting the trident overhead as it let out a fierce cry. It was challenging her. She didn't completely blame it. After all, its dinner was running away and Ava was standing in its way of recapturing it. She sheathed the dagger and gripped *Seraphina* with both hands, uttering a quick prayer to Eodran for luck and protection.

The monster crossed the space between them with two leaping bounds. The gripmaug thrust the trident to skewer her and she twirled aside. A closed fist clipped her shoulder but she ignored the dull ache and attacked back. *Seraphina* glanced off its skin but a few beads of a thick gray blood clung to her blade. She had drawn first blood! Perhaps luck was on her side after all. If the gripmaug were aware of the wound, it didn't show it. The monster lashed out again with its trident. It was trying to gore her with its three-pronged tip but she anticipated the thrust. Her father used a similar technique with a spear against the pyreken.

The beast caught her blade with its hand when she tried to retaliate. Gray blood streamed down the steel but the monster didn't let up its grip. It growled at her, thick spittle smacking her forehead and sticking into her hair. She strained her muscles to drive the sword closer to her foe. She almost didn't realize her mistake until it was too late. She dodged at the last second and only one of the trident's prongs jabbed into her leather armor. It pierced the tough leather and pain swelled in her side. She withdrew a few paces and the gripmaug trilled when it saw her injury. She only hoped that its wounded hand would affect it more than her injury would affect her. Her father had taught her that was how most battles went; dragging on with injury after injury until one could bear no more wounds. She had to be tough, to press through the pain, if she wanted to triumph.

She took a defensive stance and ignored the throbbing ache that accompanied every breath and movement. She would definitely need to patch herself up once this battle was over. The monster twirled its trident overhead and leapt forward. It brought the weapon around in a mighty swing, wielding it like a sword. Ava trained most of her life on how to face a sword in combat and was comforted by the familiar tactic. She ducked and the weapon whooshed overhead. *Seraphina* struck out and bit into its light-colored stomach with a slash. The cut was small, the thick skin absorbing most of her blow, but she had certainly scored a hit on the beast.

It hissed in rage and drew the trident back with one hand. It was telegraphing its moves, showing Ava what it would do next and where it would strike. It never tried to feint with a false attack. Clearly combat tactics were not something gripmaugs concerned themselves with. She dodged its attempt to skewer her and brought her blade down on the shaft of its weapon, striking near its hand. The weapon clattered free from its grasp and the gripmaug took a step back. Was it surprised at her disarming counter-strike? She wished she was familiar with its facial expressions. A smile spread across her own face and the battle joy consumed her.

Ava advanced to press the advantage. It turned to flee. She could let it go and call it a day. She saved the girl from the monster and, against all odds, survived a direct assault from the gripmaug. But if she let it go how many other young girls might it capture and kill? No, she couldn't just let it get away. She drew her dagger and threw it. The blade caught the moonlight as it twirled, cutting through the air. It sank deep into the monster's thigh and the monster stumbled. Ava charged, crossing the open space between them as fast as she could before it recovered enough to resume its retreat.

It must have heard her approach. Two closed fists swung at her and Ava slid to avoid the blows. The gripmaug limped as it turned to face her. A flurry of blows struck out at her as the monster attacked with three of its clawed hands. *Seraphina* was too slow to be of much use against the flurry of savage strikes and Ava was forced to backpedal, sidestep, and duck as best she could. She felt the talons tearing through her armor bit by bit. She yelped as its talons scored a hit on her flesh. It wasn't scoring deep strikes but it was enough to keep her distracted. Every time she swung her sword the monster landed a blow of its own. It didn't appear to notice the increasing number of wounds on its own body. She knew now that she should have let it escape, that she should not have underestimated the wrath of a wounded monster. Its feral instincts were taking over and she had no answer for the furious assault. Death was stalking her now, beckoning her to join her mother in the afterlife.

Somewhere in her mind came a command to slash high left. She didn't know its origin but her body instinctively obeyed. *Seraphina* sliced clean through the wrist of one of its arms and the gripmaug cried in pain. The command came again to duck and thrust up. She obeyed and

Seraphina carved a slit in another arm. And then Ava gave herself over to the commands and let them lead her in combat. Every move she made either avoided a blow or dealt one in return. The monster was weakening, its attacks slowing with every swing. And then *Seraphina* finished the job, driving deep into its chest. The monster fell to the ground at her feet and breathed its last.

CHAPTER TWENTY
The Hero of Tirgoth

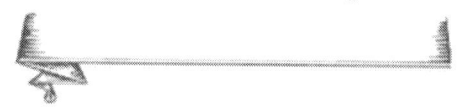

Edgar hated his new-found status of hero on days like this one. He was trying to hunt for tonight's dinner but the flock of young girls trailing him around were making too much noise and as a result scaring away all of his prey long before he would ever see it. No matter how hard he tried to beg and plead with them to leave him alone, someone always tailed him when he left his house. And before long that one multiplied into a dozen or more. He wondered if they had lookouts on every corner of his street, waiting for him to leave. There was no other way to explain their sudden, unwelcome appearance. It was beginning to drive him crazy and made it so his mother prepared meat less often for his family.

He felt his scar from the goblin attack was hideous but everyone else in the village thought differently. Many adults viewed it as the first of many battle scars, a clear sign that he would become one of the brave soldiers defending the village. The boys were all jealous of it and spent their time brooding over their lack of a grotesque scar from the attack; their sorrow increased when they realized that the young girls all adored him for it. And, in the eyes of many of those young girls, Edgar was the most eligible bachelor in the village. If he wanted to find a girl to marry, he would have no shortage of them to choose from. The problem he faced was that the girl he was in love with wasn't in the village anymore.

And somehow Edgar knew that Ava wouldn't be swooning over his scar and following him around like some lost lamb, bleating for his attention.

Memories of the pain still gave him nightmares but at least now he was left with an itchy, ugly scar instead of the searing agony he suffered. It took him eight days to recover enough from his wound to function upright for more than a few hours at a time. As soon as he could get around again, he immediately placed himself in charge of the village defense, diligently scouring the terrain around the area for signs of monsters. It had been nearly three months since he had started his vigil, and he found nothing during all of that time. The elders were begging him to return to his normal life, but the memory of the redheaded girl kept bringing him back to his vigil. He was determined to make her proud even if she never returned to see it and he knew, deep down, that he was doing exactly what she would have done if she were here. Everyone else was returning to their normal lives, forgetting about the horror of the goblins. They wrote it off as a fluke, a random occurrence that wouldn't be repeated anytime soon. Edgar wasn't so sure about that.

The one benefit to his celebrity status was the overabundance of people willing to help him improve his skills. He spent time learning to track better and became capable of seeing signs of animal presence that he would have overlooked before. He improved as a swordsman by training with a soldier, trading his expertise with a bow as payment. He even started to hit a growth spurt, adding on a few extra inches of height to pair with the muscle he was building. He was embarrassed when he thought back to the clumsy boy he had been a few short months ago. He was still probably nothing compared to Ava in terms of skill, but at least he knew he could hold his own in a battle or on a hunt.

"Where do you think we're going?" one of the girls asked. Edgar was pulled from his thoughts by the question and let out a sigh.

"On an adventure, as usual," a different girl chimed in. They all giggled at that.

"

Maybe we'll get to watch him slay some dreadful monster this time," the first girl replied. Edgar considered for a moment, trying to place the voice with a name. He decided it didn't matter, she wasn't following along because of who he really was.

"Oh, that would be exciting. The others would be so jealous."

"What was that?" one asked. Edgar spun toward them, expecting to see something fierce ready to pounce on the four of them. It turned out to be a small squirrel foraging for food. Edgar closed his eyes and counted. He would not lose his temper with them again. They weren't intentionally trying to make his life miserable. He just needed to ignore them. He turned back to the task at hand.

But he was unsuccessful in trying to tune out all of the noise caused by the trio of girls trailing him. They kept whispering and giggling every few minutes, and it seemed to him like they were trying to step on every brittle stick on the ground. He was beyond annoyed, his fury sapping some of his focus. He nearly missed the significance of a rustling bush, writing it off as another sound made by the careless girls. But, as he considered it further, he didn't remember having to step around any bushes along the trail. He stopped, cupping a hand to his ear, trying to hear the leaves rustle again.

But it was impossible to hear anything over the constant stream of conversation from the girls.

Edgar imagined his glare had become more menacing with the addition of his scar and he tested it out now on the girls. They all froze, staring at him with their next words hanging unspoken on their lips. Their eyes went wide and he smiled inwardly. He would have to remember to glare and scowl more around the girls since it seemed to be effective. His eyes darted around the area, searching for the source of the sound. A few months ago he would have deduced nothing from his surroundings but Edgar's dedicated training regimen paid off. He spotted some trampled grass a few feet away from a rather large bush. He crept forward and signaled for the girls to be quiet. The last thing he needed was for one of them to ruin his hunt even more than they already had. He notched an arrow on his bow, pulling the string taut before kicking a small stone into the bush.

He expected a jackrabbit, stag, or hart to flee from the bush. He would never have guessed that a timid drakhari was waiting in the foliage. The lizard-like monster screeched at him as it burst free from the bush, bits of leaves tangled in its rough brown scales. It wore a threadbare red shirt that failed to cover most of its upper body, and it stood a head shorter than Edgar and his followers. Its yellow slit-like eyes focused on the children and it hissed warily, a pale tongue flickering out. It had a small, scaly snout and ivory horns and its head was shaped like a hound. The drakhari clenched its claws and turned to run away, scampering into the trees with its tail whipping in its wake. Edgar fired an arrow after it even though he realized he waited too long for it to do any good. The projectile arced down and buried itself deep into the ground.

"What a hideous monster that was!" one of the girls exclaimed. Edgar was pretty sure her name was Elena.

"Are you sure that wasn't just a lizard?" asked the tall blonde. Sabine? Was that her name? It was hard to remember them all, and he didn't really want to know them better.

"A lizard man," Edgar said, silencing them all. "A drakhari, according to Ava's stories. Not a good sign."

Edgar mumbled to himself as he walked over to retrieve his arrow. He deliberately chose to ignore the buzz of conversation as it continued. He didn't want to hear how the girls thought it was so ugly or how scared they were to see a monster. He just wanted to find some dinner and some quiet to think. He gripped the arrow below the fletching and started to pull but stopped short as the importance of the encounter dawned on him. With a mighty effort he ripped the arrow from the ground and slipped it into his quiver. He ran back toward the village, still ignoring the shrieking protests of the girls behind him. It wasn't until he was halfway home that he realized they could be useful when they reached the village.

The elders might question his story if he presented it alone, but they would have to accept it as fact if he had three eyewitnesses. If it would prevent him from standing atop the stone tower for days, like Ava had before the goblin attack, then he supposed he could tolerate their presence for a few hours in order to get some usefulness out of them. It was the first time that his new popularity was going to pay off.

Edgar's mind raced as he led the way back to the village. For most of his life there was almost no monster activity around here. Now he was looking at the possibility of a second attack in the matter of a few months.

CHAPTER TWENTY ONE
A Plot Uncovered

Ava slumped in her saddle as the town came into view. She was exhausted, saddle-sore, and frustrated by her lack of recent success. The gripmaug battle was a good lead, but she spent the last few days following bad ones. She returned for the second time since her battle, riding back into the town of Albrooke. Either she was failing as a monster huntress without her father, or else someone was leaking false trails to her. But how could they know she was eavesdropping, listening through the floor in the secret room above? It made no sense. She still couldn't believe that the innkeeper, Lars, would be up to no good--she trusted the man completely--but the fact that she hadn't seen Marlene since that first night unsettled her any time she thought about it. She wasn't sure she believed the story about

Marlene going back home to live with her parents in southern Alexandria.

She wouldn't dare stray too far from Albrooke in case her father came looking for her or sent another note into town. She debated a dozen times whether or not to try and find him but she didn't know for certain where he might be if he was still alive. Yet when she decided to ride after him, Lars showed up with a note from her father, reassuring her that he was simply delayed further and to remain around Albrooke until he joined her. So she was still biding her time around Albrooke.

Ava could lead her horse back to The Speckled Duck with a blindfold on. She knew every twist and turn in this small town and was familiar with the smells she encountered along the way. There was a fish cart on the left side as she reached the proper street. To the right there was the scent of sulfur from the blacksmith's forge. She groaned as The Speckled Duck came into view, hoping this time they would be serving something more savory than stew. She hadn't had duck, roasted or otherwise, since her first week there.

She didn't go in through the front door anymore. By now Ava was familiar enough with the process and went around back, knocking on the hidden door to gain access to her room. Ava pried her usual board loose and started watching the scene down below. Two men approached a table beneath Ava, both men dressed in dark cloaks. Cowls were pulled down so far that it concealed their faces. They both told a similar story about an eyrmin being sighted to the south, in the highlands just three days from Albrooke. Ava listened as both men recited their tales and she was eager to know if it was true. But the hearty slice of roast duck in cranberry sauce stole her attention as the scent of succulent herbs and juices made her stomach rumble. If she was going on another adventure tonight, she needed to have a good meal.

Ava rushed over and sat down at the table. She grabbed a thick slice and her teeth sank deep into the tender flesh, juices dribbling down her chin. She delighted in the delicate balance of herbs rubbed to perfection on the skin, accented by the sweet sauce. She feasted on the meal as though she hadn't eaten in weeks. She finished eating and returned to her perch. Almost as if on cue, another man came across the room and spoke to someone right below her, describing the eyrmin and its last known whereabouts. But Ava wasn't paying attention to that. She was straining to hear the hushed conversations in other parts of the room. Marlene's warning, forgotten for days, echoed in her mind as she caught wind of other monsters and locations mentioned to the north. The stream of informants continued to pass under her, each one repeating the eyrmin tale. For her benefit? It had to be, but how could they know about her? Unless Lars were in on it. Marlene was right, it was all a ploy. They told her about monsters to the south and to the west. But there had never been so much as a hint of any issues to the north when she listened. At least not when she listened to the men seated beneath her. How far did this plot go? The first trail had been a good one. Was she supposed to have died facing that gripmaug? Had the note from her father been forged, too? She replaced the board and grabbed her journal, looking at the maps. She was trying to chart the travel of the first monster she overheard about when she heard footsteps coming to her door. She shut the journal in a hurry and tucked it into her belt before answering the door. It was Lars, smiling at her and wiping his hands on his leather vest.

"I had best be on my way," Ava told him, "if I want to reach the highlands in time to catch this rogue eyrmin." The smile on his face grew and he nodded. "And the duck was really good tonight," she added and his head bobbed in answer.

"Your horse is ready," he said. "I was wondering if you heard. It seems to be all that they could talk about down there and those men right under you were loud enough that the whole of Albrooke probably heard about it. Best of luck to ya. I'll send word if your father shows up, lass."

Ava thanked him and grabbed her stuff, leaving a coin in order to not make him suspicious. Did he guess that she knew the truth now? She hoped not. She headed to the stables and, sure enough, her horse was groomed and saddled again. Ava needed to put some more distance between herself and Albrooke. Fast.

She rode through the southern part of town, even though she had no intention of going south. She was certain eyes were watching and she didn't know how long they would watch her. A few miles later she turned her horse to the northeast. There was no time to waste and urged her horse into a gallop, steering clear of Albrooke in case someone was watching for sign of her return.

Later that night when she made her camp, she thought back to the things she heard. The men directly below her hiding spot said the eyrmin was south of Albrooke. The other two times she was sent to the south or the west in pursuit of another sort of monster. Ava figured that if she returned again it would have been another rare monster to the south or west. They had been lying. They all told the exact same story and they all wore the same black or blue cloaks that made them look faceless. She suspected that maybe they were all the same person, or at least the same pair of people.

Ava pulled her journal back out and studied the map again, looking for some hidden clue about the two places. There wasn't really anything in common with them, other than they were both places close to Tirgoth. That was the thought that stopped her for a moment earlier and now it made her gasp as she considered the implications. They are headed toward Tirgoth. She was certain of it! These false trails were a deliberate distraction to keep her far from the village. Which meant that she needed to hurry if she wanted to reach Tirgoth in time.

CHAPTER TWENTY TWO
Unmasking Dreams

Sleep evaded Ava that night, even though she was exhausted. When she squirmed closer to the fire, she was too hot. She was too cold if she moved further back. The sounds of nocturnal animals and insects echoed in her ears. A small pebble pressed into the small of her back, into her hip, her ankle. Ava tossed and turned and stifled yawn after yawn with her fist. She would have pressed onward, but the moonless night would have endangered her horse. So she silently raged at every annoyance that kept her awake until the fire had burned down low.

Thoughts of her father danced in her head. She wished he were with her, standing watch during the night or simply sleeping nearby. He should have been in Albrooke long ago. It was not too far from where they had separated. Even if he needed to ride to the western shore and back, he could have been here by now. Her father would never get lost, so that couldn't be an explanation. The only possibilities were death or capture, and Ava wasn't ready to face the idea of a world without her father. She had hardly known her mother and she was able to accept that fact, but her father was both her inspiration and her comfort in this world. Without him, would she ever become a full huntress of monsters?

She rolled over and her hand touched something cold and smooth. Her fingers closed around it before she realized what it was. Waves of emotions burst through her, mingling with the fear and tension already bundled inside her.

Her father stood outside a small cottage. He swayed and stumbled forward, knocking the door inward as much as opening it. His feet dragged upon the floor as he entered the cottage. A woman, slightly older than him, knelt on the floor to his left. Her head was bowed and her hands clasped together, praying to Eodran. A dozen candles burned around her and she took a deep breath before looking up at Tristan. The dim light masked the streaks of gray that threatened to overrun the vibrant red hair of her youth.

"Why do you insist on following that foolish ritual," he asked in a tone that rivaled the frigid air. "When has this supposed deity, Eodran, ever answered your prayers?"

"Every day, Tristan," she said, rising to her feet. She brushed the dirt from the knees of her black breeches and turned to face him. "Every day that you and our daughter are still alive is another day that I count my prayers answered."

He said nothing, swaying as he stared at her. He was younger than her by a handful of years and his black hair was still free from signs of age. Ava was playing with a doll in the other room, smoothing its woolen hair while biting her lower lip.

"Tristan," she said, "you need to take Ava and leave. Tonight."

"Kicking us out, Kenna? I knew you'd do it sooner or later," he slurred, advancing toward her. He was swaying where he stood, and now he advanced toward her. He raised a fist into the air, his face bright as a ripe tomato.

"I'm doing it to protect you," Kenna answered, although Ava barely heard it.

"I'm starting to think what they say is true," Tristan said, "that you hunters are in league with the abominations. That it's all some big ploy and pretend to belong to the Order of the Light but really are sworn to the Order of Might. The king said so himself at the dinner feast tonight and not a person there objected."

"You really believe that?" she asked, her gaze softening. Ava could feel the pain in her mother's voice.

"Why else would you want us gone?"

A sob caught in Ava's throat and the doll dropped from her fingers. Hot tears trickled down her cheeks yet neither of them turned toward her.

Her vision flashed a bright white, followed by darkness.

Ava clutched her father's waist as he rode away from the small cottage. Her arms were too small to wrap all the way around, but she held his cloak for added support. The wind whipped stands of her crimson hair behind her as they rode along, leaving her mother behind. Ava knew what was coming. She experienced this dream before. A scream would send them back to the house and her mother would be there, dead, in a pool of her own blood. Ava willed her eyes to open, to end the dream, but the scene continued to unfold before her.

The clouds rolled across the sky, covering the light from the stars as Ava and her father rode onward. The wind whistled through the valleys between the hills and whipped the hood of his cloak back to uncover his face.

"Mommy," Ava whimpered, stretching a thin arm toward her home, fingers wiggling as she tried to grasp the house. Her father looked back and his eyes followed the line of Ava's arm. A large shadow, nearly imperceptible in the moonless light, slipped around the side of the house and disappeared into the doorway. Her father tugged on the reins, stopping the horse at

the crossroads. A scream rang through the air. The silence that followed rang in her ears and she squirmed closer to her father and tightened her grip around him. The horse continued forward as if oblivious to the danger closing in upon them. A second scream brought them to a halt and her father turned the horse back toward the house standing between two hills.

Her vision flashed a bright white, followed by darkness.

When her vision returned she was standing in the small room once more, her eyes burning and cheeks wet. The floor beneath her feet was warm with a thick, sticky liquid. Red filled the room around her, contrasting starkly against the black and white backdrop. A pair of figures were on the ground in front of her, one sitting while holding the other in his lap. One crying, the other bleeding. Her father clutched her mother in his arms and she could feel the life ebbing away from the woman. Her vision blurred and she lifted tiny fingers to wipe away the moisture. Crimson hair blended with the crimson liquid flowing from open wounds. Pain lanced her heart and the sobs flowed freely from her throat. Her father howled in anguish and Ava sensed the final moments descending upon her mother. Laughter, cold and harsh, flooded her mind and she clutched her hands to her ears to drown it out. Yet it grew louder, rising in intensity like an orchestral crescendo. She screamed but no sound came out. She wept but no tears fell. She ran but the scene of her mother's final, painful moments remained etched before her.

Her vision flashed a bright white, followed by darkness.

Ava screamed. An owl took flight in the waking world, yet her eyes remained closed. A wolf's howl answered her cries. Her limbs thrashed and the screams became whimpers. A final jerk of her limbs and then she went still. Her chest rose and fell, rose and fell, faster with each breath. Pale moonlight reflected off pale skin. Still her eyes remained closed. Fingers curled in, grasping the black bolt until her knuckles turned white. Through the nightmares of blood and death a voice rang out and pierced the mist that ensnared her mind. The bolt split in two and her body relaxed.

"Let me show you the full truth of that night," the voice said. Ava did not respond, yet her breathing evened out and her hands unclenched as the images rewound to the first scene.

"I'm starting to think what they say is true," Tristan said, *"that you hunters are in league with the abominations. That it's all some big ploy and pretend to belong to the Order of the Light but really are sworn to the Order of Might. The king said so himself at the dinner feast tonight and not a person there objected."*

"You really believe that?" she asked, her gaze softening. Ava could feel the pain in her mother's voice.

"Why else would you want us gone?"

A sob caught in Ava's throat and the doll dropped from her fingers. Hot tears trickled down her cheeks yet neither of them turned toward her.

"Because I want you safe. Is that such a horrible thing - to want you and our daughter to be alive? There is something coming here. Tonight. It is hunting me and I don't know if I am strong enough to kill it."

His expression sobered and Ava heard him suck in a deep breath of air. "Kenna," he said in a soft voice, "why don't you come with us if you think it can kill you?"

"It is better to face it now, on my terms, than on the run. If I flee I might survive the night, yes, but I would have to live in fear and paranoia every day. I would be constantly looking back over my shoulder until either I killed it or it killed me." Kenna drew her sword and rubbed the blade with an oiled cloth. "Don't stand there gawking like a fool, Tristan," she said, not bothering to glance up from the blade. "Grab Ava and go before it is too late."

He turned to leave and stopped along the way to Ava. He looked back, shifted the weight on his feet. He cleared his throat and Kenna looked up, eyebrows arching over her emerald eyes. "I'm sorry for what I said. Please be careful."

"I always am," she answered with a small smile, "which is why I am still alive."

A sense of warmth flooded Ava's heart as the exchange ended and her father led her out to a saddled horse. The argument was not what drove her father away alone, but rather her mother's desire to protect them from an evil she wasn't certain she could defeat. Ava expected the dream to end, yet it continued onward as before with her riding behind her father until the screams brought them back toward the cottage. Ava wasn't sure she was ready to revisit the scene of death again so soon. But she had no choice in the matter. They entered, her father crashing the door open as he charged in with Ava close behind him to find her mother lying in a pool of blood on the floor. He ran over to Kenna, scooping her in his arms.

"Kenna," he cried, smoothing her hair back as tears ran down his cheeks. "You can't die on me. Our daughter needs you." He kissed her forehead and amended his statement. "I need you."

Kenna's eyes fluttered open. Her breathing was ragged and weak. "Tristan, I do not have long before my soul departs," she whispered, "the wound is deep and I can feel the life draining from me. But there is something important I must do. Bring me the white jar on the third shelf. And Avalina." He rose up to do as she bade. Ava could hear a liquid sloshing around inside the jar, smell the fragrant aroma of frankincense, myrrh, and cinnamon seeping from under the lid.

Kenna took the jar from him with shaky hands. More of the oil spilled on her arms and into her lap but she ignored that, setting it beside her. Ava wracked with sobs as she stepped into her mother's embrace and the two of them cried together for a minute in each other's arms. And then Kenna forced herself up onto her knees. "Kneel, Avalina, and bow your head. This was to be done when you were older, on your thirteenth name day but it appears Eodran has called me into His Kingdom, the 14th Kingdom." Kenna set the lid aside and dipped a hand into the jar, the blood on her skin mingling with the oil. She took a deep breath and let the oil drizzle over Ava's head. The silky liquid ran through Ava's red ringlets and dripped down her cheeks and along the back of her neck.

And then Kenna began speaking in an ancient language, repeating the same words that had been spoken over her on her thirteenth nameday. Kenna fell to the ground when the ritual was completed and her breathing grew even more shallow than before. Her face was flush, bereft of all color. And she smiled at her daughter.

"You are destined for great deeds, my child. May Eodran's Spirit fill you and guide you in times of need, give you strength when you have none left, and light your way even though the path may be in darkness. I love you."

Ava woke with a start. It all seemed so real. She felt the warmth flowing into her as her mother blessed her and sensed the presence of Eodran descending upon her. She could still feel it now, a soft presence deep inside her just out of sight and reach. But there nevertheless. Taking deep breaths, Ava rose to her feet and circled around the camp's perimeter. Her mind raced over the things she had learned that night. She was full of more questions than she had answers, but they all seemed so trivial compared to what she observed. Her mind never thought about the black bolt again, nor did she miss its presence in her pack. She was filled with a new joy and a purpose: to find her father, rescue him, and continue to make her mother and Eodran proud of her actions.

CHAPTER TWENTY THREE
A Desert Monster

Edgar struggled to keep pace with the rest of the village. The adults sprung into action three days ago, right after Edgar related his story to the elders. Sharpened spikes were placed around the village, arrows were dipped in tar and wax to make them flammable, and the lone blacksmith was hammering out weapons and bits of armor. Other men hunted as they tried to bring in enough meat for their wives to dry out. Children were sent to gather berries and nuts from the sparse bushes and trees around the village. Everyone had a hand in preparing for an attack and, while Edgar knew he helped make this happen, he couldn't help but feel useless.

Gathering berries was an important task. He knew and understood that but there were a dozen others already working on that. But he wanted to do something more useful for the village. This was probably why he wandered toward the tower. Preparing for an imminent invasion wasn't much use if you didn't know when the invasion was coming. Ava would agree with that and approve of his decision to ignore what he was told to do and take up this important task that no one bothered to think of.

His mind returned to Ava as he ascended the stone structure. He wondered, not for the first time, where she was and what she was doing right now. She was probably off having some marvelous adventure. He was certain that she was dining with kings and sleeping in beds bigger than his room. He found himself looking forward to hearing the embellished tales, watching her green eyes flash with joy as she recounted the details of her encounters. Yet he was also glad that he would get to have a tale or two of his own to share with her when she got back. That would certainly surprise her!

Unless he was wrong about the oncoming invasion. Maybe it was just a stray drakhari that wandered in the wrong direction. He had expected the elders to suggest as much, but the shock of the goblin attack a few months ago convinced them to take these kind of things more seriously. He stared out across the land, watching the forest, the desert, and the mountain in turn during his patrol. Edgar tensed up every time he thought he saw movement. He stood there, staring out at the landscape to confirm what he saw. But every time he was rewarded with disappointment. His eyes hurt from the strain, and his back was stiff. Ava wasn't here to remain on guard duty, so Edgar was determined to do it now.

Edgar drew his sword from his sheath. It was nowhere near as nice as Ava's sword, but he got a good deal from the blacksmith. The blade felt slightly unbalanced, the tip holding a little more weight than the hilt. It wasn't enough to make a difference in his training, plus his muscles grew used to compensating for its oddity. He ran a finger along the polished iron of the sword, the cold metal providing relief on his hot skin. He gripped the leather hilt tightly, the forefinger of his right hand extending along the crossguard. His trainer hated that habit, but it felt natural to Edgar and, so far, it didn't hinder his progress with learning the sword. Edgar wondered, as he shifted into a defensive stance, what Ava would say about his grip. He was positive she would call him a silly boy and spend the next few days trying to make him see the error of his grip. That certainly sounded like something she would do.

He trained against imaginary opponents until he was unable to hold the sword any longer. The weapon fell from his fingers and clattered loudly against the stones of the tower. He ran through the same thrusts and parries, slashes and strikes at least a thousand times in these three months, yet he still knew that his form and technique could improve. The sun was setting in the sky, but there was just enough light for him to take another look around before retiring for the night.

Edgar rose an hour before dawn, moved by a gut feeling, and slipped on a light beige tunic and matching breeches that would help camouflage him as he scoured the desert. He contemplated slipping on his leather tracking boots but decided to go barefoot instead. The sand would still be cool enough beneath his feet this morning, and he would make less noise this way. Ava would have been proud of his choice of stealth over comfort. He strung his bow, slipping it and a quiver over his head, and then strapped his sword to his waist. He checked to make sure the blade was loose in its scabbard so that it could be drawn in a hurry if necessary. He wanted to be prepared in case he happened to encounter anything. He would do no good to the village if he walked into an ambush and were captured.

Edgar trekked across the sand, moving from dune to dune with a practiced ease that came from years of playing monster hunter with Ava in the desert. He kept low to the ground and used the tall mounds of sand and the occasional large rock for cover. His eyes were constantly scanning the area around him and he watched for signs of someone or something in the desert with him. He strained his ears to hear anything out of the ordinary, but he couldn't manage to discern anything apart from the squawking of vultures. It wasn't until later, when taking a sip of water from his water skin, that he realized the importance of that sound.

The large scavenger birds were circling in the air, occasionally diving to the ground. Edgar knew that it could be nothing more than a dead boar that ventured out on the wrong side of town, but he had to investigate. This could be the sign he was searching for, the reason his gut urged him out here. He changed his course and cut to the northwest toward the circle of ugly predator birds.

Edgar slid the bow off his shoulder and notched an arrow in the string as he drew near the vultures. He was close enough to see their beady onyx eyes watching every move he made. The closest ones squawked at him in an attempt to drive him away from their carrion. He ignored their annoying chatter and focused instead on finding signs of a monster in the area. The bodies of an old man, a pair of stags, and a drakhari were scattered across a dune ahead. Was it the same drakhari that he saw before? Edgar rubbed his eyes on his sleeve, unable to believe what he was seeing. He couldn't see a track anywhere in the sand apart from his own. He noticed the vultures were circling around, the bravest ones making an occasional dive toward the corpses, but none of them landed. Then Edgar noticed the talon of a vulture half-buried in the sand beside the old man's body.

Edgar remained where he was, concealed behind a rock. He watched the bodies and waited for a vulture to drop down and claim a piece. He knew that they were cautious birds, but eventually one would give in to temptation and try to steal a morsel. Edgar was determined to be there when it did in order to see what was truly going on in the desert.

The midday sun peaked in the sky, and Edgar was starting to get light-headed from the heat. Beads of sweat trickled down his face, and his skin glistened in the sunlight. He knew he needed to head back to the village soon. He only brought a small waterskin and no one had followed him out this way. It would be hours before anyone thought to look for him and likely at least a day, if he was lucky, before they would find him if he passed out now. He let out a frustrated sigh and rose to his feet. It was time to head back to Tirgoth, empty-handed apart from a suspicious pile of bodies. And then a bird dove.

It happened so fast that Edgar wasn't even certain of what he saw. Before the vulture reached the bodies something burst out in a spray of sand, and snatched the bird with a massive stone hand. Grains of sand swirled in the air, a random sandstorm surrounding the hunter that lay in wait. Edgar caught a glimpse of it before it was completely hidden from his vision. It was huge. Three times the size of the men of his village. It had arms as thick as Edgar and hands as big as the rock he was crouched behind. It had no eyes that he could see, just deep black holes bored into its head where eyes should be. He had never seen it before but he had heard enough stories to know that whatever this thing was it spelled trouble for Tirgoth. Especially if it caught them by surprise, as it had the vulture.

Edgar forgot all about firing an arrow at the monster and fled back across the desert. All effects of heat and exhaustion were forgotten as he rushed toward the village to warn the elders of what he witnessed. His bare feet seemed to skim across the sand as he ran. He was too afraid to look back and see if the monster was following him, but his imagination was wild enough to keep the creature on his heels the entire run back and it motivated him to run faster than he had ever run before.

Edgar burst into the elders' meeting without waiting for an invitation or even an acknowledgment. He doubled over and panted to catch his breath. He looked up at them, wide-eyed with his chest heaving. They stared at the sight of a dirty, exhausted young boy in the middle of them. Edgar finally sucked in enough air to speak, looking around with his flushed face.

"Monster in the desert," Edgar said, pausing to regain his breath, "thought you should know." He slumped to the ground, weariness from the heat and his run rendering him unconscious.

CHAPTER TWENTY FOUR
The Second Threat

The entire village was alive with renewed activity by the time Edgar regained consciousness. Someone had carried him to his house and left a large pitcher of water beside his bed, but he ignored that as he stepped outside. He watched men run toward the western edge to meet the monster before it grew too close. He wondered if the elders had sent someone out to see what they would be facing. Knowing them, it was likely that they were blindly preparing for the encounter which meant it would be up to him to fill them in on the magnitude of the task before them.

He hurried along the dirt path, falling in line with a few older men as they crossed the village. The elders were holding a meeting along the outskirts and dozens of men stood in a line, armed and ready for battle. Edgar cut his way to the front of the group, eager to hear the tactics for facing that stone beast.

"Edgar," one of the elders said. The man frowned as he came into view. "Why aren't you back home?"

"I am here to help," Edgar said, sliding his bow from his shoulder. Some of the men around him started laughing, but he noticed that none of the elders were so much as smiling. Instead they just watched him with somber expressions on their faces.

"Go home, Edgar," Damien answered. "This is not your fight to face."

The head elder chimed in before he could argue. "We need you back in the village."

"But I can help. I killed a lot of goblins in the last attack!"

"No one doubts your ability," the head elder answered with a small smile, "nor your courage. That is why we are relying on you."

"To do what, exactly?"

"To keep everyone safe, in case we are unable to succeed."

"Oh," Edgar said. His shoulders sagged in disappointment. Their request seemed to make some sense to him, but that didn't change his burning desire to stand on the front line of the battle. This was his home and he wanted to be there to stop any monster that thought it could terrorize the village. He turned to go but remembered that they might not know what they were going to be facing. He looked at the elders, slinging the bow back on his shoulder as he told them, "The monster that is coming is big and scary."

"They all are," Bartz said with a laugh. Edgar clenched his fists, his complexion turning crimson as others joined in with the laughter.

"You don't understand," Edgar demanded as he stepped forward. But the elders had turned away from him, resuming their conversation from before. Their actions were clear: he was dismissed. They had listened but hadn't found his information to be of enough importance to take seriously. He struggled to fight back the tears as he walked back toward his house. Deep down he was afraid that everyone was going to die because no one would believe how massive this monster was.

Edgar patrolled around the outside of the town. He was trying to see if moving helped to keep his mind and emotions under control, but it seemed to him that it was only making things worse. He jumped at every sound, his mind interpreting the slightest noise as a sign of battle in the distance. He spun toward shadows seen and unseen in the corners of his eyes. Each time he raised his bow, ready to fire at nothing. Edgar was strung as tight as his bow and it was beginning to wear on him. He decided that he should go back to town and sit with the women and younger children so that he would be ready to defend them when the sand monster broke through the village's line of defense.

He tried to ignore the sounds and shadows as he headed back. He thought he saw movement again but, this seemed to be off in the distance. Edgar stopped and stared at the pair of mountains to the north. Was he imagining that movement too, or did he truly see something? He was about to dismiss it as yet another delusion when he saw the movement again. He ran toward it, determined to get a good look.

As he approached he could see that this monster was massive, at least as big as the sand monster was, with legs as tall and as thick as Edgar. Its skin had a rocky hue that allowed it to blend in almost perfectly with the mountainside as it stamped its way down a worn path. It had dull brown eyes the size of saucers and no nose, just a pair of finger-sized nostrils that flared with every breath it took. The monster's pear-shaped head was bald and Edgar thought the skin on top looked like rough, weather-worn leather. It dragged a tree trunk behind it with one hand, with thick limbs still attached to the trunk, and the other hand carried a massive rock. Edgar turned to run and warn the elders, but he heard the cries of battle start and knew it would be too late to change things. If that giant stone monster was already here they would never disengage to come and face this threat.

Edgar was going to have to face the mountain troll on his own.

He figured he had two things working to his advantage: the troll was moving very slowly, and it didn't know Edgar was here yet. He hid his bow and quiver and ran to the village, hoping to grab a few surprises to help ward off the troll until the villagers killed the desert monster. He tried to think back to his times playing with Ava, to the little comments she frequently made about various monsters and their weaknesses. He thought he remembered Ava saying that a mountain troll was afraid of fire and Edgar knew, from his months training with the soldier, how to prepare a batch of fire arrows. He was going to give this troll a nasty surprise and show it that Tirgoth was not a place for it to take lightly.

Edgar was disappointed to learn that the elders didn't order any batches of black tar to be made. Ava told him it was the best way to start a fire, pouring it onto your enemies while standing far above them on a castle wall and then lighting it with a torch. He knew that he couldn't carry the glowing coals from the blacksmith's furnace, nor would the arrows be lit long enough to be useful if he lit them in town. He was about to give up when he considered the tallow from the butcher's shop.

Would a glob of tallow burn long enough to reach the troll?

It was a long trek back to his bow and arrows. He navigated the streets of the village, lugging a heavy bucket of tallow in one hand and a lit torch in the other. Edgar hoped that the troll didn't pick up speed on its journey, otherwise he might arrive too late to deter the monster. He stopped to switch the bucket to his other hand, the weight making his shoulder dull with an achy pain. He needed his arm to be loose enough to draw the string on his bow and any numbness could affect his shot. He would only get one chance to frighten the monster and avoid a head-on confrontation.

The troll was at the base of the mountain, lumbering toward the village when Edgar arrived at his bow. He set down the bucket and wedged the torch upright between two rocks before slipping the quiver across his back and picking up his bow. He rolled the top of his arrow in the tallow, getting a thick coating along the head before sticking it in the flame. Black smoke coiled in the air and the smell of roasted pork filled Edgar's nostrils. Edgar turned to the troll. He took his aim carefully, as he drew back the string. He fired off his first shot, the burning head piercing into the troll's shoulder. It stumbled back a few steps and dropped its boulder. The monster swatted at the fiery projectile with a ham-sized hand.

Edgar had another arrow notched and on its way before the troll could get the first one removed. This time the arrow struck just below the troll's left kneecap. The monster danced around, moving far faster now than it was before. It turned to head back up the mountain when a stream of fire cut off its retreat. Edgar didn't have time to consider the fire's source as the troll spun back toward him. Fear danced in its eyes as it stomped toward the village of Tirgoth and the young archer. Edgar launched three more arrows into the monster but the fire was doing nothing to startle it. Clearly the troll feared whatever made the stream of fire more than it feared his arrows. Was it a dragon up there? One of the elders? Edgar tossed down his bow and drew his sword to face the troll. He knew that his odds of survival were slim but he needed to attempt to slow the troll down some more or else there would be a massive slaughter in the village. It was his duty because he was the only one who could do something about it.

He braced himself for the battle, adopting the same defensive stance he had seen Ava practice for years. As it got closer he realized just how small he was compared to the monster. He would be lucky to land a sword strike on its belly button, and that feat would require him to jump and swing his sword. His face paled and he tightened his grip on his sword, resigning himself to his fate. He found himself saying a prayer. Edgar had seen Ava do it hundreds of times and, somehow, he knew that she would do that now if she were the one facing the troll. The burden of fear was eased as he prayed and an aura of calm flowed through him. Then his prayers were answered as he heard the sound of a horse approaching.

CHAPTER TWENTY FIVE
To Kill A Troll

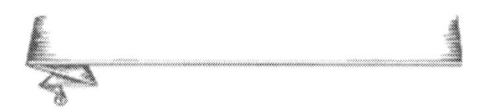

Ava was silent as she allowed her horse to walk along the deserted roads. She was looking for a sign of Edgar. Surely he would be out here even if no one else was brave enough to be. He was a better and braver warrior than he would ever realize. She caught herself watching for him, waiting to see his sandy blond hair and that crooked grin. And then she heard a something roaring in pain. She spurred her horse into a gallop, covering the ground at a rapid pace. Something was under attack on the north side of the village and Ava hoped she wasn't too late to save the people she had grown up around.

She nearly fell out of her saddle when she saw him. She was certain it was Edgar facing down a massive troll, alone but unwavering. Yet at the same time it wasn't Edgar - at least not the Edgar she knew a few months ago. He was holding a sword with the familiarity of a soldier and wasn't the little boy she had chased anymore. He had become far more interesting to her, but first she needed to help dispose of the problem in front of them and it looked like a big, mean, and ugly problem. It was three times her height with massive fists. Its skin was gnarled and bumpy, and was the color of parchment that had been left out in the sun too long. Small, sunken eyes squinted as they searched for the human prey that it was facing.

Edgar smiled at her when he saw her approach. Her breath caught in her chest as the troll chose that moment to swing the tree trunk in its hand like a large club. Ava cried out to Edgar and warned him of the attack. He ducked to avoid the blow, the wind from the swing messing up his hair. Ava glared at the monster that dared to attack the boy from her village. She dismounted from her horse and stood side-by-side with Edgar to face the troll together.

"Try to keep it at bay with the fire from your torch," Ava called over to him. "It fears fire more than anything. That should help to even the odds against it, even if it does hold the higher ground."

"It won't work," Edgar said. "I already tried scaring it with fire. Something on the mountain scared it back down with a large stream of flames."

The troll worked up the strength to unleash another massive attack. It flashed a monstrous grin at them. Small pebbles on the ground shook as it rumbled toward them.

"Circle around it," Ava said to Edgar as she prepared to dodge its attack. "I'll keep its attention on me."

Ava smiled when she noticed that he obeyed her request without questioning it. Not everything about Edgar had changed and she hoped that part always stayed. She was prepared to face this troll and it would soon learn that she was not a girl to be taken lightly.

Ava threw a dagger at the troll and the blade drove into its bare chest. It roared at her and brought the tree crashing down where she stood. Ava avoided the attack. She stabbed the back of its hand with *Seraphina*, drawing green blood as she tore through its skin. The troll grunted in pain and unexpectedly swatted at her with the back of its injured hand. The air escaped her lungs and she was slammed into a rock. The troll held her in place with the wounded hand. The troll's blood was sticky, hot, and smelled like a murky bog. It made her want to retch but she focused instead on squirming to free her sword arm.

Ava noticed that Edgar was behind the troll now. He climbed up onto a tall rock without the monster realizing it. Ava sunk down toward the ground, her face beginning to disappear beneath its hand as she worked her way free from its clutches. The last thing she saw before the hand obscured her vision was Edgar leaping toward the monster's head, sword arcing down at its exposed scalp. The troll's hand retreated moments later. The monster used it to swat behind its head as it staggered in a circle. Ava rose to her feet, looking for signs of Edgar as she strode toward the reeling troll. She was relieved to see his head pop up from behind a rock.

"Fire," she heard Edgar shout. Ava darted in close to the troll and stabbed it with a quick thrust of her sword before retreating to safety. She looked over her shoulder and saw he was right: the village was on fire.

"Edgar, where are the elders?" she asked.

Ava dodged another wild swing of the troll's weapon, rolling to safety. "Fighting a large sand monster in the desert," she heard Edgar respond as he launched an arrow that caught the troll on its jaw.

Ava feinted at the monster and swung *Seraphina* in a wide arc. It staggered back, wary of the blade. It roared in defiance and swatted at another arrow that Edgar launched. Ava swung a strike at its knee and hopped away in time to avoid its thick hand. Ava was about to dart in for another attack when a bloody blade emerged through its chest. Edgar twisted the sword before pulling it free from the dying troll.

"Come on," Edgar called out as he ran past the monster. "We need to get back to the village and try to stop this fire."

Ava hesitated for a moment, staring at the writhing form of the troll. She raised her sword, intent on finishing the monster and claiming a trophy from the adventure, but Edgar called out to her again.

"Ava," he said without looking back, "it is perfectly capable of dying without us being here to help it along. Come on."

She resigned herself to following his directions and slipped *Seraphina* back in its sheath. She ran to catch up to Edgar. The fires burned tall in the village, the grass thatching on the houses roaring ablaze. Ava wondered at who, or what, was behind the attack. What was strong enough to control a troll, a sand monster, breathe fire, and spread false leads in Albrooke? Ava spent the entire run back trying to puzzle it out. She knew what her father would guess but that was probably just his thirst for revenge.

Ava spotted women and children running through the village, splashing pails of water on the raging fires. Their efforts were in vain; the water was barely making a dent in the spreading inferno. At least they were trying, Ava thought as they marched past them. But she had bigger mysteries to worry about so she didn't concern herself too much with the problem. The villagers never gave the two youths a second glance as Edgar and Ava cut a path straight through to the other side of the village.

The fires burned stronger on the eastern side of Tirgoth and the heat around them increased with every step. Sweat soaked through Ava's clothes by the time they came to a stop. Edgar took three steps forward and paused. He jumped back in time to avoid a wave of molten flames. Ava gasped when she saw the origin of those flames.

"Flynn?" Ava said. She could hardly believe what she was seeing. Wasn't Flynn dead? The pyreken injured the prince and then the king sent his guards because the prince died. Yet here he was, presumably alive and well. His tall figure stepped out in front of them, his red and orange robes singed along the edges. A pale red glow radiated around his staff as he slammed the butt into the ground. His eyes found hers and a sinister smile crept onto his lips.

"Hello, Wife."

CHAPTER TWENTY SIX
The Real Threat

"We were never married," Ava said, crossing her arms over her chest. Ava studied his marred face, the results of his fateful encounter with the salamander, and determined that his appearance finally matched his ugly personality.

"A minor detail," Flynn said. He waved a hand to dismiss the matter, "that will be resolved as soon as I am through destroying your home."

"You are supposed to be dead." Out of the corner of her eye she saw Edgar creeping off to the side. Ava knew she needed to keep Flynn talking, focused on her so that he wouldn't see the boy sneaking away. She took a step closer to the prince and fought the urge to draw *Seraphina*.

"Sorry to disappoint, beloved," Flynn said with a smile. "It was a rather genius idea. I only wish I had been the one to think of it."

"So it was your father's plan to tell us you died?" she guessed.

"Ha! That doddering old fool? Hardly! He wouldn't recognize a good plan if it dropped into his lap." Flynn frowned at her and raised his staff to the side. "But speaking of good plans, how about this for a consolation prize?" Flynn stepped aside and shoved a bound figure to the ground in front of him. Her father was in the prince's custody! Several big, red patches of skin showed her where he was burned severely and one of his arms hung at an abnormal angle. In spite of his injuries he was struggling to get to his feet. He was stopped when a pair of glowing red manacles appeared, encircling his hands and feet. Ava guessed that Flynn was binding him with some kind of magic.

"You've gotten stronger since I saw you last," her father told her. She almost laughed because he sounded unconcerned about being restrained. He hadn't stopped struggling, though, and she wished she could rush toward him and embrace him. But if she did that, Edgar might get detected and then they might all be in trouble.

"Strong enough to melt your innards with a thought," Flynn bragged, assuming Ava's father was talking to him. "And I have you two to thank for my newfound power."

"How so?" her father asked. Ava met his gaze for a moment and he nodded his head ever so slightly. He was trying to tell her something. Perhaps that she should try and sneak behind the young Pyromancer. She inched her way around him and listened while her father goaded the prince for more information.

"I wanted to hurt you so bad after I woke up from the pyreken attack," Flynn said. "And then this dark, shadowy figure appeared beside my bed. It promised me power, more power than I could dream of or imagine--which is quite a lot, mind you--and a chance to avenge my injury." Ava noticed the color left her father's face at the mention of the shadowy figure. "It wanted me to kill both of you, something about needing to clean up some unfinished business, but I convinced it to let me keep your daughter as a pet."

Ava had rarely heard her father curse, but he let out a stream of obscenities now that made her blush. Although she couldn't see Flynn's face from this angle, she was almost certain he was wearing some sort of sneer. She reached down to pull *Seraphina* from its sheath, but pain lanced through every part of her body as soon as the blade slid free from its sheath. Her sword dropped to the ground and clattered away. Ava fell to her knees. It was a struggle to keep from collapsing completely. She had never experienced pain like this, not even when the gripmaug stabbed her. She let out a cry of agony in spite of her best efforts to remain silent. Flynn laughed.

"What are you doing to her?" her father demanded. Ava could hear the hairs on his skin sizzle every time he tried to move.

"Teaching my pet to obey," Flynn said casually, as though he was doing nothing more than scolding a young pup that was being trained.

"Leave her alone," her father said. He cried out in pain as soon as the words left his mouth. It took Ava a few moments to realize her own torture subsided. She could feel something other than that burning torture pulsing through her body. She crawled forward, trying not to watch or listen as her father succumbed to intense pain. Her father was strong, and she admired that in him, but she doubted even the strongest person would be able to remain silent under that burning magic.

"What is it your god, Eodran, teaches," Flynn remarked idly. "Spare the rod, spoil the child? I know, that is just a paraphrase but the gist of it is in there. Well, when I am through with her she will be quick to obey my every desire because she will understand the consequences if she displeases me."

"You... are... a... monster..." her father gasped. His face was red and his entire body quivered from the pain coursing through him. He slumped to the ground, chest heaving as

Flynn released him. Ava moved faster, sensing that another bout of pain was coming her way soon. "You may have... obedience... but never her... love."

"Love?" Flynn laughed and shook his head in disbelief. "What do I need with a worthless emotion like love? You can't conquer kingdoms or destroy armies with love. The only things I need are power, discipline, order, and fear."

Ava was right behind him now. She rose slowly from a crouch and drew a dagger from her belt. Every movement was deliberate and she took special care to make no sound in the process. The slightest mistake could cue the prince in on the danger and then she would miss her opportunity to end his hold over them.

"An empire built out of fear will crumble," her father said. Ava raised the dagger overhead.

"Who will dare to stand against me?" Flynn said, sweeping an arm to his side. The handle of her dagger turned red-hot and it burned her hand. She fought through the pain, driving her hand forward, but the point met an invisible wall of resistance inches away from Flynn's skin. She dropped the dagger to the ground and clutched her scorched hand.

Flynn spun to face her. The look in his eyes frightened Ava and she tried to back away but her legs wouldn't move. He struck her face with an open hand. The blow left a red mark and tears blurred her vision. "How much longer before you learn that I am invincible now? With this new power at my command there is nothing that can stop me. No one that can defeat me. Nothing that can surprise me. The sooner this lesson sinks in, the better it will be for you."

Ava heard her father groan in pain again. Flynn grabbed her jaw, holding her head straight as he stared into her eyes. She tried to shut her eyes to avoid looking at him but his magic burned the insides of her eyelids when she did that. Her emerald eyes blinked open again, the stinging sensation lingering in her memory. Her father writhed on the ground behind Flynn.

"Let's see if my pet has learned her lesson yet," Flynn said. "Her poor father is in pain. With a simple request I can end it for him. Ask me to kill him, my pet."

"Never," Ava spat without hesitation. The burning pain returned to her body and she felt it coursing through her insides like a serpent. She could see red tendrils beneath her skin as it probed through her. A scream escaped her lips as it brushed up against her heart and lungs. Ava felt violated by the powerful magic but there was nothing she could do. She couldn't blink anymore, much less escape from Flynn's grasp. Her father cried out in pain, convulsing violently on the ground.

"I can keep him alive for days like this," Flynn whispered. His sour breath repulsed Ava. "Either way I will kill him. The only question is when. You will be doing him a kindness by commanding his death, my pet. Just say the word and it will all end for him. His suffering will be no more."

"I'll die before I give in to a soulless serpent, you cowardly bastard."

His smile faded, replaced by a deep scowl. He turned toward her father and redirected his full attention on the prone man. Ava had never witnessed anyone suffer as much as her father suffered now. His lips opened but no sound came out. Ava wondered if Flynn might actually be right, that death might be the kinder option. It would be unfair to subject him to such torture just because she refused to let go and Flynn showed no signs of remorse. She hoped that some miracle would intervene and strike Flynn down. She waited, watching her father writhe in utter agony, until she could not watch anymore.

"Flynn," she said in a weak voice. Her mouth was dry as he stopped. The prince turned toward her, his eyes alight with a dark triumph.

"You have something to say, my pet?" Ava opened her mouth to speak but Flynn shook his head, pointing at the ground. "Get on your knees and beg me to do it." She complied but her muscles were only able to move slowly, like a puppet on strings. She told herself it was all a bad dream. She would wake up soon and everything would be okay. Flynn would be back to being dead and their village would be unharmed. She would find that she was still in the castle. Or even in Albrooke. Anywhere but here.

But she wasn't waking up.

The burning sensation returned and this time it was isolated on her legs. She fell to her knees with a cry of pain. Then she felt a strange power at work, stealing control of her every muscle. It took control of her voice, her mouth uttering words she'd never say in a million years. "I want you to...." How could she ever want her father to die? She fought against the magic as it worked her tongue and lips. Ava strained to resist every impulse that would condemn her father. And then the words came out, "know I will never give up, never give in. I will defy you until my final breath if need be. I am Avalina, a monster huntress, and you cannot control me." The fire within her died down. She could feel her limbs again, move her fingers of their own accord.

Flynn's face burned brighter than the flames surrounding them. Clearly that was not what he expected to hear. "Fine, my pet, you leave me no choice. Watch as your father suffers because you are too stubborn to see sense." He raised his hands in an exaggerated manner, making a spectacle of the coming torture. An arrow whistled as it sliced through the air, aimed at Flynn's throat. It stopped just short of him, the tip touching his skin and he laughed. But his laughter was interrupted by Ava's dagger as she drove it into his back. Flynn staggered forward, eyes wide and the blood drained from his face. He stopped Edgar's attack but hadn't realized she broke free from his control when she had defied his attempt to control her tongue. And that proved to be his final, fatal mistake. He fell to the ground and breathed no more.

Ava ran over to her father and knelt beside him. His skin was gaunt and his breathing haggard, but he was still alive. Ava wept tears of joy over him, not caring anymore who saw her do it. He was alive and that was what mattered most.

A crack of lightning made Ava look up. Dark clouds appeared overhead without warning and covered the village in darkness. Thick, black smoke spewed from Flynn's mouth and spiraled toward the clouds. The transparent shadow of a shrouded figure hovered in the air, staring at them with a chilling look. Her skin was crawling as though she was staring Death in the face and then it vanished as the smoke dissipated in the air.

The clouds were gone as fast as they had appeared and everything seemed to go back to normal.

But Ava knew that things would never be normal again.

CHAPTER TWENTY SEVEN
Monster Huntress

Ava still knelt beside her father, clutching one of his hands in hers, when Edgar came into view. He ran toward them, sandy blonde hair dancing in the wind. His eyes looked them over for injuries, and the scowl told her they looked as bad as she felt. It took Ava a few moments to remember that Edgar was originally with her when Flynn appeared. He ran away, escaping unnoticed by the possessed Pyromancer prince. Which was how he had been able to get that perfect shot off with his bow, which distracted Flynn long enough for Ava to end the threat. She at least owed him a thank you, but the words jammed in her throat. Ava rose to her feet and took a few steps toward the boy before falling into his arms, unbidden tears streaming down her cheeks.

It seemed like today was the crying sort of day, whether she liked it or not. "You don't need to heal me with your tears, you know," Edgar said. And then he held her while she wept, being the silent presence she needed for that moment.

Ava was glad the nightmare was over. She just wished she could move past all this unpleasant sobbing. She found his strong arms to be strangely comforting, and, if she was completely honest with herself, she was enjoying the way he stroked her hair while he held her. But she couldn't ever tell him that.

Then again, maybe she could.

"Edgar, I..." she started to say, looking up at his face. For the first time she felt an urge to kiss him, to kiss him in the way she saw wives kiss their husbands in the village. So she did. She could feel his body tense, sense the surprise that ran through him for the briefest of moments before he enveloped her in a warm embrace. Part of her wanted to keep kissing him but she knew that they needed to get help for her father. There would be plenty of time for kissing later. He would just need to earn those kisses.

They each grabbed an arm and dragged her father into the closest house that was still intact. Neither one of them said a word. There was no need for words right now. That didn't stop the butterflies from fluttering around her insides. Edgar blushed every time their eyes met. Ava found that to be quite endearing. They worked together and somehow managed to get her father into a soft bed, covering him with warm blankets and starting a small fire in the firepit. Her father still looked terrible but his breathing was getting stronger and Ava was able to find a pulse. He was going to live even if it took months for him to recover. That thought made tears return to her eyes but this time they were of joy.

The soldiers and elders struggled to keep the sand monster at bay. Quite a few lost their lives, including three elders. Things looked grim in the end. It broke through their defensive lines and headed toward the village when it stopped. The monster disappeared into the sand and didn't emerge again, although they surrounded the spot for hours. Ava guessed that it probably went back to its lair when Flynn died, his control over the monster broken. From their exaggerated descriptions of the unknown monster, combined with Edgar's honest description, Ava was guessing they had met a stone golem. Their weapons had been useless against its stone body and even water did little to slow it down. It was a lucky break that it didn't keep on heading toward Tirgoth when Flynn died. If it had, there wouldn't be a village left to rebuild.

Her father stayed unconscious for a few days. Ava spent most of her time at his side. She could be found holding his hands while exchanging stories with Edgar. She was surprised to hear about his own adventures and found that she was more than a little jealous when he told her about girls trailing him. That newfound popularity of his was going to come to an end now that she was around. She was going to make certain those girls would stay away from him whether he wanted them to or not.

Her father woke up five days after the battle, coughing uncontrollably. The color had returned a little to his skin and his wounds were slowly healing. Edgar shared a smile with her and nodded before leaving the room. Ava embraced her father and felt his arms holding her close. She promised herself she wasn't going to cry. Her father was strong, much stronger than Flynn. He wouldn't cry at a time like this. But as she released him from their hug she was surprised to see tears trailing down his cheeks.

"Was it everything you imagined it would be?" her father asked in a weak voice. She knew what he meant.

"No," Ava whispered. "It was exhausting, I found out people hate us, and I was scared to death I was going to lose you forever." Ava paused, looking at her father. His eyes struggled to remain open, even though he had been unconscious for days, but she could still see the strength of steel in his eyes. "But that doesn't mean the job isn't an important one."

"You want to continue training as a monster huntress?" her father asked, shaking his head. "You are just like your mother," he whispered. "She felt the same way about it before she died."

"Mom was a monster huntress?" Ava asked, feigning ignorance. He had told her about it before, many times. Her father didn't know that she had found the annals and therefore, found many more stories about her. But she always loved hearing him talk about her mother and seeing his face light up at her memory. That was one thing a book could never do.

"She was. The best one in all the land, and I wasn't there to support her when she needed me the most."

"You were off hunting some other monster?" Ava asked. She was eager to learn more. Her father rarely spoke about her mother and there were so many things that she wanted to know. She knew from the book and her dreams that her father hadn't been a hunter yet but she wanted to hear it from his own lips.

"I wish that had been the case, Avalina. I wasn't a hunter when she was alive. I was a noble in the king's court at Hárborg. On the day she died I accused your mother of some unspeakable things. Then you and I rode off, leaving her alone to face a monster that was coming to the house." Her father let out a deep sigh, looking into Ava's eyes. "It took your mother's death to make me realize the error of my ways. I had thought she was a monster and I had started to hate her. But it turned out that I was the monster that day. She was a hero, and I loved her.

"I had caught a glimpse of the monster that killed her that night and I swore to hunt it down and destroy it no matter the cost. I traveled with you across the country for a year, but it always managed to elude me. It had gone into hiding somewhere but I couldn't find out where. So I headed back toward the kingdom of Hárborg and brought you here, to Tirgoth, where I could make sure you were safe. After all this time I thought that we were safe. I thought it was gone."

"Was that what you were looking for when you left?"

"Yes," her father admitted. "I wanted to find it and get my revenge. The thought consumed me but I was chasing down a phantom. I had given up on finding it by the time we got to Hárborg castle."

"What happened after you told me to ride to Albrooke?" Ava asked him. "Why didn't you send me a note to let me know you were alive?"

"I was overpowered and captured by something that had command of dark magic. But I wasn't taken back to Hárborg. They took me to an odd tower, miles north of here beyond the mountains, and I was held prisoner there by Flynn until his plans were in motion. I had no idea the prince had truly been dead but I suspected he was amplifying his own power somehow. And then, when Flynn told us about the source of his power, I knew that the monster that killed your mother had finally decided to come after us."

"I saw it," Ava said, thinking back to the figure in the smoke when Flynn died. "It felt like I was staring Death in the face."

"That is because you were looking at a lich, Avalina."

"What is a lich?" she asked. It was time to finally learn more about her enemy if she was going to be hunting it in the future.

"A monster that is more dead than alive," her father said, closing his eyes. "They first surfaced in the Wizard Wars. Some of the wizards grew hungry for more power and forged dark pacts with demons, trading their soul for increased power. They feed off magical power, sapping the wizard's soul until it becomes their puppet. A young wizard like Flynn was the perfect choice because he was eager for power and revenge. I would guess that, by the time he got here, it was no longer Flynn we were facing but rather the lich controlling him from afar."

"We must find this lich and kill it!" Ava exclaimed, rising to her feet. Her father grabbed her arm, shaking his head.

"I admire your passion, Avalina," he said, "but right now the best thing we can do is to rest. And help the village rebuild and recover." He leaned back on his pillow, his eyes heavy. "Besides, there is only one person I know of that knew how to kill one and her journal has been lost for years. I don't know what I would have done if I had encountered it, but there is no sense in chasing it without knowing its weakness."

As much as she didn't want to admit it, she saw the sense in what her father was saying. The lich could wait, at least for a few weeks. She was going to tell him that he was right but he had already fallen back asleep. Ava sighed, shaking her head. He was safe and going to live and that was what was important right now. She decided to leave him alone for a while, so he could get the rest he needed to recover. Whose journal could he have been talking about? Could it have been her mother's journal that held the secrets? She would have to ask him later but she knew she would need to do it in a manner that wouldn't raise his suspicions. If he thought that she was planning to go after it he would find a way to keep her here with him until he was able to go himself. But she knew, from his injuries, that it might be a long time before that would happen and they needed to track the lich while the trail was still warm.

Ava sat on the top of the tower, staring off into the distance when Edgar found her. He sat down beside her without saying a word. She found his presence to be reassuring, a reminder that she was not alone. Her thoughts continued to dwell upon her parents and what she learned today about the thing that killed her mother so many years ago.

"Ava," Edgar said at last. His words broke her mind free from her thoughts. He was looking at her with the smile she had seen hundreds of times growing up. "Want to play Monster Hunter?"

She couldn't help but smile back at him. "Sure," she said, getting to her feet. "After what we've been through, that would be great!" The lich could wait at least a few hours.

"Okay, I'll be the troll," Edgar said.

"No," Ava said. Edgar stopped and stared at her.

"You want to be the monster this time?"

"Of course not." She could not stop herself from laughing at the daft boy. "I need my hunting partner with me. To watch my back and help keep me safe."

"Then what are we hunting?" The frown on his face formed lines on his forehead.

"I hear that those girls following you everywhere aren't really girls," Ava said in a hushed voice. She got close to Edgar's ear, whispering to him. "They are really doppelgangers taking on those human forms to blend in without raising suspicion." Edgar's eyes widened in understanding and the smile returned to his face.

"You know what I heard about doppelgangers? They turn to stone if you dump buckets of cold water on their heads."

"There is only one way to find out," Ava said as she descended the tower.

If you enjoyed this epic fantasy, please leave a review with your book retailer of choice, so he knows what you liked and didn't like about the book and can make the next one better for you.

About the Author

David Wiley is an author of science fiction and fantasy stories, choosing to write the stories that he would love to read. His first fantasy novel, Monster Huntress, will be published by OWS Ink, LLC. in April 2018. His novella, A Merchant in Oria, is set in the same fantasy world but follows a different cast of characters on an adventure that challenges the notion of what it takes to be a hero.

His short fiction has previously been published in Sci Phi Journal, OWS Ink, and King Arthur anthologies by Uffda Press and 18th Wall Productions. David resides in central Iowa with his wife and son, and spends his time reading, writing, and playing board games.

Learn more about David at his website https://authordavidwiley.wordpress.com/

OWS Ink, LLC Fantasy Books Coming Soon...

A reckoning is at hand, and Gillian will be judge, jury, and executioner.

Moss, clay, and blood--that's how her life began. She's nothing but a doll until Mab, Queen of the Fae, gives her not only life, but a mission. Gillian must track down the rogue fae in the Americas and bring them under Fae Law.

And they have no idea what they're in for.

Moss and Clay is the delicious introduction to the Mab's Doll series by Rebekah Jonesy. This dark yet snarky urban fantasy adventure will leave readers longing to see the justice Gillian metes out.

Meet the next generation of the ancient Aos Si Fae today!

The Dark Archer Robert Cano-
Coming July 2018

All he wanted was the safety of his princess. What he received was eternal torment.

And now, completely bereft of a soul, a wraith with no ties to humanity, Bene wanted nothing more than death. A release from the twisted existence that had been forced on him.

Trapped between life and nothingness, perhaps if he could reclaim his soul he could find the death he so desperately desired.

Along the way Bene finds rare solace in the company of Feorin. A satyr war hero who had grown tired of the centuries long war with the Fae and finally walked away from it into exile. A lonely life of peace until he met Bene. And Moriactus, a dragon who cares nothing for the world, and only wants to destroy the wraith and all he cherishes.

Soul Purge A.L. Mabry-
Coming October 2018

How many times can you watch your love die?

The gift of remembering your past lives and always finding your soul mate is a heavy gift to bear. Especially when you cannot change the outcome.

Be sure to join us at ourwriteside.com to learn more about the many amazing books coming soon!

Other Books by David Wiley

A Merchant in Oria by OWS Ink, LLC

Firion is a young merchant descended from generations of merchants. His first big break comes along when he sets out to trade with the wealthy dwarven kingdom of Oria. He has always dreamed of visiting this grand kingdom, having heard his father describe it in detail a hundred times while he was younger. But when Firion arrives in Oria, he is jarred by the details present that contradict with the image etched into his mind. Something dark and sinister seems to be afoot in Oria, but Firion knows he is no hero. He is just a simple merchant, and what can an ordinary person do in the face of danger and deception?

The First Martian Church of God by David Wiley published by Sci Phi Journal, Q1 2016: The Journal of Science Fiction and Philosophy

Monsters: A TPQ Anthology

After Avalon

Tales from Our Write Side: An Anthology from OWS Ink, LLC

King of Ages: A King Arthur Anthology
Morgan Chronicles

Quickfic Anthology 1: Shorter-Short Speculative Fiction

Mystic Signals - Issue 26

Made in the USA
Lexington, KY
01 May 2018